I0724075

TIME IS NOW

ANTHONY AMADEO

TIME IS NOW

ANTHONY AMADEO

WORKBOOK PRESS LLC
187 E Warm Springs Rd,
Suite B285, Las Vegas, NV 89119, USA

Website: https://workbookpress.com/
Hotline: 1-888-818-4856
Email: admin@workbookpress.com

Ordering Information:
Quantity sales. Special discounts are available on quantity purchases by corporations, associations, and others. For details, contact the publisher at the address above.

ISBN-13:   978-1-953839-25-1 (Paperback Version)
                978-1-953839-26-8 (Digital Version)

REV. DATE: 04.11.2020

Table of Contents

Dedication • • • • • • • • • • • • • • • • • • • 03

Chapter 1 • • • • • • • • • • • • • • • • • • • 04

Chapter 2 • • • • • • • • • • • • • • • • • • • 07

Chapter 3 • • • • • • • • • • • • • • • • • • • 10

Chapter 4 • • • • • • • • • • • • • • • • • • • 15

Chapter 5 • • • • • • • • • • • • • • • • • • • 21

Chapter 6 • • • • • • • • • • • • • • • • • • • 28

Chapter 7 • • • • • • • • • • • • • • • • • • • 35

Chapter 8 • • • • • • • • • • • • • • • • • • • 47

Chapter 9 • • • • • • • • • • • • • • • • • • • 54

Chapter 10 • • • • • • • • • • • • • • • • • • • 61

Chapter 11 • • • • • • • • • • • • • • • • • • • 69

Chapter 12 • • • • • • • • • • • • • • • • • • • 74

Chapter 13 • • • • • • • • • • • • • • • • • • • 80

Chapter 14 • • • • • • • • • • • • • • • • • • • 84

Chapter 15 • • • • • • • • • • • • • • • • • • • 91

Chapter 16 • • • • • • • • • • • • • • • • • • • 95

Chapter 17 • • • • • • • • • • • • • • • • • • • 106

Chapter 18 • • • • • • • • • • • • • • • • • • • 111

Chapter 19 • • • • • • • • • • • • • • • • • • • 120

Chapter 20 • • • • • • • • • • • • • • • • • • • 125

Chapter 21 • • • • • • • • • • • • • • • • • • • 134

Chapter 22 • • • • • • • • • • • • • • • • • • • 139

Chapter 23 • • • • • • • • • • • • • • • • • • • 147

Chapter 24 • • • • • • • • • • • • • • • • • • • 155

Chapter 25 • • • • • • • • • • • • • • • • • • • 165

Chapter 26 • • • • • • • • • • • • • • • • • • • 170

Chapter 27 • • • • • • • • • • • • • • • • • • • 174

Chapter 28 • • • • • • • • • • • • • • • • • • • 185

Chapter 29 • • • • • • • • • • • • • • • • • • • 194

Chapter 30 • • • • • • • • • • • • • • • • • • • 208

Chapter 31 • • • • • • • • • • • • • • • • • • • 215

Chapter 32 • • • • • • • • • • • • • • • • • • • 219

Chapter 33 • • • • • • • • • • • • • • • • • • • 225

Acknowledgements • • • • • • • • • • • • • • • 230

TIME IS NOW
BY
ANTHONY AMADEO

"MANY LIVES, ONE ETERNITY, GOD KNOWS ALL."

Multiverse theory, dimensions, time travel and realities

Other books by Anthony Amadeo:

HUBEARIA

GUARDIANS OF HUBEARIA

ANOTHER DAY IN NEVERLAND

For more information visit us at www.hubearia.com

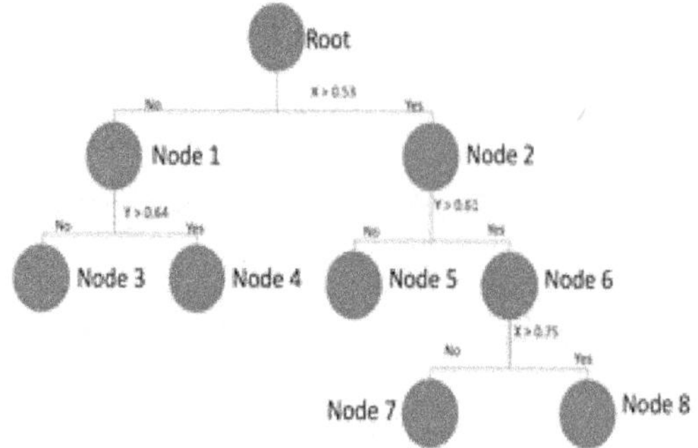

"I believe in everything until it's disproved. So, I believe in fairies, the myths, dragons. It all exists, even if it's in your mind. Who's to say that dreams aren't as real as the here and now?"

John Lennon

"I'm not afraid of death because I don't believe in it. It's just like getting out of one car, and into another."

John Lennon

"Know that the only distinction between past, present and future is only a stubbornly persistent illusion."

Albert Einstein

DEDICATION

To my Mom and Dad, you are in my thoughts and in my heart every day. To my little best friend Pluto, who crossed over the rainbow bridge to be with his big brother Amadeus, thank you. And also, to my rescue princess Savanna, a big thanks.

To my family, children, grandchildren and my friends who inspire my stories.

To my wife and best friend Helene, for being there with encouragement, patience, making me laugh and help me every day in my writing. Most of all for all your love—Always and forever.

CHAPTER 1

Halloween night, 1988, Farmingdale NY

It was a foggy cool fall night in a remote cemetery:

"Allen, this is crazy, I'm cold and this place is too scary" Come on Jodie it's Halloween, you know it's my favorite holiday. Renee and Mitch your good right?" "Sure, Allen, I love walking through a cemetery at night, why not it's a blast, don't you agree Renee?' "Where else would you want to be on Halloween." "Here is a good spot, Jodie set down the blanket right by this gravestone. Mitch you open the wine." "What time is it?" "It's 11:45 he should be here any minute. I see a light now that must be him." Allen flashes his light. "Allen, how much are we paying this guy?" "Three hundred but it will be worth it, this guy is the real deal. This is going to be awesome best Halloween ever, trust me." A tall thin man in a black raincoat and black gloves, a drawn thin face with partially grey beard, approaches. "Allen this guy looks freaky." "Don't worry, it's all fun, a little scary but cool, you will see. "Allen." "Otto, right." Otto nods, "Are you ready?" "Yes, just tell us what to do." "Money first." "Now you all sit in a circle. I will channel the spirit from the grave. You can ask any questions of him. He will answer through me, this will last as long as the spirit stays. Only one question at a time, no other speaking or movement. Once the spirit enters my body, I will not be in control the spirit will. I will begin." Leo stands raises his hands upward and begins to chant.

"adducere ad me, et spiritus ortus tui
adducere ad me, et spiritus ortus tui
adducere ad me, et spiritus ortus tui"

Otto repeats the chant over and over again. After five minutes, Allen whispers to Jodie, "This is so cool but nothing is happening." Just as Allen is speaking, a soft wind begins to swirl around them.

Leo continues his chant and suddenly stops. He stands still but his body begins to tremble as he falls to his knees. His eyes close he begins to speak "I'm so thankful that you have called upon me. I have waited for this day for so long." Allen speaks, "Who are you? Are you a spirit? As they wait for a response the voice deepens, "Questions, I have not returned to answer questions. Who are you to ask me questions? I am who I am. You are pathetic nothings that are looking for some entertainment and I will not entertain you but I will entertain myself." Jodie and Renee start to panic. Jodie, "I'm scared let's get out of here now! As Jodie speaks the swirling increases, Otto stands shaking violently screaming, "No! No!" He starts to move backwards then turns and runs. The swirling wind engulfs the four of them pushing them together as they are trapped. A face appears in front of them a smiling evil face moving his lips as he drains the breath out of them. All four desperately try to break away to no avail. As they watch in horror unable to move, a crack in the swirling wind begins to widen and an opening appears. An entity materializes smiling, as he sucks the life out of them. The entity laughs, "Trick or treat."

The next day, Sargent Gulli of the County Detective Unit pulls up and parks his car. He walks to the yellow tape surrounding a section of graves. "Okay what do we have?" A young woman covered in a protective suit walks over to him. "Four bodies side by side but no signs of any marks. No blood, no wounds, nothing at all." "What is the cause of death?" "We don't know." Gulli smiles, "What do you mean you don't know?" "Look Sarge sorry but there seems to be no reason that we can see. I'm sure when we get the coroner's report it will clear this up. Only one thing sarge, a marking on each female body, a carving. Let me show you." Gulli bends down and carved into both women's chest is, nunc tempus est "So, we got two women carved and all four bodies with no cause of death. What about the bottle of wine?" "No Sarge, it's clean but again we will need a full report. There was another set of foot prints so it looks like there was one other person at the scene." "Okay, that's our killer. Now you are giving me something. I'm assuming no witnesses, no camera's, it's a cemetery, I get it. This is all I need four young bodies drop dead together in a cemetery for no reason but at the same time someone carved this crap in the women. You can't make this shit up. Okay, we need to get all video of the whole area around this cemetery. All cameras, industrial buildings, anything we can find. We need to identify all the victims. Hopefully we can identify the car the killer came in or were they all together. We got a lot of work to do, you know the routine, let's get on it. Once this gets out, there will be a lot of heat looking for answers. They all have ID's let's get a work up on them and Jamie run a complete check on these few graves, see what the connections are. Find out the what the hell that carving means. Check this stone first. they are just about on top of it. Gulli bends over the stone and reads out loud Stevie Bracken, 1947 to 1967. Alfred, the coroner walks over to Gulli, "I took some Latin, Nunc tempus Est means time is now."

CHAPTER 2

Two months earlier, 1988

Jimmy, Jennifer and their two sons Daniel thirteen and Steven ten, stood over the graves of Daniel (Danny Amendola) and Steven (Stevie) Bracken. Sal, Ray along with their wives and kids stood silently. Danny's brother Alex and his wife Joan stood with their two sons Alexander and Anthony. Father Thomas finished a prayer as they all said, "Amen." Jimmy bent down and picked up two stones placing one on each gravestone. He wiped the tears from his eyes and watched Jennifer, Alex, Ray and Sal do the same. Jimmy turned to Jennifer, "It's hard to believe that it's been twenty years since they were killed in the club." Daniel turned to Jimmy, "Dad, how did they die?" "It's a long story Daniel and someday I will tell you but not right now." Jimmy asked Ray to take the boys back to the car he needed a minute with Father Thomas. "It's funny the way life turns out. I know I owe a lot to Danny; he saved my life." Father Thomas asked, "That night at the club he saved you?" "No not that night it was a year later." "Jimmy, a year later Danny was already dead." "That's right. I know this sounds crazy but he saved my life. It was in Viet Nam. I was there about ten months when I was on a search and destroy mission. We were looking for Viet Cong in a small village. I was part of a squad and we had just captured a VC prisoner. He was wounded and we were heading back to camp. We were under attack from VC and were moving through the jungle. I moved away from the rest of the guys because I was trying to contact the base. As I was on the radio it suddenly went dead. I saw a light appear in the dark jungle and in the light, it was Danny. I thought I was hallucinating as Danny told me to move away now. Come to me now. He kept saying it, so I did what he said and I started to run to the light towards Danny. As I ran, I heard a loud whistle sound and then an explosion. It was a mortar round hit a few feet from where I was. I felt a pain and then I went down. I was told that if I was a few more feet in the other direction I would have been killed by the blast. Somehow Danny came to me and saved me. I was evacuated to a hospital in Cam Ranh Bay. I was treated for months before being sent home. I was going to the VA for rehab and that's where I met Jennifer. She was working as a nurse there and we became friends. We had a lot in common, being there the night that Danny and Stevie were killed. She was broken up about it but it was good we were able to talk about it. She told me, she was so sorry about what had happened. She was never really with Carlo they just went out a few times. She tried to tell him not to bother her anymore but he was persistent. He kept calling and always coming over. He was intimidating and had a reputation of being connected to the local mob. She didn't know he was going to be at the club that night. In a way Jennifer was relieved that Carlo would spend most of his life in jail. After a while Jennifer visited me even when she wasn't working. We became friends and then we started to date and the rest is history." Father Thomas smiled, "That is a miracle what happened." "I guess it was Father. I never talk about it because I know the shrinks would recommend therapy or worse for me, but that's what happened." Danny's brother Alex came over, "I never heard you tell that story. That is great to hear and I believe you. Danny died trying to save Stevie but Stevie died anyway. In his death he came and saved you. Danny was a special person and we all miss him so much. He never had a chance to live his life but he helped you live yours." "I suffered from shrapnel wounds and a couple of broken legs but with Jennifer's help I was able to get through it. If it wasn't for Danny, I would have died or at best been crippled the rest of my life. We have a great life together; we live in a great neighborhood and we have wonderful neighbors. We have an elderly couple next store to us that have been like grandparents to our kids. You know Father, I have some crazy dreams over the years about both Danny and Stevie. It's almost like I have dreamt about different lives. It's hard to explain but it just seemed like my life could have turned out very differently. Danny and Stevie always seem to be in my dreams." "That's understandable Jimmy because what you went through that night, losing your two friends and then Viet Nam and all you have been through. It's a testament to you that you have survived and have such a wonderful family, friends and life. I spent a lot of time in a remote part of England working in a monastery. I worked with a very special monk named Brother Aiden. While working with him I witnessed many amazing events. He believed in good and bad messengers which were angels that altered the lives of many. In some cases, they saved people lives by interceding and changing their course. He believed in alternate universes that can send one from one path in life to another. Just like what happened to you, with Danny appearing to you and saving your life. He in some ways was a good messenger that saved you an altered your life for the better. I knew a person like Danny who came to me for help when he was at a crossroad in his life. With the help of Brother Aiden, I think we saved him and many other people from a very bad fate. One never knows how and when these messengers change our lives." "Father did you ever meet Danny" "Jimmy, that is a question I cannot answer."

CHAPTER 3

Stevie Bracken is six feet tall, dark hair, handsome, well built, a sweet smile that always worked for him. As Stevie looks into a puddle of water he smiles, "I can't believe it happened again, another chance, another life. How these pathetic idiots hire the one person who could have made this happen. Welcome to my world my darling. I'm ready to have some fun. Now I need somethings to get started." Stevie walked to the train station sat and waited. The Long Island Railroad would bring him where he wanted to go. He hopped on board and sat down in the back of the car. After ten minutes he hears, "Tickets." Stevie walks back and opens the train door and stands in between the railroad cars. The door opens and the conductor says, "Ticket." Stevie ignores him, turns his back to him and moves close to the edge. The conductor comes close to him again saying, "Ticket" Stevie in one motion reaches in his pocket and then quickly grabs the conductor pushing him out of the train. Stevie smiles, saying out loud, "That was easy." Stevie exits the train at Penn Station walks up the stairs on to thirty-fourth street. He starts walking up to the theatre district. He is smiling as he walks briskly enjoying the evening air. He enters a large parking garage and picks an area and sits on a car patiently waiting. He nods to a number of people as they walk by going to get their car. An hour passes and then Stevie sees what he is waiting for. A single man in his middle twenties wearing a very expensive suit passes Stevie by. Stevie slowly follows him. Just as the man reaches for his keys and clicks the remote opening the car, Stevie makes his move. He surprises the man punching him in his lower stomach. As the man doubles over in pain, Stevie shoves him in the back seat. He jumps on top of him punching him merciless. After the man is unconscious, Stevie grabs his throat and chokes him making sure he is dead. Stevie gets behind the wheel and drives off. He heads uptown towards the fifty-ninth street bridge. He gets off and continues on Northern Boulevard. After driving a few miles, he pulls over on a quiet street. He smiles as he takes a small pen knife off the key chain and exits the car. He quickly switches license plates. He gets back in the car and drives off. He heads onto the Grand Central Parkway east out towards Long Island. He is enjoying his ride as he blasts the radio on a classic radio station. He drives out to eastern Long Island on the Expressway singing along with the song. He continues to a desolate spot, pulls over shuts the car off. He takes the body and puts it in the trunk. He gets back in the car and closes his eyes.

The next morning, Stevie pulls up to a diner in Center Moriches. He goes inside to the men's room and cleans up. He sits at a booth and orders a large breakfast from a middle-aged woman. She smiles at Stevie as she pours him some coffee. He notices a small TV behind the counter in the corner and a few people gathered around it. Stevie asked the waitress, "What's going on?" She looks at Stevie, "Oh that, it's all over the local news, some maniac pushed a conductor off the train last night." Stevie shook his head, "That's horrible, who would do something like that." The waitress replied, "Some sicko for sure. The poor guy is in a coma in ICU it doesn't look good. This is a sick world we live in buddy." "I agree with you a very sick world." After he ate, he opened the wallet he took, stacked with one hundred-dollar bills. "Can you break a hundred?" "Sure" Stevie left a generous tip and left. He stopped at a small hardware store and bought a shovel, flash-light and a few other supplies. He drove east and headed for a secluded area. He waited till dark. He dragged the body and dug a shallow grave. He then drove off until he felt far enough away, he pulled over into a quiet area. He looked through the wallet, "Richard Gardner, well thank you Richard, it was my lucky day picking you out, good for me not so good for you my friend.

Jimmy and his wife Jennifer live in a nice middle-class neighborhood in Plainview NY. They have two boys Daniel and

Steven, a small ranch house with a dormer upstairs with two extra bedrooms. Last week they visited a cemetery where Jimmy's boyhood friend Danny Amendola is buried. Jimmy and Danny grew up together with Ray Freed, Sal Ritello and Stevie Bracken. Jimmy has remained friends with Sal and Ray and see each other all the time. Danny and Stevie died many years ago.

One night after dinner Daniel says "Dad, can you tell me how your friends died so young?" Jimmy smiles at Jennifer nods his head and says, if it's okay with Mom?" Jennifer makes a frown, "Well he is thirteen, okay with me. They go into the living room and sit down on the sofa."

One night we all went to a dance club; Stevie was dancing with a girl she was very pretty." As Jimmy said that he looked at Jennifer and smiled. "She was very pretty: did I just say that already?" "Yeah Dad, twice." Okay, as the night flew by, we were making plans to meet at mid-morning and were going to Jones beach to spend our Saturday. Where else would you go on a Saturday in the summer on Long Island? It was getting late and the place had really thinned out. There were about three or four couples on the dance floor. It was getting to that time when we would hit the closest diner, stuff our face with some hamburgers and head home. I was happy that Stevie was so into the girl, he was no problem at all. It was nice to have a night out with no problems, all is good. Danny came over to us, the girl he was dancing with gave him her phone number and he was happy. Now we were waiting on Stevie. He was slow dancing to what was the last song of the night. We decided as soon as it was over, we would grab him and hit the road. As the music stopped Stevie walked over to us, arm and arm with the girl. I pulled Stevie over and told him to get her number because we were ready to go. He was cool and knew it was time. He took the girl by the hand to a corner; they spoke a while and he was writing down her number. Just as he was writing down her number two guys came from what was I guess the back door. One of them pulled the girl by the arm and away from Stevie. I knew right away this was not good. I knew Stevie was into her big time and he would not let this go. I told Uncle Sal to get the car and get ready to pick us up so we get out of there real fast. Uncle Ray grabbed Uncle Sal and they went to get the car. I was watching Stevie waiting for him to do something stupid but he didn't move. He just watched as the girl and this guy were in a heavy conversation. I told Danny to come with me and we would get Stevie out of there. Danny and I went over to Stevie and I told him to be cool and let's get out now. Stevie smiled and said he was good, he just wanted to wait just to make sure she was okay with this guy. Stevie seemed calm, so I started to relax a bit and said I would wait with him. The girl waved at Stevie and mouthed to call her. Stevie smiled and nodded his head. We both turned and started for the door, thank God, no problem. I guess my instincts were wrong. I thought this was going to get ugly but just another Friday night out with the guys. As we walked away and were a few feet from the door this jerk yells out, "You better get the hell out of here, you blank." Stevie stops short, he starts to walk towards this guy. I see where this is going, so me and Danny get in front of Stevie and tell him, "No, don't be stupid just forget it and let's go." Stevie stops looks me in the eye smiles with that angelic look on his face and says, "You're right let's go home." I take a deep breath and move away from Stevie towards the door. The rest happened so fast it was surreal. Stevie instead of following us turns back at the guy and goes right at him. I was way too slow to react. I believed Stevie was coming with me and in a second, he goes the other way. Danny goes after Stevie and he tries to get to Stevie to stop him. Stevie punches the guy in the stomach and they both fall to the floor. Danny gets in between to break it up and a second later, as I tried to get to them, I hear "Pop, pop, pop" The guy gets up and runs out the door. I see blood pouring from Stevie's chest and Danny is lying right next to him. It all happened in seconds, I fell to my knees, grabbed Stevie and Danny and screamed to call an ambulance. I cradled them in my arms pleading with them to hold on. About fifteen minutes later the ambulance showed up but it was too late; Stevie bled out and Danny died in my arms. They had no chance the bullets tore them apart. Look Daniel I know this is a hard story to hear but I'm sure you would have heard it somewhere down the line. I know you were always asking questions so I rather you hear it from me and not someone else. This the real story something I have had to live with. They were like brothers to me and they both died that one awful night. That's why in one respect I was willing to go into the army. I wished for a way to get as far from that night as possible. Well you know that old saying be careful what you wish for because you might just get it. I did get my wish but I had no idea that wish would send me to Viet Nam. Well that's a story for another time. Okay buddy how about you go upstairs and watch some TV." "Okay Dad, I don't know what to say but thanks for telling me. Love you Dad." "love you to Daniel." Jennifer came over to Danny and sat next to him. She put her hand on his shoulder, "You think we will ever tell him that I was the girl that Stevie was dancing with?"

CHAPTER 4

November 1988

Stevie is feeling good and decides to celebrate. He drives to Freeport Long Island and goes down by the water. There are a number of bars, clubs and restaurants. It is a cool night but the area is still busy. Stevie picks out a restaurant named Seven, seems like a hot spot. He goes by the bar and orders a scotch and water. He whips out a hundred-dollar bill and lays it on the bar. He looks around and smiles nodding his head very pleased with himself. He is considering what he wants to do "Do I pick a pretty little thing, a more-sexy one, or maybe just a very ordinary one. What should I do with that lucky girl?" Just as Stevie was in deep thought a very pretty girl bumps into him and stumbles forward. Stevie reacts quickly and catches her before she falls. "Oh, I'm so sorry." "No problem, are you okay" She looks at Stevie and smiles, "I'm good, these stupid heels. I just bought them and they are brutal, I can't walk in them. Just so you know I don't drink, so I'm not drunk." Stevie smiles back, you say you don't drink but you are at a bar?" "No, I'm at a restaurant and I had dinner with my friend." "Where is your friend?" She just left and I like this band, so I decided to stay awhile longer. Why am I explaining myself to you?" "No explanation necessary, my name is Stevie." "Hi I'm Lisa, it's nice to meet you." "Can I get you a drink, a soda, coffee?" "How about an ice tea no sugar?" "You got it." Stevie smiles to himself thinking, "Sometimes what you are looking for just comes to you easy but this is ridiculous. What to do with this pretty girl? How much do I want her to suffer? Questions, questions what to do?" Lisa looks at Stevie, "Hello earth to Stevie, did I lose you?" "Sorry, I just was thinking about something, not important. So, Lisa where are you from" "I live in Hicksville, where are you from?" "I moved here from Arizona a few months ago and I am kind of local." Stevie spot a high-top table across the room, "Would you like to sit a while and talk?" "Sure." They sit at the table and they talk for half an hour. As Stevie listens to Lisa talk, he feels a little strange, "You know in another life, I think I could actually like this girl. "Something about her, she makes me feel good and she is definitely attractive. Nice long hair, big brown eyes and a great body. It's really a shame that I have to end her life. I wish I could think of a reason to let her just leave." "Stevie you are doing it again." "What?" "You seem to go off somewhere. You know what it's getting late I think I'm going to go." "Hey, I'm sorry I have a lot on my mind. I apologize, let me walk you to your car. You never know outside these places you can get some sicko waiting out there." "I don't know about that but sure you can walk me out, that would be very gentlemanly of you." "Okay then let's go." Once again faith seems to be helping Stevie as Lisa's car is in the back of the parking lot. The area is not well lit. As they walk, Stevie takes Lisa's hand and she does not resist. They approach her car and she begins to take out her car keys. Stevie starts to reach into his back pocket. He carries a nylon dog choker for these occasions. Just before he pulls it out, he hears, "Lisa hey, wait up." Lisa turns," "Hey Billy what's up, I didn't see you in there." "Sorry to bother you but can you do me a big favor I need a lift home. I know this is a bad time I don't want to interrupt but I have an early day tomorrow and I need a ride. My buddy hooked up with this girl and ditches me. I am really sorry." Lisa says, "Sure no problem but can you give me a minute?" "Okay, of course, I'll just wait over there." Lisa turns to Stevie," Hope you don't mind but he is my friend and we live in the same apartment building. How about I give you my number and if you want you can call and maybe we can get together?" Stevie hesitates thinking of his next move but then says, "Yeah, sounds good. I'll call you and maybe we can have dinner or something." Lisa smiles, "Great I would like that." She then kisses Stevie on the cheek and yells to Billy, "Okay, let's go." Stevie watches them drive away thinking, "I should have killed both of them, shit! Oh well a date sounds nice, maybe a fine dinner, some wine and she will be my dessert."

Westbury Motor Inn Westbury, Long Island:

Stevie puts down his bottle of beer and calls Lisa, they have a very pleasant conversation and make a date for dinner Friday night. Lisa gives Stevie her address and directions to her home. Friday Stevie gets dressed in a sharp new shirt, shoes and slacks he bought at Macy's, thanks to his buddy, Richard Gardner's money. He puts his choker in his back pocket. He heads out and drives to get Lisa. Stevie stops by a local florist and picks out a small bouquet of flowers. Stevie is feeling good and in some weird way he is excited to see Lisa. He knows what his intentions are but still he's looking forward to being with her. Stevie pulls up to the apartment flowers in hand and rings the bell. Lisa opens the door and she looks great. "Come on in. I will be just a minute. Beautiful flowers thank you, that was sweet of you." "Well that's me. Where would you like to go for dinner?" "I was thinking Apple Annie's it's a great place, food is wonderful and not expensive." "Sounds perfect." They go to dinner and everything goes great. Lisa tells Stevie all about herself and Stevie tells her about his life in Phoenix, Arizona. Of-course none of it is true but Stevie loves to tell stories and he is good at it. Stevie is as charming as can be. He has two sides and on one side he is very likable, funny and the girls always are drawn to him. His other side is something new and that is pure evil. After dinner they drive back to Lisa's. Once again great conversation and chemistry between them. They go inside and Stevie sits on the couch as Lisa goes for some wine. Stevie starts to think now it's time to take care of business. Just as Stevie is thinking of his next move Lisa hands him the wine and sits next to him. Stevie can't resist and by instinct he kisses her softly. She returns the kiss and in seconds they are all over each other. Lisa suddenly stops and says, "I think we should slow down. I'm sorry but I'm not going to go to bed with you. I mean, I like you a lot Stevie but it's just too soon." Stevie sits back thinking that's it. This shit is over it's time to do this bitch in. He begins to reach for the choker in his pocket. Lisa puts her head down muttering, "Sorry Stevie." She turns to Stevie and puts her hand to his face. "How about we get to know each other. Spend some time and see where this goes." Stevie looks into her eyes and begins to relax. He feels strange and is fighting off the urge to hurt her. The evil in Stevie is strong and just as he is about to act, Lisa speaks again, "How does that sound?" Stevie sits back quite confused. She looks at Stevie, "Let's talk some more before you leave. What do you do for work?" Steve still confused starts to stutter a bit, "I'm in sales." Almost unwillingly Stevie engages in conversation with Lisa. After a few minutes of telling her all his made-up work stories he asks her what she does. "I work for a law firm. I am a researcher and coffee and donut server." She laughs and Stevie asks her what she does as a researcher. "I find people and information about them. It's pretty boring but could be interesting as well." Stevie thinks about this and says, "If I give you a name or two, can you find them for me. I have a couple of friends that I lost touch with when I moved to Arizona. We were very close and I would love to find them." "Sure, I can do it. Write down their names and I will look them up and get all the information I can find. "Great, thanks I really want to find them." Stevie writes down on her pad, two names, Jennifer Amoroso and Jimmy Cetano. Oh, maybe one more if you can Danny Amendola. "Thanks Lisa, I guess I'll get going. I'll give you a call tomorrow, okay?" "I'll look forward to it." Lisa kisses Stevie again. As he walks to his car he thinks "I think that meeting Lisa and keeping her alive for now, was meant to be."

A few days go by and Stevie is spending more and more time with Lisa. He somehow enjoys her company and is drawn to her. She makes him laugh and he feels good when he is with her. He has urges for violence but then she has a way of calming him. After spending a full day and evening with Lisa he has to leave. On his way back to his motel he decides to stop at a corner bar in the town. He sits at the bar and orders a scotch and water. He feels a rush entering his body. In his mind he hears a silent voice but he seems to understand the message. He starts to think of Lisa to help calm him. It works but just for a few minutes. Then he feels something pushing Lisa out of his mind. He could feel his body temperature rising and his head begins to throb. He feels a rage that is hard to control. He gets up throws some money on the bar and walks out. He starts walking to his car fighting off this feeling. As he comes closer to his car, he sees a couple in the back of the parking lot arguing. He walks up behind them without being noticed and kicks the man in the groin. The woman is stunned and before she can scream Stevie grabs her and covers her mouth. With one hand he reaches in his back pocket pulls out his choker and wraps it around her neck. In a minute she is gone. He turns to the man who is moaning and crawling away. He comes behind him and with his choker strangles the man. He calmly puts both bodies in the car. One in the back and the other in the front. He takes both wallets empties all their cash. He then rips the shirt off the man and using his knife he carves into the man's chest. He does the same to the woman in the back seat. He locks their car and drives off in his car. As he is driving, he feels a calming sensation and a strange satisfaction that please him. He drives down by the water and throws the car key into the water. He drives off putting some classic rock station and continues back to the motel. Two days go by and Stevie calls Lisa and makes a date for that night. That evening on the way over Stevie stops and picks up some Chinese food. He goes to Lisa's door and she opens it. "Surprise, I have some Chinese food for a change is that okay?" "Sure, love it come on in." Stevie and Lisa sit and eat dinner. They share some wine and enjoy a pleasant conversation. After dinner they sit on the couch. Lisa turns to Stevie, "Hey did you hear about the two dead people the cops found in a car downtown Huntington?" "No, I didn't hear about it." Lisa looks at him, "It's been all over the local news. They said they had some crazy carvings on their chest.

I mean how sick is that?" "You know Lisa there are a lot of crazies in this world, so nothing surprises me." "Yeah I agree. You want to watch a movie there's a new one on tonight I haven't seen, is that okay?" "Sure, why not. I hope it's not too scary?" "No, it's an action flick." They sit back and watch the movie and Stevie enjoys it. After the movie Lisa gets up and shuts the TV, "I almost forgot, I have the information on your friends, I'll be right back. I wrote down their address and information for you. Your friend Danny died twenty years ago in some bar shooting. I'm sorry about that. Your other friends Jennifer and Jimmy have been married to each other for fifteen years and live in Plainview." Stevie looked stunned and sat back in a daze. "Hey Stevie I'm so sorry about your friend. I should have told you that a little better. I'm so sorry." Stevie's demeaner changed. He was feeling that same rage he felt a few nights ago. His head started to throb and he was feeling thoughts pushing him to act. Lisa realized Stevie was real upset, "Stevie, I'm going to put on some coffee, maybe that will make you feel better." Lisa went into the kitchen. Stevie watched her leave the room. The message he was getting was loud and clear the bitch served her purpose. He now had the information he wanted. She was of no more use to him. He slowly stood up. He reached into his back pocket and pulled out his choker. He started towards the kitchen and stopped to watch Lisa making a pot of coffee. He began to move forward but then suddenly stopped. He turned and quickly left the apartment. He rushed into his car and drove away. All these thoughts raced through his head. Danny died the same night he did. "That prick killed us both. All because of that bitch Jennifer. Jimmy my good friend, he betrayed me and marries her. I will make them pay. Now it's my turn to get my revenge." He drives back to the motel contemplating how he should get even with them. Stevie was able to push out all the other thoughts that seem to be filling his mind. He now had his own agenda nothing else mattered but Jennifer and Jimmy.

CHAPTER 5

Detective Gulli is sitting at his desk and calls out to Jamie. "What do we have so far? I need to go over this again. We have four bodies and nothing to go on. No DNA, no prints, no witnesses and no visual. Plus, how the hell do you kill four people without a struggle, no poison, no drugs, nothing. What does he do hypnotize them? This guy has to be the luckiest son of bitch or he is a real smart killer. There were no cameras at the cemetery, I get that but nothing shows up on any cameras. Now we got another body in Manhattan carved up with the same shit and once again they tell me the same. No camera in the bar, no witnesses and no DNA or prints, nothing. Jamie this is pissing me off. A killer who takes cash we have a motive, robbery. If that's it then why the carvings and in Latin no less. Maybe he is a broke priest that went nuts. Normally a serial killer doesn't want the money but that doesn't mean he is not a serial killer." Jamie sits on the desk, "Why do you say he, you sure it's a guy?" "Well history tells us that Serial killers are loners who stalk strangers at night to later snatch, torture, and sexually assault them before finishing the deed. Male serial killers, according to the researchers' theory, are "hunters," who follow their prey. Women are different they tend to kill acquaintances, people who surround them. They are often caregivers, and are well-educated. Consider "Jolly" Jane Toppan, a young nurse who lived in the northeastern US in the second half of the 19th century. She killed at least 31 people, many of whom were in her care. She used poison, and relished watching them die, reportedly even lying down by their side as they were entering the netherworld." While men largely attack strangers, previous studies have shown that about 80% of women serial killers know their victims. "Wow, listen to you Gulli, you sound like a professor, I'm impressed." "Yeah that's me professor of serial killers. Look if you follow history it repeats its self and the more you do your homework the better your chances."

As they continue talking, they are interrupted by a female officer, "This just came in a double homicide downtown Huntington and it looks like the same MO." "Shit, come on Jamie let's go."

Plainview NY

Jennifer yells to the boys, "Come on dinner is ready." "Hey, what about me?" "You are invited to my darling." "Okay darling, I like that. I'm starved." "You say that every night." "It's your wonderful cooking that does it to me." "Dad's buttering up mom, he must be in trouble." "No smarty, I speak the truth." "Okay sit and let's eat, say grace Jimmy." "Grace." "Okay funny man now say it for real." After dinner they sit around the living room and Jennifer says, "How about we all watch a family movie, maybe a Disney film." "Pass, I have homework to do." Okay Danny what about you Stevie?" No, I'm good I'm going upstairs a watch some wrestling." "Disney film, what are we the Brady bunch?" "I was just trying to make it a family night. What's wrong with that?" "Nothing you are great mom and one beautiful wife. I have an idea, why don't we bring that bottle of wine over there and go into our room and make our own movie?" Jennifer smiles and heads to the bedroom.

Stevie stared at the house and watched the lights go out in the front room. "I wonder what the happy couple is doing right now. Maybe my good friend Jimmy is screwing my sweet Jennifer, how about I break up their little screw session and pleasure myself. Oh wait, they have two sons, I don't want them to be orphans, so maybe I will save them that sorrow and kill them too. You know what they say, the family that dies together stays together. Maybe this is not the right time besides Jimmy won't be that easy. He could be hard to take care of. I need a little more time to find the right moment. Plus, I do enjoy watching over them. When the time is right, I will know it"

A few days go by and Stevie decides to call Lisa. For some reason he misses her. "Lisa it's Stevie. I'm sorry I ran out on you but I was hit hard about Danny. I had no idea he died we were like brothers growing up. Danny, Jimmy and me went everywhere together. I should have said something before I ran out. I'm really sorry." Lisa hesitates, "Yeah I get it. It had to be a shock. I should have told you a little better than I did. It's okay Stevie, I do understand. How you been? I was kind of worried about you." "I'm okay, I just needed a little time to take it all in. I also wanted to thank you for getting me the information. It's not your fault it was bad news." "Well at least you can find your two other friends. I guess you were surprised they are married?" Stevie started to anger but held back, "Yeah, that was a surprise but it's all good. I can't wait to see them. I am going to surprise them soon." "I'm sure they are going to love seeing you after all these years." "Not as much as I'm going to love seeing them. How about I give you a call and we get together this weekend?" "Sounds great, I'm looking forward to it." "Okay, I'll speak to you soon."

A few days go by Jimmy and Jennifer are in the kitchen. Jimmy comes behind Jennifer and softly kisses her neck. "Stop it or I'll never get this ready." "It's just Sal and Ray they want us to watch the old video that Sal found. It's a party he had at his house when we first married. It was his mom's birthday and we were all there." "Oh yeah, the party in the back yard with the DJ, I remember we had a great time. I still need to give them some food you know Sal and his food." Sal and Ray come and they watch the video. After the video we sat around talking and remembering old times. Ray says, "Remember when we were eighteen and John got his new Chevy Impala Super Sport." Jimmy looks at Jennifer, "Jennifer you didn't know John's mom, she was a great lady. She was old time Italian mom and would treat John as if he was ten no matter how old he was. One summer Ray, Sal, Danny and me went in John's brand new 1965 Chevy Impala it was a beauty. Dark burgundy with black interior and bucket seats. He kept it immaculate. We park it in a Jones Beach lot and walk under the tunnel to the beach.

We spend the day enjoying the sun and water. Summer's at the beach, at that age, was heaven. It was getting late and it was time to go. We pack up our stuff and head back to the car. Danny leads the way and as we approach John's car, Danny stops us as he is looking in the window. He says this isn't John's car. John is still not at the car; I say of course it's his car. Danny says no this car is some crazy custom one it has no seats. John runs up to the car and opens the door. He starts cursing out loud screaming they stole my damn seats. We all are in a daze, How the hell did they steal his seats. Well sure enough that's what happened they stole the two bucket seats. We go over to the guard house and he tells them what happened. They say they will make out a police report. After all that is done, we are trying to figure out what to do now. John's trying to see how he can drive the car with no seats. The guard suggests a milk box that he had. So that's what we did. John sits on this milk box and we sit in the back seat and on the floor. As we are driving home, we can't help but crack up how stupid he looked driving sitting on this box. A brand-new car sitting on a box driving it, it was hysterical. Now he comes into Plainview where we all live just a few blocks from each other. Danny says to drop him off first because his street is first. John says hell no you are all coming home with me. I'm not facing my mother alone. When she sees this, she will go crazy. You guys have to be there. We all agree, so in a few minutes, John pulls up the driveway. His dad is outside watering. He shuts the hose off and comes over. John's dad was a cool guy we all liked him a lot. He was the total opposite of his mom. He was very calm and cool. John goes right over to him and tells him what happened. He is stunned he couldn't believe it either. He takes it well and says that John has insurance and they will cover it. He will get new seats put in and it will be okay. Now John's mom is at the door, she asks what's going on. She steps out and John's dad goes up to her, telling her don't get excited but something happened to the car. She pushes him out of the way and looks at the car. She says, what happened the car looks fine. John tells her to look inside and opens the door. She looks in and says absolutely nothing. She stares at it for a few minutes and asks John where are the seats? John says they stole them. Then all hell breaks out "look at what they did to my son! Look what they did to his car." I mean she is screaming at the top of her lungs. She is in a housecoat and goes into the middle of the street screaming. All the neighbors start to come out. I'm sure they thought someone was murdered. Everyone starts to calm her down and after a few more screams she stops. She then looks at John and asks him did he lock the car? John was honest and says he wasn't sure. Well now she goes off again. She starts screaming my son didn't lock the car. How could you not lock the car? A brand-new car and you didn't lock it. She screams over and over again why didn't you lock the car? Are you happy now, look what you did? I hope you are happy. John couldn't take anymore and he starts screaming back. Yes, I'm happy they stole my seats. I left it open so they could steal my seats. Jen I'm telling you this was insane watching all this. John's mom was a classic character." All the guys couldn't stop laughing it was a great memory. Jennifer says, "You were good friends with John what happened?" "Nothing really, he moved to Westchester and we kind of lost touch. I should give him a call." Ray says, "Jimmy tell Jennifer the time we got in to the accident in Manhattan." Yeah, another John's mom classic. We were drinking at a few bars down in Little Italy. We had Ray's old Chevy. We were driving on Canal Street at an intersection, this car comes from nowhere and hits Ray in the back side. The car spins around. The car that hit us takes off so we push the car towards the sidewalk. Thank God none of us were hurt but Ray did have a bump on his forehead. The cops came and once again we were lucky, they might have known we were drinking but they didn't say anything. Now, it's really late and we have no way of getting home. We decide our only option was to take the subway to Penn Station and take the Railroad home. We get to Penn Station and we missed the last train out to the Island. The next one won't be till six AM. We then take turns calling our parents. We told them we had a small accident and we are all okay.

We tell them about the next train out so we won't be home until morning. We all do okay with the calls, of course all our moms were upset but thank God no one was hurt. Now its's John's turn to call. He tells us to come by the phone booth to listen in. He tells us his mom will go nuts. His only hope is if his dad answers and he won't have to speak to his mom. John makes the call and his dad answers. He explains what happened and when he would be home. John was relieved and just before he hung up, he hears his mom yelling at his dad. His dad tries to tell his mom not to worry but she gets on the phone. John tells her the whole story and his mom starts screaming at him. John holds the phone out for us to hear her. She is screaming it was his fault and to get home right now. He tells her how could it be his fault he wasn't driving. Does not make a difference to her she just keeps screaming at him. She tells him he has to be home within an hour. He tries to explain again they missed the last train out and the next one won't be until six. She doesn't care and keeps screaming come home now. John can't take anymore and starts yelling back, that he will fly home or maybe he can call the Long Island Railroad and get a special train sent because his mother wants him home right now. This show goes on another ten minutes and finally she hangs up. We take the train home and then a cab to our houses. John tells us the next day when he got home, she wasn't at the door waiting for him. So, he took his shoes off and slowly tip toed by her bedroom to go upstairs to his room. John was happy she wasn't at the door and he must have got lucky that she was still sleeping. As he quietly went by her room, he hears her screaming and he gets hit in the head with one of her shoes. The next one misses as he ran up the stairs and locked the door." We all kept on laughing and it was great as always getting together with the guys. Jennifer was the perfect hostess and she made us coffee. We had some cake and talked for a long time. The guys left, "Thanks honey, you were great." "I love listening to you guys I don't mind at all. I'm going to check on the boys." "I'll close up down here."

Stevie watched Sal and Ray leave. He felt strange, "I miss those guys. If it wasn't for that night and that prick Carlo, I could be with them. He took my life away. I have to call Lisa and see what she could find out about Carlo. He has to still be in prison, I would think but I need to be sure. I loved Jimmy and the guys and I wish there was a way I could be back with them. I need to get the hell out of here and I need to think this shit out.

CHAPTER 6

Gulli and Jamie were driving back from the Coroners, "The same shit. Absolutely nothing again. Two more bodies and no evidence in the car, the clothing, nothing. You tell me Jamie, how is this possible. We got us a serial killer that is like a ghost. He leaves nothing, he swoops in kills, carves them up and disappears. Leaves nothing to go on. Once again, no witnesses, no video, prints, DNA, a big fat zero. So now we got seven bodies. Every time he strikes it's the same, doesn't leave a clue. How could he be so perfect and so lucky." "You know Gulli the report on the grave sites might be something. The four gravestones around the Victims were all normal, nothing unusual. The site that they were almost on top of was Stevie Bracken." "So." "This guy was killed in a bar like twenty years ago. I'm thinking some kind of revenge thing going on. I checked all the victim's and they have no connection at all. "So, we still have nothing? Or am I missing something." "He was killed along with another guy named Danny Amendola. I got excited about that, so I checked him for any connections but." "Let me guess nothing?" "Yup." "You know Jamie I have a good friend who I was in Viet Nam with. I kind of remember him telling me that he lost a couple of friends in a bar fight around that same time. Who knows, maybe there is some connection? Look it's a long shot but I will give him a call and see. At this point we got nothing to lose.

Later that evening Gulli calls Jimmy. "Hey Jimmy how the hell are you doing?" "Great Gulli, everything has been good. The kids are doing well and Jennifer is good. I haven't heard from you in a while. You doing okay I hope?" "Yeah I'm good just been super busy. You know I'm working this case and I have to admit that is one reason I'm calling. I thought maybe you can help me. "Help sure but what can I do.? I'm no big-time murder detective like you. Just busting them Gulli, anything I could do to help, no problem."

"Well, I'm on this murder case and I have four bodies dead on a grave site. They are lying on one particular grave. The name on the stone was Stevie Bracken." "Wait, Stevie Bracken you got to be shitting me? This is bullshit right?" "No, I wish I was. I know you had a couple of friends that were killed in a club but I couldn't remember their names so I figured I give you a call just to see. Sounds like this is your friend?" "Yeah, Gulli it is. This is weird, what are the odds that the bodies are on his grave. Honestly, I don't know what to say. Are you thinking there is some connection or just a coincidence?" "Not sure Jimmy, but that's why I thought you might help. I was thinking you can come down the station and I can show you the files on the bodies and see if you can see any connections. Look Jimmy this really a big reach but I got nothing. Between you and me I'm sitting on seven bodies and not one damn clue. If there is any way you can shine some light on this, well it's worth a shot." "Sure Gulli, I will help. Whatever you need. It sounds to me this is some kind of serial killer?" "Yeah, it sure looks that way." "Wow, this is awful. I can come down tomorrow around twelve is that okay?" "Great Jimmy, I will see you tomorrow and we can go over the files."

Jimmy sits down on his couch and stares into space. "Jimmy you okay? Looks like you saw a ghost? Who was that on the phone?" "It was Gulli I know this sounds crazy but he wants me to come down to the precinct to help on a case." "What kind of case?" "It's a murder investigation. You know those bodies they found at the cemetery." "Yes, it's been on the news but what do you have to do with that? Something I should know Jimmy?" "Yeah, it was me I'm a killer and Gulli caught on to me. All kidding aside, the bodies were lying on a grave. The grave stone was Stevie Bracken." "Your old friend that Stevie?" "Yeah, I know this is crazy right? What are the chances it's his grave they land on? Gulli wants me to come down and go over the files on the bodies to see if I can make some kind of connection. There are other victims and he is grasping at straws to find some clues." "Jimmy is this a serial killer?" "Looks that way. I'm going down to meet him tomorrow." "You want me to come with you?" No. I'll be fine. I don't think it will take that long. When I get back, I will fill you in."

Next day Jimmy goes down to see Gulli. "Thanks for coming in Jimmy. It's been crazy around here. They put together a task force on this case. I've been in meetings all morning. Captain Marvelous is heading up the investigation but that's another story. I kept you away from that bullshit this is just between me and you. Look here are the victims, I broke down the most important information on them. I want you to read this over and see if anything rings a bell. I'm looking for any connection to your friend and any reason at all." "Okay Gulli, I got it." Jimmy spends the next half hour going over the files. "Gulli, I'm sorry but I don't see anything. I never heard of any of them. They had to be like babies when Stevie and Danny were killed. The only thing strange is they land on his grave. I mean, what are the odds on that?. Stevie was a good guy he never would hurt anybody. I just don't see how it could be a revenge thing going on. Maybe Carlo the guy who shot them could there be something there?" "No, we checked him out he still is doing time and has a long way to go."" Is there anything else I could help you with? "No Jimmy, I'm sorry I wasted your time but I need to try everything I can. Give my best to Jennifer and let's get together soon." "Sure Gulli, sounds good. I hope you catch this nut." "Yeah, me too."

Later that afternoon an officer comes over to Gulli. "Sarge I got this guy who wants to talk about the murders. Says he has information on the victims." "Send him into room two. I'm sure this is another waste of time but bring him in." "Okay, what information do you have? I'm all yours." "I was there the night those four people were found dead." Gulli sits up and gets in his face, "Say that again." "I was there with the four people that were killed. "You were there and you saw them get killed?" "No, I did not see them get killed. I left and did not know anything until I saw it on the news." "Why have you waited for so long to come in. We have been looking for any witnesses from the beginning" "I was scared. I thought you might suspect me as the killer because I was there. I swear, I never did anything to them. I left and didn't see anything." Gulli picks up the phone and calls for Jamie to come in. "Jamie, I want you to listen to this. "We are going to record this conversation is that okay with you?" "Yes, I have nothing to hide." "State your name and address for the record." Otto gives all his information. "Now Otto tell us exactly what happened that night." "I was hired by Allen Bishop to perform a service Halloween night at the cemetery." "Wait perform a service what kind of service? This some devil shit or sex thing? "No, I am a channeler. I communicate with the dead." "Okay let's get one thing straight Otto! I am up to my ass in this investigation and if you think you can come in here and waste my time with some bullshit story, you are mistaken. I will throw your ass in jail and throw away the key. Now tell me exactly what information you have and cut the crap." "I am telling you the truth. I communicate with the spirits of the dead. I call on them to speak through me. I do this for a living and I am very good at it. I have performed this ritual for over twenty years. Allen hired me with a large sum of money to do this for him on Halloween. This is not normally what I do, but the money was tempting and I had nothing on for that night. He told me he was a big fan of mine and researched me. He was convinced I was the real thing and I assure you I am." "Okay sorry, I lost it I am under a lot of pressure on this case. So, tell me what happened after you met them." "I met with them at the location that Allen set up. I do not know why he picked that particular grave site but it was not important to me. I met them at 11:50 the time he wanted. They were drinking some wine but they were not in any way drunk. He paid me and I began. I called on the spirit at hand. Once I summon the spirit, they speak through me. At that point I have no control. The spirit says what they want. I am just a conduit, a connection.

From the start something was different about this entity, it was strong. I can't explain it but it was far more in control then I ever felt before. It immediately went beyond me as a channel he began to take control. It felt like pure evil and it frightened me. I never experienced anything like that before it was a horrible evil force spreading first through me and then all around me. I panicked and ran. Yes, I just ran and didn't stop until I got to my car and drove off. I went straight home. I haven't been out of my home since. I swear, I never hurt anyone and I didn't see anything. I was way too scared to look back. I tried hard just to put it out of my mind but I couldn't. I thought of reporting it or even to call Allen but I couldn't do either. When I saw it on the news, four found dead, I was so scared, I didn't know what to do. Last night I decided I had to come forward." Gulli sat back and looked at Jamie shaking his head. "Okay Otto, as crazy as your story sounds; I believe you are telling the truth. Do you think this spirit killed the four of them? "I know this makes no sense detective but all I can do is tell you what happened." "Look Otto we will bring you some coffee, I need you to relax and give us a little time before you can go. You okay with that?" "Sure, thank you, I'm very upset." Gulli and Jamie walk out to talk. "What are you thinking, Gulli? "I have been doing this a long time but this is crazy shit. Do I think a ghost kills four people, seriously not in my life time? Do I think Otto could murder four people one third his age, no I do not? So where does it leave us? Back to square one. If Otto is telling the truth which I believe he is. That means someone else got to them and I don't think it is some ghost. We have to run some checks on our buddy Otto and if all comes back clean, we will have to cut him loose." "I agree and I'll get to work on him."

Stevie goes to Lisa's apartment. "I have an idea how about an early movie tonight and then a bite to eat?" "Sounds great, Stevie. I'll be ready in five." Stevie sits down and he starts to think. "You know this girl is as sweet as I remember Jennifer to be. She is just as pretty and I like spending time with her, I almost feel I want to spend more and more time with her. Maybe I should forget about Jennifer and all this shit. Lisa told me Carlo is still doing time, so I can't get to him, yet. I'm tired of sitting out by Jennifer's house and watching her and Jimmy. I can't make up my mind on what to do. Sometimes I feel like just forgetting about them and then other times I see myself putting them down for good. They get me pissed off and Lisa makes me feel good. She calms me and I like that feeling. At times I feel calm and then something happens and I have this wave of what I need to do. I have a reason that I'm back and that is what I must follow. I'm not sure if I know anything about why I'm back. I was in limbo in a dimension of emptiness. A cold dark nothing and then I'm pulled into another reality that now I live." "Sorry I took so long but I'm ready. What do want to see?" "Anything you want. It's up to you. Then it's my turn and I have a surprise for you." "Great, I love surprises. There's a funny movie at the Huntington theater." Sounds good, let's go."

After the movie, "Okay, Stevie what's the surprise? "Well it's not a surprise gift or anything like that but I know you love pizza and I'm going to take you to have the best pizza you ever had. It's my favorite place you will love it." "Pizza okay I'm up for that and it is a perfect surprise, let's go, I'm starving. Where is it maybe I know it." "It's in Brooklyn, the Spumoni Garden. Have you been there?" "No, Brooklyn?" "I hope you don't mind. My mom's brother my Uncle Carmine came from Brooklyn and we used to go visit him when I was a kid. He used to take us there and I loved it. I stuffed myself with pizza and then the spumoni was incredible. I haven't been back there in a lifetime." "Yeah why not sounds fantastic let's go." Stevie takes her there and they have a great time. They eat and talk for hours. "Tonight, it was not crowded because it's cold. You have to see this place in the summer it will take hours to get some food. Maybe when it's warm we can come here and then I'll take you to Coney Island. That's another place my Uncle would take me. I loved the Cyclone the first hill is like straight up and you go flying down. It's incredible. The Parachute it was great too. Have you ever been there?' "No but I know about it. I'm a Long Island girl never spent any time in Brooklyn." "Okay then, that's what we will do." Lisa looked at Stevie but didn't say anything. Stevie sensed maybe he was going too fast for her. Maybe she had no intentions of being with Stevie in the summer. Stevie drove back in silence. He needed some time to think.

CHAPTER 7

The days flew by and Jennifer was getting ready for their visit upstate with her parents. Her parents had a second home in Roscoe NY. It was beautiful up there. A rustic cabin on a lake. It was cold this time of year. They had a fireplace and it was a great setting for the Holiday season. "Hey mom, can I bring my Nintendo?" "No Daniel, I told you not this time. We are playing family games. It's going to be fun, trust me." "Can I bring my playboy magazines?" "You are very funny Jimmy; I can't stop laughing. Now let's get the car packed before it gets late. It's a four-hour drive." "Yeah Jen, tell me about it. I do the driving remember. I hope they have cable up there now. Last time I had like four stations to choose from." "Oh, my poor baby, how terrible for you." About an hour later they are finally on the road. They drive onto route Seventeen heading northwest. "It's a great scenic drive in the daytime but at night it's real boring. These roads are so curvy and dark." "Well I'm sorry I had to work today and we got a late start. You know Jen, we could have left tomorrow, in the morning." "I know but Saturday there is a lot of traffic and it takes forever. At least now we missed all that traffic. Babe, you know I get excited and I can't wait. I love going up there and seeing my mom and dad. We spent so many summers and holidays up there. It makes me feel like a kid again. Plus, the boys are fast asleep and we don't have to hear them bitchin, how long before we get there?" "I hear that. I'm okay with it. "You know that I love time travel stories, right babe?" "Yeah, I know Jimmy. How many times you going to tell me that? "Look, it's a boring drive, can I tell you about the ones I just read about?" "Sure, maybe it will keep you awake." Okay, you're so sweet that's why I love you so much." "Tell me the stories already." I just read about A guy in October 1969, identified only as L.C. and his business associate, Charlie, were driving north from Abbeville, Louisiana, toward Lafayette on Highway 167. As they were driving along the nearly empty road, they began to overtake what appeared to be an antique car traveling very slowly. The two men were impressed by the mint condition of the nearly 30-year-old car, it looked virtually new and puzzled by its bright orange license plate, which said only "1940." They figured that the car must have been part of an antique auto show. As they passed the slow-moving vehicle, they slowed to get a good look at the old model. The driver of the car was a young woman dressed in vintage 1940s clothing, and her passenger was a small child likewise dressed. The woman seemed panicked and confused. L.C. asked if she needed help and, through her rolled up window, indicated yes. L.C. motioned for her to pull off to the side. The businessmen pulled ahead of the old car and turned onto the shoulder of the road. When he and Charlie got out, the old car had vanished without a trace. There was nowhere the vehicle could have gone. Moments later, another car pulled up. The driver told L.C. and Charlie that he had seen their car pull off to the side and the old car simply vanished into thin air." "That's crazy, right?" "Yeah, I guess." Here's another one check this out. Two British couples vacationing in the north of France were driving, looking for a place to stay for the night. It was 1979. As they drove, they noticed signs that seemed to be advertising a very old-fashioned circus. The first building they came to look like it might be a motel, but the men standing in front of it told the travelers that it was an inn and that a hotel could be found down the road. Further on, they did find an old-fashioned building marked "hotel." Inside, they discovered, almost everything was made of heavy wood, and there were no modern conveniences such as telephones. The rooms had no locks, only simple wooden latches. The windows had wooden shutters but no glass. In the morning, while the travelers were eating breakfast, two police officers entered wearing very old-fashioned caped uniforms. After getting what turned out to be very bad directions to Avignon, the couples paid a bill that came to only 19 francs, and they left. After two weeks in Spain, the couples made a return trip through France and decided to again stay at the interesting if odd but very cheap hotel. This time, however, the hotel could not be found. Certain they were in the exact same spot (they saw the same circus posters), they realized that the old hotel had completely vanished without a trace. Photos taken at the hotel could not be developed. And a little research, revealed that French police officers had stopped wearing caped uniforms in 1905. These are real stories." "Well, I'm not so sure how real?" "Come on Jen, give me a break. You don't believe anything. I got one more for you. In 1932, German newspaper reporter J. Bernard Hutton and his colleague, photographer Joachim Brandt, were assigned to do a story on the Hamburg-Altona shipyards. After being given a tour by a shipyard executive, the two newspapermen were leaving when they heard the drone of overhead aircraft. At first, they thought it was a practice drill, but that notion was quickly dispelled when bombs began exploding all around and the roar of anti-aircraft gunfire filled the air. The sky quickly darkened. Hutton and Brandt realized they were in the middle of a full-blown air raid. They quickly got into their car and drove away from the shipyard back toward Hamburg. As they left the area, however, the sky seemed to brighten and they again found themselves in the light of a calm, ordinary late afternoon. They looked back at the shipyards, and there was no destruction, no bombed-out inferno, no aircraft in the sky. The photos Brandt had taken during the attack showed nothing unusual. It wasn't until 1943 that the British Royal Air Force attacked and destroyed the shipyard, just as Hutton and Brandt had experienced it 11 years earlier. Last one, A time travel case of Rudolph Fentz. Back in the 1950s, a guy with mutton chop sideburns and Victorian-era duds mysteriously appeared from nowhere in the middle of Times Square.

The man looked startled, according to eye-witnesses, and was eventually run over by a car and killed. When his body was searched, 19th-century money was found as well as documents dating from 1876 that didn't appear to have aged a day. From these documents the man's name was found, Rudolph Fentz. Attempts were made to track down his family, if he had any. A Mrs. Rudolph was later tracked down who just so happened to be the widow of Rudolph Fentz Jr. (the mysterious dead man's son). Rudolph Jr., so the story goes, recalls how his father simply disappeared one day in 1876 and never returned." "How about some nice music?" "I don't want to wake the kids. You don't think any of this can be true?" "I don't know." "If you could time travel what would you rather do. Go back in the past or go into the future? Come on, Jen, just play along." "Okay, I don't think I would want to see the future, so I would rather go back in the past." What about you?" "Yeah, I feel the same. I mean it would be kind of cool to see the future but it could not be the way you would hope it will be. I would go back to the past." "Any particular time?" "Maybe go back and visit my mom and dad. You know I would go back to that night in the club. Maybe I could save Danny and Stevie. I loved those guys they were like my brothers." I Know hon, I'm so sorry about them." "Thanks babe. I know I get carried away with this time travel stuff. I'm sorry if it gets boring." "I never get bored listening to you. I kid around but I love just listening to you and your stories." "That's why I love you so much. You are the only one that would put up with me. How about a kiss?" "Forget it, keep your eyes on the road and watch out for the other cars." "What other cars, I think we are the only nuts on the road. Everyone else is asleep. Well maybe I spoke to soon there's a car coming up behind us and he is flying. He must be in a rush to see his in laws, I bet." "Funny man." A split second later the speeding car turns into Jimmy forcing him off the road. Jimmy fights the steering wheel trying to keep the car under control. The impact was too much and the car spun down the hill off the road. Jennifer and the boys were screaming as the car smashed sideways passenger side first into a tree. The impact was devastating the car was almost bent in half. Jimmy was pinned behind the wheel and barely conscious. Jimmy could barely breath or keep his eyes open. Just before he blacked out, he saw someone looking in the window.

It was a man, looked at Jimmy and smiled. Jimmy closed his eyes and everything went black.

"Jimmy, how you feeling? "Gulli, thanks for coming." "I'm so sorry, Jimmy. I can't believe this happened. I don't know what to say." "There's no words, Gulli my life is over." "Don't say that Jimmy, please." "I got nothing to live for. My wife, my kids are gone Gulli. I just want to go back to sleep and never wake up." Gulli watches him and then holds Jimmy as he cries along with him. After a few minutes, "There's just no way you can imagine a horrible accident like this could happen." "No Gulli, this was no accident. He hit me on purpose. There is no doubt in my mind. He came right at me and turned his car into mine. It was intentional. He wanted to run me off the road." "Intentional are you sure? That makes no sense, why would anyone do that? ""Look, I'm not nuts. I know how it sounds but the car came up on me and turned into me. It was one hundred percent intentional. He hit me and forced me off the road. I tried to keep control but I couldn't, the impact was too much. I lost control and hit the tree. What I'm telling yo, is the truth. How I'm alive is ridiculous. I should be dead and they should be alive. Why me and not them. They're my life, Gulli my everything. Without my Jen I have nothing. My boys they were so young. I can't deal with this." "Okay Jimmy, I know this is brutal. Listen I have to ask, did you get a look at the car. Anything that could help me track it down. I want to get this guy and bury him for you." "No, it happened so fast. I think it was a black car pretty common mid-size. I gave this information to the local cops and they said they were all over it. They were really good about it. I could tell they want to get this scum bag. The next thing I tell you I didn't tell them. I don't want anybody else to know this either. The last thing I need is a psychiatric test. All they been doing is running tests. Every time I turn over here, they come. MRI's, Cat-scan, blood, I'm sick of it. The one thing I remember before I blacked out was that I was pinned in and couldn't move. I see this face, a guy coming to the window and I thought thank God someone to help. Instead of helping he just looked at me and stared right at me. He smiled. I'm telling you the bastard smiled at me and then I went out."

"He smiled? Shit this has to be some sicko. Jimmy are you sure he smiled? "Positive, it was clear, he smiled. This is not the only thing that is weird. I know you are going to think I'm crazy but the face was my old friend Stevie Bracken.' "Stevie Bracken the one that was killed twenty years ago? The same Stevie Bracken that was the grave site the four bodies were found? "Yes, and yes!" "Look Jimmy, it was dark you were probably in shock and your mind could play tricks on you. This is very normal under the circumstances." "Yeah, I knew you would say that and that's why I didn't tell the cops that. You don't think I thought the same thing. I've gone over and over this since I been lying here. I am convinced it was real. I am sure it was him. He looked right at me and smiled, an evil smile. If I close my eyes right now, I can still see him as clear as I'm seeing you. It was real." "Okay, but how can that be? He is dead, has been for twenty years. Do you think it was a ghost but can a ghost drive a car into you? Jimmy, I hate to say it but I think you were in shock and were hallucinating. It's the only thing that makes sense." "I know, I'm well aware of what you are saying but I know what I saw." "Listen why don't you get some rest. I want to check with the cops that are handling the case and see what I can find out. I will come back as soon as I can. Is there anything I can get you before I go?" "Yeah, how about you leave your gun so I can end this nightmare?" "Stop it Jimmy, just get some rest and let me do my thing. You have my number, call if you need anything at all. I love you brother, stay calm."

Gulli stops by the desk and asks for the Doctor that is treating Jimmy. "Doc, I just wanted to see if you can give me an update on Jimmy's condition. Look I'm a good friend and I'm also working the case." Gulli shows his shield. "Well he is actually doing very well. He has a number of bruises and a fractured rib. Other than that, he is in excellent condition. Considering the accident and losing his family he is lucky to be alive. All his tests are normal and he should be released soon. We will just keep him awhile and monitor his condition. Need to make sure no concussion symptoms or any other problems show up." "What about any brain damage or anything like that?" "No, we did a brain MRI and it was negative. No damage. Like I said he is very lucky." "Yeah, losing his wife and kids, very lucky, Doc."

Gulli stops in at the local police department and finds out that the car that hit Jimmy was found. It was stolen and banged up. They are running tests and agreed to share the results with Gulli.

The next day Father Thomas comes to visit Jimmy. Jimmy sits up in the bed, "Father Thomas thanks for coming. I didn't expect to see you here. It is very nice of you come." "I heard what happened and just wanted to see you and see if there is anything I can do." "Father thanks but there is nothing anybody can do. I don't want to sound bitter but I am lost. My wife and kids were everything to me. They were my family, my life. They were my world. Now they are gone. I don't know how I can go on. I've lost everything." "Jimmy, I am so sorry. It was just a little while ago I was with you and your family. I know it is so hard to accept what has happened. This was a tragic accident and there are very little words that can help. I am a priest so I believe they are in God's hands now at peace." "Father, I don't want to interrupt you but I know what you're saying and it doesn't help me right now. Father, this was no accident, this was intentional. I don't want to go over this again because you will think I'm crazy. The fact is it was intentional.

"Jimmy what are you saying, intentional please tell me." "Okay Father but when I'm done, I know what you will be thinking. I was hallucinating and possibly lost my mind." "Please Jimmy, tell me I promise I will just listen and not judge you." Okay here goes." Jimmy tells Father Thomas the complete story he told Gulli and the fact that he saw his old friend Stevie smiling at him. Yes Father, the same friend that was killed over twenty years ago. His face was pure evil. I don't know any other way of explaining it but just evil. My buddy detective Gulli was in to see me and he is helping out on the case. I don't think he believes me but he is a great friend and trying to help. When he was here, he told me he is working a murder case where four bodies were found on a grave site. The grave site they were lying on was my friend Stevie's. How weird is that? I mean four dead bodies on his grave site and then I think he ran me off the road. Killed my family and then smiles at me. He's dead, how does any of this make sense. Is this one big coincident and my imagination playing tricks with me. Look Father, I know what it sounds like but I am sure he was there. It wasn't my imagination he was there." Jimmy watched Father Thomas sit back in the chair and shook his head. "You see Father, I knew you would think I am nuts." "No Jimmy, I am not thinking that at all. I came here today because I wanted to see you before I left. I came to see if I could give you some consolation, some hope, some comfort. I had no idea that you would tell me this horrible tragedy was intentional. I knew about the four bodies. I know about the carvings in Latin. I did not know they were found on your friend's grave site. The reason I am leaving I have been called upon by my old friend Brother Aiden. He lives in a monastery in a remote part of England. I am not sure exactly the reason but I do know it is of grave concern. Brother Aiden is one who has dealt with these occurrences before. His methods have pushed the boundaries and he did lose his standing with the church. As a matter of fact, his case went right to the Vatican and I have been told that the Pope himself made the final decision. The Monastery, which he is part of, works outside of the church and is not recognized by the Vatican; it is in fact a separate entity. Originally Brother Aiden was part of the Monastery called North Umbria during its "golden age." It was the most important center of religious learning and arts in the British Isles. Brother Aidan took the name in honor of the founder, Saint Aidan." "What actually does this Monastery do and believe in?" Father Thomas put his hand to his weathered face and strokes his thin grey hair, "This is kind of a grey area, they are very secretive. They allow no visitors except on an individual dispensation from their governing body, which no one knows anything about. From what I've learned over the years, they believe, practice, and study a combination of "Divine utterances." To make this as easy as possible, Brother Aiden believes and practices methods of inviting messengers or angels, who at times, act in helping change and alter events. The Bible and associated texts have been widely received as divinely oracular by various religious sects, where verses can be interpreted as supporting desired ideas of "God," reincarnation, spirit communing, extraterrestrials and the afterlife. To answer your question in the simplest of terms, Aidan and the Monastery he resides in, study and practice this combination of beliefs." "Father I am confused, what does this have to do with me?" "From the information I have received there has been numerous murders in England and Italy having the same carvings. These murders have been committed at the same time in many different parts of these countries. Therefore, they cannot be done by the same killer. I'm not sure why Brother Aiden wants me but he must have his reasons. I have worked closely with him in the past and he felt he can always count on me to be truthful and helpful. These murders seem to be the start of something the Church has been prophesying for centuries. A final battle of good and evil." "Once again Father what does it mean for me?" "Brother Aiden believes and has worked with good messengers or if you prefer angels that can interact with human destiny. He has worked on altering realities. He believes and has worked with these messengers to open different portals to alternate realities. Jimmy, I have studied this subject matter for many years. In 1954, a young Princeton University doctoral candidate named Hugh Everett III came up with a radical idea: That there exist parallel universes, exactly like our universe. These universes are all related to ours; indeed, they branch off from ours, and our universe is branched off of others. Within these parallel universes, our wars have had different outcomes than the ones we know. The study of quantum physics began in 1900, when the physicist Max Planck first introduced the concept to the scientific world. Planck's study of radiation yielded some unusual findings that contradicted classical physical laws. These findings suggested that there are other laws at work in the universe, operating on a deeper level than the one we know. I have certain conflicting memories of the work I have done. It is very complicated but to simplify it the best I can. I believe I have witnessed Brother Aiden call upon these angels to help humans cross over into other dimensions or realities in which the outcome of their lives was different. Now I realize this sounds very strange but it is true. The belief is that there are portals that bring us back in time where we can change a direction or a decision that changes an event. Once the event is changed it's a domino effect that can alter the future events. When this occurs, there is an alternate reality which can be very different from the existing one that we know. There is belief that there are many alternate realities. For example, your friend Stevie and Danny were killed in a club over twenty years ago. If you went back through a portal of time and changed that decision to go to that club on that night, it is possible, that they would not have been killed. This would then have created an alternate reality. In one reality Danny and Stevie would be alive. In the other reality they would not. If they were alive this would alter the events of so many different lives." "Father are you saying that we can be living in different realities at the same time?" "Well yes but again this is a theory and a belief. Brother Aiden has dedicated his life to explore this belief. He has gone so far that he was cut off by the Vatican. His exploration in calling on messengers and angels to combat evil went too far. The Pope himself made the decision to remove him from the church. The monastery to was exiled from the church. I have worked with Brother Aiden without the church's knowledge. Brother Aiden has dealt with evil or dark messengers in many different occurrences. These evil messengers bring violence and horrible crimes against humans. The bible teachers us that All humanity is now involved in a great controversy between Christ and Satan regarding the character of God, His law, and His sovereignty over the universe. This conflict originated in heaven when a created being, endowed with freedom of choice, in self-exaltation became Satan, God's adversary, and led into rebellion a portion of the angels. He introduced the spirit of rebellion into this world when he led Adam and Eve into sin. This human sin resulted in the distortion of the image of God in humanity, the disordering of the created world, and its eventual devastation at the time of the worldwide flood. Observed by the whole creation, this world became the arena of the universal conflict, out of which the God of love will ultimately be vindicated. To assist His people in this controversy, God sends the Holy Spirit and the loyal angels to guide, protect, and sustain them in the way of salvation. The devil's first major battle in his war to gain control of two universes (physical and spiritual) away from God ended in a resounding defeat (Luke 10:18). The Bible reveals, however, that he will soon launch three more major assaults against him. The last battle the devil initiates will be the final one that any spirit or human will ever start. Brother Aiden fights these battles in individual cases. What I'm most concerned with is what is happening now can be the beginning of a final battle. If this happens it will put us all in jeopardy. If this is still isolated cases and not the beginning of the end as we know it, then we have a chance to change events." "Wow! Father you are making my head spin. I am not sure what to think. Please tell me in the simplest of terms how does this affect me?" "Okay Jimmy, I believe that if we can get to Brother Aiden, he can possibly help you to enter a portal and possibly change the events of the night you were attacked. If that could be done you can enter a different dimension, a different reality where your family could be saved. I must warn you there is no guarantee we can get to Brother Aiden. I am not sure if we do meet with him, he will help you at this time. He seemed so concerned with what is taking place he might not be able to help you. Even if he will help you there is no guarantee it can be done." "Father, this all sounds like a science fiction book. I don't know what to say." "Of course, I understand. I will be leaving for England day after tomorrow. If you decide to come with me, I will take you to Brother Aiden. I will do my best to see if he can help you. I certainly can use the company. I am getting a little too old for this type of traveling. Think it over and I will speak with you tomorrow." "The doc said, I should be released tomorrow. I have a lot of thinking to do. Let's talk then"

CHAPTER 8

As Gulli is looking over the reports he turns to Jamie. "In some way, Jimmy made me think there is a connection with these murders and what happened to him. The problem is that the pattern just doesn't fit. A sicko serial killer carving his victims in Latin and someone smashing into Jimmy trying to kill him. Every M.O you can think of this has to be two separate incidents. Then Jimmy says he sees the face of his dead friend Stevie smiling at him. You put that together with the four bodies we found lying on this same friend Stevie. Well maybe there is some connection." "You believe Jimmy that this is dead friend is doing this?" "No, what I am saying there could be a connection. Maybe some kind of a revenge thing but every time I go there, I come up blank. The most logical thing is that Jimmy was in shock and for some reason Stevie came to his mind. Both incidents were traumatic so he connected them together. I know Jimmy a long time. We went through hell together in Viet Nam. I saw how he handled himself. He never panicked he always kept his cool. I'm talking under heavy fire, buddies getting killed. He made tough quick decisions involving life and death. If he says this was intentional, I believe him. The Stevie part is a puzzle. Do we have new reports and new information?" "No Gulls, nothing. It' been quiet maybe our killer is done for now. Still the same on the reports, no evidence and no leads. Our friend Otto was a big letdown. We thought the fifth person there was the guy. Otto seems legit he checks out. Has no connections to the victims. None prior to their meeting that night." "Okay, Jimmy is getting released tomorrow. I'm going to drive up and see how he is doing. I'll check in with the detective up there see if they have anything new." "Get some sleep tonight. I will talk to you tomorrow."

Stevie laughs as he lies on his bed." I loved Jimmy's face when he saw me smiling at him. Jennifer and the kids were definitely dead.

I have to admit didn't need to kill the kids but what are you going to do, shit happens. Jennifer, I would have preferred to do her in a better way. I just couldn't help myself. When I was watching them, I was so pissed, I just had to get it over with. Her happiness was making me sick. The perfect wife, perfect mother. Well she was a bitch who got me killed. I know I went off base and that was on me. I know I was supposed to send a message but I don't give a shit. I had to do it. I was going to wait but I snapped. Next time I will do it your way. This was my moment and I needed to get it done. Now it's back to work. Where shall I go. Lisa has been such a pleasure but maybe her usefulness is over. She is such an easy target. She presents no challenge at all. I think I'll go see her and let faith take its course. I should check on Jimmy and see if he is finished. I am pretty sure he was done too." Stevie rolled over and picked up the phone. "Lisa, what are you doing? Have any plans for tonight?"

Gulli was almost at the hospital. He couldn't stop running through the recent events, over and over. "Nothing on the car. It was stolen and there were no prints. Once again, no leads, no evidence, a big nothing. Well this fits in place with all the rest. This leads me to believe that this is connected. Whoever this is has been super lucky or very good covering his tracks?" Gulli goes in Jimmy's room. "Well look at you getting dressed. Looks like they are letting you go." "Yeah, I'm out of here." "How you feeling." "I'm sore but the Doc said I'm good to go. I'm glad you're here. Any news from the investigation?" "No, sorry Jimmy. The car was stolen but there are no prints, no evidence to go on so far." Father Thomas was in to see me yesterday. He was very kind and concerned. He told me some wild things that he has seen. I don't think you will believe any of it. I am not sure myself what to believe. The crazy thing is the bottom line he wants me to go to England with him." "Some type of vacation to get away from things?" "No, not exactly. I really don't know if you want to hear what he says. You will think we are both crazy." "Try me Jimmy. I want to hear it." "Okay, Here goes."

Jimmy tells Gulli exactly what Father Thomas told him yesterday. After he was done, Jimmy looked at Gulli, "I know this is so out there I must be nuts going with him. Here's the thing I have nothing here. My life is over. I lost my wife and kids. I have nothing to lose. I realize this is a fantasy but Father Thomas says he has witnessed these events himself. He is a priest I don't think he is lying and don't think he is crazy. I know he is old but there is something about what he says gives me a drop of hope. To me a drop no matter how small is better then what I have now. Staying here is killing me. I have to try something and as nuts as it sounds it's all I have. "I get it. Yeah, it does sound far out. Father Thomas is getting on in age and maybe his memory is playing tricks. I have to admit if I was in your shoes, I would probably do the same thing. Who knows maybe he is right? I have read about some of what he says and just maybe he can help. If you go back in time do me a favor and keep me out of Viet Nam." "Funny, I'll do that." "Have you heard from your old buddies?" "Yes, Sal and Ray were here late yesterday. They wanted to stay over but I told them I was being released today. I also told them I had some relatives in Italy that I was going to visit. You know, just to get away. I couldn't tell the truth. I only told you, that's it. Bad enough you think I'm nuts I didn't want them to also." "Before I go is there anything I can do to help?" "Yeah find Stevie Bracken and kill him again. Hopefully this time he will stay dead." "Jimmy, I don't know what to say but be careful and stay safe. If you need me just call. Love you buddy."

Next day Jamie calls to Gulli, "Otto is in room one." "Detective, I don't know why you want to see me again. I did not do anything to those people. I would never kill anyone. I never would hurt anyone. I was honest with you and told you everything that happened that night. I shouldn't be a suspect. I didn't do anything." "Listen Otto, you were the last person to see them alive. You will be a suspect until we can solve this case. That being said do I think you killed them, the answer is no. Just relax and take a breath. I want to go over the night again.   When you said you summoned a spirit what does that mean. Did you see him or it? "No, I felt it's presence. I was its conduit to speak to them. When this happens, I retreat into an altered state of consciousness. They could speak with the spirit. I don't know what is said. I cannot hear anything. I know you and many others think this is a scam. To be honest, I would guess ninety-five percent of so-called channels are scams. I and a few are not. This is a gift, that I have had since a child. I could be at a funeral and out of nowhere I would hear a voice. I could hear the spirit talking to me. I first thought I was a little crazy but after time I realized what it was. I studied and honed my ability. Yes, I have turned it into a career and I have done very well. I never dabbled in the dark side. I do it to give people closure and comfort. Knowing they could see their loved ones again. You know spiritus or channels are even in the bible The Bible has a story about a case where communication with the dead actually happened. King Saul did it. The spiritus at En-Dor put him in touch with the prophet/judge Samuel." "Okay Otto, I believe you believe what you are telling me." Tell me again why did you just stop and run away?" "Simple, I was scared. I never experienced anything like that before. I have had some unusual experiences but this was different. The spirit who I channeled was dark and evil. It was powerful to. It is hard to explain but it was taking over my body. I could feel it. It seemed to be coming alive and it broke through my state of consciousness. I panicked and ran. I didn't look back. I ran to my car and left." "When you say it was powerful and coming alive. Do you mean it was materializing like into a living entity, A real person?" "No but I don't know. As I told you before I never have gone to the dark side. There are ones and groups that do." "What do you mean?" "Well, there is a group a society who practice that type of channeling." "You mean like some type of a cult some sort of witches, voodoo, black magic?" "No, not like that. This is a secret society that believes in bringing up all the evil and destroying all the good. They believe that the Devil's ability to manipulate what comes from beyond the grave. The devil has appointed the <u>antichrist</u> who gathers "kings" in a placed called Armageddon. These kings, loyal to the antichrist, will gather their armies to wage war against the people of God. This society has representatives all around the world. Once they have gathered all their leaders in one place the final battle will take place." "So, this group is bringing back an evil dead army to take over the world?" "Detective I know this is all very hard to digest or believe. All I can tell you is what I know. I have been approached in some subtle ways to partake in their doings but I always refused. I cannot give you specifics because there are not any. As I said they are very subtle. The fact is they exist to what extent I really don't know." "Otto what does "Mageddo et nunc, EA incipit" mean to you?" "The final battle is now, it begins. Why do you ask?" "Otto, do you think you could have summoned one of these dead beings to life? Do you believe that could happen?" "Detective, I don't believe I could be responsible for something like that." "I'm asking you if it is possible, yes or no?" "I don't know." "Thanks for coming in. Do not leave the area you can be called in for more questioning. I do want to thank you for your help." Jamie looks at Gulli, "This case just gets weirder and weirder. I agree with you I think Otto is telling the truth. The problem is where are you going with this, are we looking at a dead zombie as our prime suspect?" "I know Jamie this case is getting more like a horror movie.

"Good morning Father, why did you want to see me? "Good morning detective. I wanted to talk to you about a letter I received from a friend of mine in England. "Sure, Father have a seat." "Thank you, this letter mentioned a number of murders that were happening over there." "Father, I only work the Island. I would love to go to England but I don't see the department picking up the tab for the trip." Father Thomas smiled, "Yes I am sure that would be a problem. The murders that have occurred have the same carvings in Latin. They believe it is more than just one serial killer. Some of these murders were hundreds of miles away. Some were in Italy, all around the same time. I thought you should know because I believe it's possible that in some way they might be connected." "That is very kind of you to let me know. This is something that I was not aware of. The coincidence is very interesting but I'm not sure how they can be connected. I'm going to have to look into this to see how the dates match up. It's possible some type of copycat murders are happening. Any other information in the letter I should know about?" "Well, that is a little difficult to explain. My friend believes that this is the beginning of a very trying time for all of humanity. I won't go into details because that would almost be impossible to explain. The simplest form of this is that the church believes there will be a final battle of good and evil. This can be the beginning of that time." "Are you talking about Armageddon and Revelations from the bible?" "That is possible but there are many other prophecies. Do you really want me to continue with this detective?" "Yes, Father please do." "There are some who believe the devil orchestrates the calling up of evil messengers to bring horror to mankind. This begins with individual acts like these murders. Sending a message that evil has risen and tempting God to interfere. After these evil messengers work as individuals then they are summoned to a special location where the devil appointed administer coordinates a savage attack on mankind. This administer is the leader of a society that believes in the devil and do his bidding. It is a secret and dark society that exists today. The elite members are thought to be located somewhere in Italy. Detective, I know this might sound like some rambling of an old priest but I assure you this is believed to be true. Not all members of the church believe in this but there are many who do. I'm going to England to see what I can do to help in this matter. I am mostly consulting more than anything else. I have worked in this field for many years and my dearest friend believes I can be of some help. I believe that they are trying to attain a meeting with the Pope himself on this. I asked Jimmy to come with me. I think it will do him good to get away. He could be a welcome traveling partner. There is also a possibility that we can help him if it is at all possible. I will not take up your time on how we might help Jimmy at this time." "Okay Father, you have given me a lot to think about and I appreciate you coming in. I am not the most religious person so I need to do some research on my own. I know you said they believe these murders are connected because of the carvings. Our killer has seemed to commit random murders without those carvings. Well, I'm just thinking out loud. I do agree with you on Jimmy. It can't hurt for him to get away for a while. I hope you have a safe and successful trip. Take care of my buddy. Father if there is anything else you think I should know please let me know. Here are all my numbers call me anytime." "Thank you, detective, I will."

CHAPTER 9

"Jen, where are you? I have a surprise for you." "I'm up in the bedroom." Jimmy runs up the stairs. "What are you doing?" "I'm packing what does it look like." "What kind of clothes are you packing?" "Winter clothes fool, it's cold upstate this time of year." "Well stop packing the winter clothes and pack your bathing suite. Some of your sexy sun dresses and your favorite flip flops." "What are you drunk? Why would I pack those to go upstate to my parents? Have you forgot where we are going?" "No but we have had a change of plans. Instead I have here two tickets to Cancun, Mexico. I spoke to your Dad and told him my plans. They are headed down here to stay with the boys and we are going to Mexico. I booked this fantastic all-inclusive hotel, for all the drinks and food we want. Just so you know it is eighty-five degrees there now. Like I said, pack your summer things." "This was okay with my parents? "Yeah, they loved the idea. They said we deserve a vacation by ourselves and they would love to have the boys to themselves a few days. I got a great deal on the vacation from my old army buddies' wife. His wife works for a travel agency and they had this special offer because they are promoting this brand-new hotel in Cancun. It's the first of a new chain where everything is included. They have a limited amount of the reservations and she got us two. This is going to be great. Look I know you love going upstate but we can do that anytime. This is a once in a lifetime thing. Are you okay with it?" "Jennifer empties her luggage on the bed. "Get out of my way I have to get my summer outfits. Am I okay with it are you kidding? I can't wait to get on that plane. This is fantastic, come here." "Jennifer pulls Jimmy and gives him a big kiss. I love you, you sweet beautiful husband.

"Jimmy this place is beautiful. The ocean is like perfect blue and I love the sun. I can't believe we are here. What do you want to do first, Pool, ocean, check out all the things to do?" "How about you come over here and join me on the bed? How does that sound?' "Great I would love to but first I want to go to the pool. The sun will be going down soon and then we can come back here. Please!" "Okay no problem."

Later that evening: "Babe, I'm starving what should we eat." "Well, they have a Chinese restaurant, Italian, French, German, Mexican of course, and Japanese. What does my darling desire?" "How about Japanese?" "I knew you would say that. I made a reservation at the Japanese for about ten minutes from now." "You are the best Husband in the world." "You got that right. Come on get going, don't want to miss the reservation."

"Wow this is fantastic. Look at the fountains, this is like being in Japan." "Here comes the chef. He is going to cook right in front of us. This is like a show, better, we eat and have fun."

A few hours later: Walking by the different little ponds, all lighted with different colors. A dock and walkway leading to a private hut in the pond. Jimmy and Jennifer enjoying a margarita as they sit, facing the beautiful winding pool. A warm sultry breeze gently passing through the palm trees. A large yellow moon shines above the ocean. A Mariachi Band walking the grounds and entertaining the guests. "Honey, I love our life and I love the boys but the way I feel right now I just want to stay here forever." "I know Jen, this is like a dream. One thing the Chef was Mexican, and so were all the waiters. It supposed to be a Japanese Restaurant. I mean the food was great but I thought that was a little bit strange. "Seriously, we are in Mexico, hello husband." Jimmy laughing, "Look I have to find something to complain about. It all has been so perfect, it's crazy." "Don't look for trouble just enjoy it. They have a tour bus going into the shopping district downtown Cancun, can we go tomorrow?" "For you sweetie, of course. Now that will give me something to bitch about. I'm just kidding, I will be fine with it. Besides you can't go on vacation and not shop. Right now, I honestly don't want to think about anything else. I'm in paradise with my beautiful wife, that's all I need." Jennifer leans over and kisses Jimmy slowly and whispers in his ear, "I think it's time to go back to our room."

"Wake up sleepy head. Come look at this view. It's so beautiful here." "I love it. I love being on vacation. I love it all. I always loved going on vacation. When we were eighteen Danny, Sal, Ray and me went up to the Catskills. We drove Sal's big ass Pontiac convertible. We get up there after driving in the hot sun for hours and were dying to get into the pool. Instead of going straight to the pool Sal says we have to wash his car first. He said he has to have a clean car to pick up girls. We wanted to kill him but we did it just to shut him up. We all go down to the pool except Sal. We're in our bathing suits hanging out at the pool. We're talking to these girls and finally Sal arrives. He is wearing this white safari like outfit. He comes over and sits. We introduce him to the girls and five minutes later he leaves. Ten minutes later he comes back with a different Hawaiian outfit on. We just shake our heads and the girls were laughing. He says outfits are very important when you're on vacation and we have no class. Later he leaves again and the girls invited us to their room later that night. Sal is very wary about this. He says it could be a set up. He's read about these things. It's a trap and when we get there, they have guys waiting to rob us." "You're, kidding, right?" "No, come on, you know Sal, he's paranoid. We go up to the room, of course Sal has a completely different outfit on. We go up to the door and we're just about to knock. Sal says to wait. He goes to the door and puts his ear to the door and tells us to keep quiet. We look at him like he's crazy but we let him do his thing. Then he gets down on the floor and tries to look under the door. We tell him enough let's just knock and go in. We knock and the girls let us in. Sal comes charging by us and starts looking in their closets, the bathroom, and under the bed, no lie, Jen. The girls think he is crazy but we all had a good laugh." "Then what happened?" "Can't say, it's a guys thing you know. The next day we go to the pool and are hanging out with the girls. Sal comes running out and yells here I come and dives head first into the pool. I'm sure he wanted to impress the girls. The problem is that he dove into the shallow part of the pool. It was a foot or so of water. He comes up with this huge gash on his head and bleeding like crazy. We get a towel on him and rush him to the hospital. As I told you I love vacations. Jimmy watches Jen laugh like crazy and then he hears,

"Jimmy opens his eyes smiles and looks straight at Father Thomas, "What the hell, where am I?" "Jimmy we are on the plane. You must have been dreaming, you were out for quite a while. Are you okay?" "I'm sorry Father, I guess I was dreaming. The strangest thing it was so real. I mean it wasn't like any other dream I have had. It was so real. I could taste the food; I felt my wife and it was like she was never killed. It sounds crazy but I could swear I was there and not here. Father, I was never in Mexico but I could see the Hotel perfectly. I can describe it in perfect detail. I was at a Japanese Restaurant and I can see a Mexican Chef. I saw the pool; I heard the band and I could still taste the food." Father Thomas smiles, "You know some people believe there are alternate realities. In one reality you would be here with me and in another, you could be with your wife and sons. In my life, I have witnessed and seen some very unusual things. I have worked with Brother Aiden on this very subject. I believe that there are ways to send one into different realities. This is one of the reasons that I wanted you to come with me to see him." "Father, exactly what are you saying? Do you believe this Brother could help me cross into another reality where my wife and sons are still alive?" "Look Jimmy, I don't want to get your hopes up on something like that. I shouldn't have said that. I want you just to meet with Brother Aiden and see if he thinks he can help you. He has a way of seeing things a little different then we do. Just try to relax and let faith take its course. I know you will have many questions but for now let's be patient." "Patient? Father I lost my wife and my kids. I lost my life. I would do anything to have them back. I have no idea why I am going on this trip with you. I don't care about any of this. For some reason I have this feeling that you can help me. Help me some way to find some answers to what has happened to me. When you say things like this alternate realty can be true, that gives me some kind of hope. Please understand I want to help you and do what I can. The real reason I'm with you is that I believe you know something that could help me. This Brother Aiden and this monastery work is some kind of deep mysterious dealings that I don't have a clue about. Please anything you can tell me that gives me some type of reason to go on, please tell me. Don't worry about getting my hopes up because that is all I have."

"Okay Jimmy, I will tell you some things that I and Brother Aiden believe. There are some portals, openings that lead to an alternate reality and dimensions. There comes a time in just about all of our lives that we make decisions that send us in one direction. If we could go back and change that direction it could alter our lives dramatically. Look at it like a crossroad, if you take one path you would go in one direction. If you choose the other path it's a totally different direction leading to a different destination. These different destinations have many different results. Let say the crossroad you took ended in a bad destination it would be wonderful if you could go back and choose the other road. Well Brother Aiden has worked on this theory for many years. In life once we have chosen one path we cannot go back in time and change directions. The scientific community would and are seeking ways of connecting these realities or dimensions their way. Brother Aiden believes in the spiritual way to connect these realities. He believes on the calling of messengers or angels to help us achieve this gateway to a different reality. There are many problems that go along with this happening. Once an evil destination has been achieved there are dark forces or evil messengers that work to prevent this from happening. This is the on-going fight between good and evil. Also, if the crossing into another reality was accomplished there is no guarantee the results would be the way we want it to be. For instance, in your case you lost your family in the horrible car tragedy. If you went back and changed the path or decision not to go on that trip, we do not know how the results would turn out. It's possible you stayed home and this maniac that you say tried to kill you did it in a different way. That could mean you could have been killed. We are not sure that if you crossed into another reality or dimension you would have that same memory. These are all unknowns. What complicates matters is the letter I received from Brother Aiden. He did not go into detail but there is a big concern that some of what I have been telling you has been happening. He believes that there is a dark society that has been at work in calling on dark messengers to help in bringing the evil from the depths of hell to wreak-havoc on the world. With the final battle to control the world. This society some have called it the Illuminati or the Priory of Sion but in truth I don't believe it has a name. Some say they have a tattoo with the face of an owl on their chest. The owl is not for wisdom but representative of the devil and his schemes.

I am not sure if he can take the time to see if he could help. We go back along time so I will ask him as a favor to me. I do believe he will help. I will ask you to trust me. You have a lot to think about. Once we are there you can speak with Brother Aiden. He will explain all the risks, the unknowns and the possible results. I think we can help each other. I need your company and assistance on this trip. Hopefully this trip could help you find some closure, in one way or another." "Thanks Father, I appreciate your honesty and advice. I have nothing left but hope. If there is even the slimmest of possibilities, I will do whatever it takes. I am not sure of how this fight between good and evil works but I never would back away from fighting against any evil. I have been through hell before in Viet Nam, so I would not let that stop me from trying to get my family back." "Then we are off to the monastery and a meeting with destiny."

Rome Italy: Small Italian restaurant one kilometer from Via

Vittorio Veneto and the US Embassy.

"Has everything been to your liking?" "Yes, Salvatore, as always." "Can I get you some more wine or a liqueur?" "What's that one that tastes like chocolate?" "Yes, I know exactly the one. I will be right back. Should I close the door for some privacy?" "Yes, thank you." "Oliver, you know it has begun?" "I'm aware." "Will he be pleased?" "You know he is never pleased. This is like a small seed that has been planted. He wants a full garden. "Have the arrangements been made?" "Yes, the meeting will be at the summer villa. We have notified all the members and they have responded. How many seeds have been planted so far?" "A total of nineteen. All of them as we orchestrated except for one." "What do mean except one?" "There was a separate calling in the U.S. we did not orchestrate. He left the correct markings but we knew nothing about it." "A copy-cat?" "Yes, I would imagine." "Has he been caught?" "No." "Well, I guess that just adds a little more seed to our garden. I will have one more contact with him before the final meeting. It is not pleasant contacting him. You never know what the outcome will be. He has a thirst that cannot be quenched. This is what he has been waiting for from the beginning. He will return as a king of all the world." "If all goes well?" "If it doesn't, then we all pay the consequences, of course. All these seeds are a diversion to the real plan." "Yes, we have set in motion so many different fires they will be engulfed in trying to solve, they will not see the big picture. From sickness, to food shortages, water contamination, serial killers all over the world. We have our members in place and we will bring the world to its knees. He will see the final battle and the he will rule as he prophesied. He then will finally be pleased." "Gentleman, sorry to interrupt but I have your after-dinner liqueur." "Thank you, Salvatore."

CHAPTER 10

"Lisa, you look fantastic." "Smooth talker Stevie, right? Bet that's what you say to all the girls." "No, you're the only Lisa I know." "Come on in. I want you to meet my cousin Charlie. He is visiting from Buffalo." "Hi Steve, I'm glad to meet you. Lisa told me we are going to the race track. I'm so excited, I have never been to one. I know they allow betting so I have my lucky rabbits foot with me. How many races are there? Are all the horses the same color? I mean can you tell them apart? How much do you have to bet? Are there different horses in every race?" "Slow down there Charlie that's a lot of questions. Lisa can I speak to you alone?" "Sure, come in the kitchen. What's the matter everything all right?" "I didn't know we would have company today? I mean I kind of thought we were going to spend the day together." "Oh, I'm sorry, Charlie kind of surprised me. I really didn't know he was coming today. I didn't want to just leave him and I didn't want to cancel our date. I didn't know what to do so I just asked him if he wanted to join us. As you can see, he was pretty excited about coming." "Yeah, I could tell, he is definitely excited." "I'm sorry Stevie, I'll just tell him we would rather go alone." "No, it's okay, I'm good with it." "Thanks, you're sweet. He does get a little clingy and he does ask a lot of questions. He also talks a lot. We grew up together when we were kids before his family moved to Buffalo. He really is a sweet guy if you just give him a chance. He kind of grows on you." "No problem, let's get going, it'll be fun. Just the three of us." Lisa smiled," Thanks." Stevie watched Charlie walk to the car. He had a bad limp on his right side, so he walked kind of slow. Stevie just smiled and thought, "Maybe I'll just push him in front of the horses to get rid of him. No, I don't think that would be appreciated by Lisa." As they drive off Charlie leans forward from the back seat. His face is almost in Stevie's ear. "Steve, do you know any of these horses?" "Not personally." Stevie smiles. "No silly, you Know what I mean. Do you know who might win?" "Well, if I knew who would win there would not be much fun watching them. The answer is no. I just look at the program and pick a horse." "I see, can you help me pick a horse? I could just pick a number or maybe a color. They do wear different colors"" "You mean the horses?" Lisa taps Stevie," Don't be mean, be nice." "Yes Charlie, the jockeys wear different colors." "How much money did you ever win? Do you normally win when you go?" "The answer to your first question is not much and the second question is no." "I hope I win. I'm a bit of a sore loser. I like winning and really don't like losing, especially money. Losing money is really bad. I went to bingo up in Buffalo with my aunt and I lost all night. Not one time did I get bingo. Could you imagine all night just watching other people winning?" "I can't imagine sounds like a bummer of a night. What about you Lisa, do you like winning or losing?" Lisa just looked at Stevie and shook her head. "I'm just asking, I think me and Charlie would like to know?" "Winning." "Okay then, let it be known we all like winning." "I hope we will be able to get in. Do you think it could be so crowded they might not have any seats left?" "Don't worry Charlie, there will be plenty of seats.

"Wow, this is cool. What a beautiful Race track. I love watching the horses run. They are really fast, right Steve?" "Yes, they do run fast, Charlie." "Lisa, I'm going to get a drink. I really need one bad. What would you like?" "Just a coke would be great." "Lisa turns to Charlie, "What can Stevie get for you?" "Oh, a milk shake or maybe an ice cream soda." Stevie looks at Charlie and then at Lisa, thinking, "You got to be kidding me with this guy. A milk shake, seriously." "Okay, got it. I'll be right back. A few minutes later. "Sorry, Charlie, no go on the shake but here's a coke." "That's alright, thanks. I'm trying to decide on what horse to bet on. I thought me and Lisa could go partners and bet as a team. You want to be in with us, Steve?" "No, I think I will do my own betting." "Okay, but can you recommend a horse? Does the horse have to win? I heard you can bet on the horse to finish second or third? Is that right?" "Yes, it's called place and show." "Well that makes it a little easier to win. I like that because I don't like losing. Now, what horse do you think me and Lisa should bet on?" "I don't know, Charlie why don't you just close your eyes and pick one." Lisa could tell Charlie was driving Stevie crazy, "Charlie, pick a number from one to twelve. I'll do the same and then we will bet on both of them. If we win, we split the money." "Yes, that's a great idea. Stevie realized he was letting Charlie get under his skin and he didn't want Lisa to get turned off on him. He decided to try to be nice. "Lisa, are you okay being here?" "Yeah, it's fine. I've never been here either. I think it was a good idea to come. "I want you to not worry about us we are fine. Please bet and do what you like to do." Stevie smiled and said to Charlie, "What do you do for fun up in Buffalo?" "Well, I belong to the Moose lodge. We have social dances and bingo. All kinds of things." "Moose Lodge and you live in Buffalo. So, I guess your part of the herd?" Stevie laughed and Lisa had to chuckle at that. Charlie seemed confused, "Herd, I don't know about a heard?" "You know Charlie Buffalo, Moose, herd." "Oh, yes, I never heard that before. I guess I'm part of a herd." "Okay then, I'm ready to bet. You guys ready?" "Yes, the number one is mine and the nine for Lisa." "Great how much, and to win, place or show?" "One dollar to finish third." "One dollar apiece?" "Of course, silly." "Okay, I will go and place the bets." "Steve, would you mind if I came with you? I would like to see how it is done." "Sure, Why not." Stevie walked with Charlie right behind him as he thought to himself. "I can take him in the bathroom and choke him to shut him up. The problem is what do I tell Lisa. For some reason I care about her and I don't want to blow it. It's only one day and hopefully he shuffles off back to Buffalo." Stevie patiently explains how to bet step by step. He listens to Charlie go on and on about all types of crap. The day goes by and he gets to spend some time with Lisa in between answering Charlie's questions. The crazy thing is Stevie is having a good day with hitting two exacters and a few straight winners. Charlie is not happy as he and Lisa have lost six dollars apiece. Just after the seventh race Charlie has a mini meltdown. "This is just awful, again our horses finished seventh and ninth. I hate losing, I just hate it. I'm so upset." Lisa smiles at Charlie, "It's not that bad. We still have a couple of races to go. Our luck can change." "Look Charlie, I'll pick a horse for you and Lisa, this race. Give me your dollar and leave it up to me." "Okay Steve here. What's another dollar?" Stevie winks at Lisa and smiles, "I'll be right back." Stevie places his bets and waits there until the race ends. He sees the seven-horse won, which he didn't bet on. He goes back to Lisa and Charlie and with a big smile, "Charlie it's your lucky day. I bet an exotic bet and hit a triple for you. Here is twenty-five dollars for you and twenty-five dollars for Lisa." "Oh my God, are you serious, we won? This is fantastic, oh what a great day. This is so wonderful, I am so happy, I never won anything close to this. Thank you, thank you, Lisa we won." Charlie gives Lisa a big hug and then goes right at Stevie. He grabs Stevie and gives him a huge hug. "Would you pick another horse for us Steve in the next race?" "You know Charlie, I think we should quit while we are ahead. I say we head out and go have some dinner, on me." "I agree with you. I would rather leave now a winner then take any more chances. I'm starving." As they walk to the parking lot Charlie is chatting away how he had such a great time. Most of all how much he loves winning. Lisa pulls Stevie by the arm and talks in his ear. "Amazing how you bet one race for us and win fifty dollars on a dollar bet. That is just so lucky and fortunate for Charlie." "Well, first of all it was a two-dollar bet and those triples pay off big." Lisa kisses Stevie on the cheek, "Sure Stevie, and thank you, you made Charlie so happy." "Just plain luck, Lisa."

Back in the car:

"Steve, did you read there could be a serial killer around? This stuff really scares me. I read that there were four people found in a cemetery Halloween night. There were some others killed too. I read this in the morning paper that you get around here. My goodness how scary is that. I will tell you one thing while I'm down here I will not go out alone. I don't think you and Lisa should either. I say let's just stay home until they find the killer. I think the daytime would be safe but nights oh no. I think most serial killers would kill at night. Don't you think I'm right?" "Makes sense, you would think." Stevie was not happy about where this conversation was going. "Lisa, where would you like to go for dinner?" "Oh, I'm fine with any place you think is good. Italian would be nice." "Italian, yes that sounds just yummy. I love Italian food. You know that Buffalo has a large Italian community. There are tons of Italian restaurants all around Buffalo. I have to admit I have had my share of Italian food. What about you Steve? You like Italian food? Do you think it's safe being out tonight? We should eat real soon so we can get home before it's too late. Did I mention I am starving?" Stevie looked at Charlie in the mirror thinking," Of course your starving, as he looked at Charlie's round chubby face. He wasn't that tall and very chunky. He wore wide frame glasses but wasn't ugly kind of a cute roly-poly dude. "Don't worry Charlie I know a good Italian restaurant not far at all. I promise I will not let anything happen to us. I don't believe all that serial killer stuff you read. They just want to sell newspapers. They probably OD on drugs or something." "No Steve I read they had some kind of carvings on their bodies. How sick is that? You know I do feel safe with you Steve. I am not going to let that spoil my night or my visit. You know Lisa is my favorite cousin. She is more like a sister. I love her to pieces." "Ahh, Charlie you are so sweet. You are my favorite cousin too. I wish you lived down here. Then we could see each other all the time. It would be just like if we were kids again." "Stevie almost went off the road when he heard that. "Well you know I don't think there are too many if any Moose Lodge around here. Plus, you are a part of the heard up in Buffalo, right Charlie?" "Oh, you're wrong. There are plenty of Moose Lodge's all over the country. I am pretty happy up in Buffalo. You know my Mom needs me around anyway. I take her shopping all the time. We love going to the Mall. You know we have one of the largest Malls up there. You know my mom don't like driving so she counts on me to take her. You know I have thought about going out on my own but to be honest I'm scared to live by myself. Although if I could live with someone, I feel comfortable with. Lisa, wouldn't it be crazy if I came down here and stayed with you?" Lisa stuttered, "That would be great but you have to think about your mom." "True, she would be lost without me. Are we close to the restaurant? I'm famished." Stevie went as fast as he could to the restaurant. After a wonderful dinner, they walked to the car. "Let's hurry and get in the car. Walking at night now makes me nervous." Considering the circumstances somehow Stevie enjoyed the day. He felt good walking and holding Lisa's hand. Every opportunity he had he would get in a kiss. Lisa was very obliging and this made him feel great. He was even starting to like Charlie. He was defiantly annoying but there was something about him, he kind of grew on you. As they got into the car Charlie grabbed Stevie's hand. "Thank you this was wonderful. The dinner and the whole day were perfect. I have to admit I was a little annoyed when I was losing, not sure if you noticed. Then when you picked the winner for us, I was delighted. You know I love to win and hate to lose. When we get back to Lisa's how about we play a board game. I love playing board games. It will be just like we were kids, Lisa. One problem is that when I lose, I can get a little upset. I don't like losing you know." Stevie smiled, "Let me guess you like winning, right?" "Yes, Steve you're getting to know me." Lisa knew Stevie had enough of Charlie for one day, "It's getting kind of late maybe another time." "Yeah, 'I will drop you off maybe some other time." They pulled in front of Lisa's apartment and into a parking spot. Lisa took her key out of her pocketbook and said, "Charlie would you mind going in first and give me a few minutes with Stevie?" "Oh, oh yes I get it. I have been kind of the third wheel, haven't I? Well, you take as long as you need to chat and I will see if I can watch some TV before bed. I like to watch TV before I go to bed. It relaxes me and I feel better. Well, off I go and once again thank you so much Steve, I had a great time. Hope to see you real soon." "No problem Charlie, I'm sure we will, good night." Charlie went running to the door as if a ghost was chasing him. As he got to the door he turned and gave a big wave. Lisa turned to Stevie, "I too want to thank you. It was a fun day and a great dinner. I know Charlie can be a little much but you were great." Lisa pulled Stevie close and kissed him tenderly. They kissed and embraced for a while. "I better get in I don't want Charlie to panic and call the cops. Can we get together soon? I would really like that." "You bet, I will call you tomorrow and we will make plans. Lisa smiled, "No board games, I promise." Stevie drove off feeling great. It was like he was a new person. The anger and the rage in him seemed to be gone. He felt like a normal person and he was crazy about Lisa.

Later that night at the motel:

Stevie laid in bed looking up at the ceiling. All he could think about was Lisa. It was like he was a different person. He felt like the person he used to be. Everything was so confusing. All parts of memories of different lives. He had a glimpse of when he was happy and being with his friends. Having flashes of a normal happy life. Then flashes of violence, revenge and hatred. He was torn between two different people. He seems to have thoughts of different lives, different worlds. He knew where he was. He knew the area; he was in a world he knew well. Yet he felt like a stranger in his own skin. Almost as if he had all these bad dreams. He could see himself in a rage needing to cause pain. To seek revenge on an old friend. To kill for money or just for the sake of killing. Now it seems he has changed. He wants just to be with Lisa. He has no more desire to hurt anyone. He wants to live the life he should have had. He is trying hard to block the bad thoughts out of his mind. Anytime he drifts back he thinks of Lisa and he calms down. She has restored his life. He has decided to start all over again. He feels that he has been given another chance. He wants to be happy and enjoy life. He closes his eyes and drifts off to sleep, smiling, thinking of Lisa.

A few hours later he wakes up in a cold sweat. He feels sick. His body is trembling and his hands are shaking. He forces himself to go into the bathroom. He washes his face with cold water. He stands over the sink and begins to relax. He looks into the mirror and a cold-chill shoot down his spine. The reflection in the mirror is distorted. He senses a voice crackling not natural, "You were returned to perform my will. I need you to please me. You must thirst for blood to kill. You are now part of the beginning of the end. You were brought back by chance but now you must serve on my behalf. You are not who you think you are. You are an undead, caught between worlds never dead but you should not be alive. If you do my wishes you can remain. If you continue to defy me you will pay dearly. Once you continue my deeds and follow the thoughts that I place in you then and only then you can remain. If you do not obey me you will die permanently and suffer for all eternity. You have no choice but to do my bidding. Continue to destroy to kill and spread fear. You can start with the two you were with today. Kill them and mark them "EA INCIPIT" You must do what I say." Stevie took his fist and smashed the mirror. "Screw you, it's my life. I am alive and I will do what I want. I am not that person anymore." He looked at his hand it was covered in blood. He took a towel and wrapped it up to stop the bleeding, He went and sat on the bed. "That was not real. I must have had some bad food or something. That was some type of nightmare. He swung around and laid back in bed thinking of Lisa and tried to go back to sleep.

CHAPTER 11

Gulli looks at Jamie, "Did I ever tell you that you're pretty decent looking for a cop?" "Are you hitting on me partner?" "Never, we are partners and besides I'm old enough to be your father." "Well, you're not that old but yes we are partners." I'll buy the next round, Scotch neat? I think we deserve a night like this. This case is wearing. There are so many special units on this, it's nuts. I've been thinking about your friend Jimmy. He said he was sure it was his old friend that ran into him. That he smiled and seemed to enjoy his suffering. Why do you think he thought that?" "Look, he was probably in shock. Your mind plays tricks. I know it is weird that the gravestone was on the same guy. He couldn't have known that. I guess a big coincidence.?" "You believe that?" "I know, but what else? The guy is dead. Dead men don't drive. This whole case is screwy. No leads, nothing." "You and Jimmy were close, right?" "Yeah, we met in the Army. We served together in Viet Nam. We became like brothers. He is a stand-up guy. We seen plenty of shit over there. He did his job, no matter what. We all knew he had our back." "You never talk about the war?" "What is there to talk about. It sucked. We all did our best to stay alive and keep each other alive. The war was bullshit and we all knew it. It wasn't like the old-World War Two movies where we were heroes liberating countries. They looked at us as invaders. It was their land their country. Half the time you couldn't tell who the enemy was. Women, kids, farmers, Viet Cong, their army. The heat, the bugs, the damn rain. It was like hell all we wanted was to come home. When we did come home there were no parades. No welcome home signs, no cheers for the conquering heroes. They spit on us, called us baby killers. Most of the guys are still paying the price. I have a number of buddies dying of exposure from agent orange. So many couldn't adjust to a normal life." "What was agent orange?" "It was to kill forest areas that might conceal Viet Cong and North

Vietnamese forces and destroying crops that might feed the enemy. They said it was no harm to us. The shit was delivered in large barrels with color-coded bands painted around storage drums. Orange bands meant to identify the chemical. They then just called it agent orange." "Gulli, tell me one story about your experience there, just one. I'll even buy another round." Seriously, you have nothing better to do then to listen to old war stories. Wouldn't you rather go to some club, or something more exciting than sitting here with me?" "Listen to you, what am I some teenager, or party girl. I'm a cop, just like you. This is what I do. This is where I want to be. Come on, just a story. You are the only guy I know that was there. I'll tell you one of my college stories about us coeds. I know you guys like that stuff." "What are we like kids you show me yours and I'll show you mine?" "Yup, come on, a short one or long."

"That's an offer I can't refuse. After about eight months into my tour, Sargent Willie calls us together and tells us we have a new Lieutenant taking over. He was all gung-ho right out of officer's candidate school in the states. He had an attitude that he was going to win the war by himself. His first course of business was to call our platoon for a full out inspection. Sargent Willie introduced him to us as Lieutenant Burley. We hadn't had an inspection since we were in the states. We all started mumbling what a bunch of bullshit this was. The Lieutenant was wearing a baseball cap with a big letter "B" on it. He was from Boston but he explained the "B" was for Burley's rangers. Guess what? That was what we are going to be called from now on. I turned to Jimmy and said, "Oh shit what an asshole." All the guys around started to laugh. Sargent Willie called us to attention and to get in formation. The Lieutenant started to tell us that we will lead the way. Night patrols, ambush missions, whatever it took, he will lead us to get the job done. These were the worst missions that he was going to volunteer us for. We were lined up in formation for the inspection and he walks down checking our gear. He comes to my buddy Gordan where he stops and looks at his rifle, "Soldier this rifle is unacceptable." He takes the rifle and sticks it muzzle down in the sand about six inches. Then barks at Gordan, "I want to see this weapon cleaned in a half hour, now pick up your weapon and get back in formation." The Lieutenant stood face to face with Gordan. Gordan was an African American, over six feet tall and built solid. He came from a tough area and did not take shit from anyone. The Lieutenant was five feet nine, black hair, good looking, in perfect physical condition. He looked like he came out of a movie poster. As they were face to face, Gordan just stood his ground and you could see steam coming from his ears. One unwritten rule is that no one screws around or even touches another soldier's weapon. We all knew our weapons were cleaned, oiled and could pass any inspection. We had been here for long enough and knew our weapons were keeping us alive. This ass hole was trying to show he was now in control and was a tough guy. Even Sargent Willie was shocked at the action taken by the Lieutenant. Gordan looked the Lieutenant in the eye, "You stuck my weapon in the sand so you fucking clean it." Gordan's eyes were glued into the Lieutenant and you could see he was about to kill him. Burley started to respond to Gordan but Sargent Willie stepped in between them, "Lieutenant, we have to talk." Sargent Willie then ushered Lieutenant Burley into the tent. We could not hear everything that he was saying but we heard enough. He told him that is not the way to treat soldiers. If he wanted to have the respect of his outfit, he better change his attitude quickly or he would not survive over here. Sargent Willie's talk definitely worked because Lieutenant Burley came out of the tent, pulled the rifle out of the sand and apologized to Gordan for his actions.

After a few weeks went by, he did adjust to us, but that did not stop him from volunteering us for all the shit assignments. One of his self-serving, search and destroy missions, backfired on him big time. What was different on this mission was we had the use of a canine unit for the first time. The unit consisted of a trained team of a German Sheppard and his Corporal handler. The duty of the Corporal and his German Sheppard were to be up front and lead the patrol. The canine was trained to sniff, hear, and see for traps, VC, and ambush. If the dog sensed any of these he stops and points to the danger, the Corporal handler signals to the unit to take proper action. The Corporal uses hand signals to communicate. As we moved up the mountain and through the jungle bush and elephant grass the dog got excited indicating there was something in front. The dog started to slowly run heading towards the top of the hill. At that point Lieutenant Burley was positioned behind the dog and his handler instead of where a squad leader would normally be in the middle. Now our fearless leader decides to run ahead of the dog and his handler. The dog was in a controlled run, gets excited and begins to chase Lieutenant Burley. He jolts ahead and the Corporal trying to keep up with them trips and falls. His rifle goes off accidently and shoots Lieutenant ass-hole in the ass. He goes down with a loud scream. We all gathered around our fallen hero setting up a perimeter of defense. Our medic checked and bandaged the wound which was just a graze and not life threatening. He called in a chopper anyway and our leader was evacuated to the base camp at Pleiku. I'm not sorry to say that was the last time we ever saw or heard from Lieutenant Burley. We were sure that Lieutenant Burley was going to be very proud when he gets the Purple Heart medal pinned on him. Back in the states we were sure he would put quite a spin on how and where he was wounded. I'm sure it will be in a fierce battle. A few weeks later we got a replacement for Lieutenant Burley. He was a seasoned Lieutenant who immediately earned the respect of our platoon. It was after his first speech where he said it was his number one priority to get us home safe. We will do our share and only our share and we will survive. He was not here to win medals just do his job and keep us safe. He was the total opposite of Lieutenant Burley. His final words of his speech were a bronze star doesn't look good on a mohair suit. Amen." Jamie smile and sips her drink. "I can't believe you got me going on this old shit. It's ancient history. Now your turn. How about those coed stories you had?" "The ones in the dorms? Sorry Gulli, I never went away to college. I stayed here on the Island and went to Hofstra. I drove back and forth and lived with my parents." "You have to be shitting me. You tricked me." "Yeah but I did buy the drinks".

CHAPTER 12

Over the loud speaker the captain announced they were beginning their final descent into Heathrow Airport. "Father, how come we are landing here. Isn't it a long way from the Scottish border? You had told me where we are going was close to Scotland." "Yes, that's true. I had a bad experience out of the airport there and I always prefer Heathrow. I always enjoyed the bus ride up through the north. I have always met the nicest and most interesting people along the way. I hope you don't mind the long bus ride. I'm sorry I should have told you about it." "No problem I was just curious. I have been thinking of my old friend Danny. When we were at the cemetery you said some things that didn't register at the time. For some reason I have been thinking of them. That day you said something like Danny and good messengers saved lives and altered realities. I asked you if you ever knew Danny? You said that was a question you could not answer. Why did you say that?" "At that time there was no reason to answer that. To be honest even today it is a difficult question for me. I told you I have worked with Brother Aiden on many occasions in dealing with good and bad messengers. There were many times that we tried to help people back to a better life or reality. The problem is most of the times I have very little or no memories of the results. As I tried to explain that we believe there are multiple dimensions and same for the realities. If we succeeded in changing one's reality it seems we are not part of that new reality. In a way that person that we helped into a different dimension left us in another dimension. So, we have no memory of it. This is so confusing and almost impossible to explain. When you asked about Danny, I have some memory of him. He had a situation that he seemed to be caught between dimensions and realities. We tried to help him return to the one where he was happy and belonged. The problem is I never know if the results are good or bad. One of the things I told you is that there is no guarantee that the results are the one you might want. If we were successful in helping Danny it's possible, he is alive and in another dimension. The one that I exist in now, he has died at that club. We could have been successful in sending him back to change his destiny but the outcome is not good. To answer your question did I ever know Danny? I am not sure. I have memories of him but as you can see, he died so many years ago that I couldn't have known him. Are my memories an illusion, a dream, or am I in a different reality then he is?" "Oh shit, I am totally confused. I don't know what to say." Jimmy sat back thinking, "Is Father Thomas nuts. What did I get myself into? I can't begin to make any sense of what he is saying. He could just be senile and delusional. He knew Danny but maybe he didn't. He could have helped him to another dimension where he died at twenty or maybe not? This could be a big mistake coming with him. "Jimmy, I know what you must be thinking that is why I couldn't answer you at the cemetery. I don't really understand how this is all possible. I do believe that we have helped people, to return to a time where they were able to change the outcome of their life. I do believe that Brother Aiden can help you. I also believe that there are portals that lead to different dimensions and he can help you return to the dimension where you want to be. I cannot promise it but I believe that it can be done. If you don't believe in me or trust me then you should return home as soon as we land," "I don't know what to think or believe. To return home to what? I have no more home. Without Jen and my sons, I have no home or life. If there is one chance in a million that this Brother Aiden can help me enter some portal and get my life back, I want to try. At this point I have nothing to lose. From this point I'm willing to roll the dice and go along with anything you say to do. I might be just as crazy as you but I don't care. I need to believe in something so I choose to believe in you."

"WELCOME TO HEATHROW AND LONDON"

St. Marks, at Via Maggio 18, Florence, Italy

Father Cabrini put out the last candle and entered his office. It was late but Father wanted to do some paper work. It was nice and quiet just the way he liked. Father Cabrini was loved by all in the parish He has been at St Marks for twenty-two years. He just had surgery that kept him from saying mass for the last three weeks. He was now writing thank notes to the many who had sent him so many thoughtful get well wishes. He took it upon himself to write them and attach a personal thank you. He loved people and they loved him. He was seventy-four years old. His seventy-fifth birthday was coming soon. He was a medium sized man with grey hair and small round glasses. He was looking forward to this Sunday he will be saying mass for the first time in weeks. In the back of the church a large man opened the door and walked towards the front. He was dressed in black and wore a black long coat. He slowly walked around the front pews and around the left side of the alter. There was a small hallway that led to the back of the church. He walked down the hallway and approached the back door leading to the small office. As he slowly opened the door, he saw Father Cabrini at his desk cleaning his glasses. He quickly came behind the Father and in one motion pulled a wire choker out and wrapped it around the father's throat and pulled it tight. Father Cabrini tried to react but he had no chance. He died quickly. The killer took out his knife and carved Nunc tempus est he wiped his blade and slowly walked out of the church.

St Wilfred's 15 Church Ln, Ripon HG4 2ES, United Kingdom

Father Edmund walked around the church. He does this almost every night. Father Edmund is about six feet one well-conditioned who has just turned forty-four years old. He is a handsome man and very popular with the female parishioners. He coaches the adjoining school soccer team. They have been one of the best teams ever since Father Edmund arrived. He didn't become a priest until he was thirty-eight years old. He served in the British Navy for four years. He thought he would marry and raise a family someday. Before becoming a priest, he was a high school history teacher. He loved his job and his students. One day while he was on his way home from a school function, he stopped at a local store to pick up a few items. It wasn't very late but the store was getting ready to close. As he approached the counter to pay for his items, he noticed a young man enter. There was something about the man that seemed to be odd. He seemed very upset and was almost shaking as he walked through the store. For some reason he decided to re-enter the store. The clerk asked him if everything was okay with his order and he said yes. He looked for the strange man but he didn't see him. As he started to walk to the back a woman was walking quickly to check out. The man seemed to appear from nowhere and pushed the woman to the floor. He then went to the register clerk an demanded all the money. Father Edmund approached the man saying, "Don't do this. I can give you some money, just stop and think what you're doing." Father Edmund came closer to the man and in a split second the man turned and stabbed Father Edmund in the upper stomach. The woman screamed, the man took a handful of money and ran. Father Edmund fell to the floor. He was bleeding badly. The woman bent over him and wrapped a handful of tissues on his wound. She screamed at the clerk to get her a towel or something to cover the wound and to call an ambulance. He tossed her a towel and called. Father Edmund laid there and looked at the woman. He silently prayed to God to save him. He wasn't ready to die. The women stayed with him trying her best to stop the bleeding until the ambulance came. They rushed him to the hospital and he was in the ICU for five days, fighting for his life. After he was moved to a regular unit his family gathered around him. The Doctor came in and told him he was a lucky man to be alive. If it wasn't for the woman helping him, he would have died. She happened to be a trauma nurse and knew what she was doing. From that day Father Edmund decided to devote his life to God and become a priest. As Father Edmund knelt at the alter saying his nightly prayer a stranger dressed in a black long coat entered the church. Quickly and quietly he walked up to the alter. He approached Father Edmund with a wire choker in his hand. He swung the wire around Father Edmunds neck and started to pull. Father Edmund instinctively swung his elbow and hit the attacker in the stomach. The attacker moved back and Father Edmund turned and punched him in the head. The attacker went down and the choker fell to the floor. Father Edmund reached for the choker. The attacker pulled out a large knife and lunged at the Father. He was quick to defend himself and grabbed the attacker's hand. They both fell to the ground. The Father was trying to wrestle the knife away. They both rolled over and the knife then penetrated the stomach of the attacker. Father Edmund looked at the man took off his shirt and wrapped the wound as best he could. He then quickly called for the police and an ambulance. When the police came Father told them what happened. The EMT's were getting a stretcher ready for the attacker. He could barely move but he reached into his pocket. He pulled out a small pill put it in his mouth and swallowed. In a few seconds he convulsed and died. They all were shocked as it happened so fast. The Inspector asked Father Edmund if he was trying to rob him? Father explained he did not think so, he was just trying to kill him. Inspector asked if he knew him and again, he said no. The inspector asked some more questions but it seemed this was a random attack, with no real motive.

Rome:

Oliver sat back in his chair and listened to the report from Jacob. "It was a very successful night. Five priests were killed. One in France, two in Italy, two in the UK. one failed. He was not successful somehow the priest fought him off. He was stabbed with his own knife. Before the police could talk to him, he did what he was told and killed himself. Do you think he will be pleased? "He is never pleased but we are moving on as scheduled. I will be arranging the final meeting at the Villa in Pompeii. All the messengers will be summoned there as he wishes. We all will witness the rise and the final conflict will begin. He will pull people from all four corners of the earth. World leaders will side with him, and they will attempt to annihilate God's people. What we are doing is a small warning on what is to come. Our messengers will be given their weapons of destruction. As it is written you cannot attack God but we will destroy his saints. His army of believers will be sacrificed as he will await the Lamb. As we speak, I am sure the Vatican is realizing what is happening. They will be divided because so many are not true believers. They will be helpless. All is in place and now we will go to Pompeii and make the final arrangements." "Will he be there?" In some way I am sure. He has anointed one as his sole messenger who will rule until the final battle."

CHAPTER 13

Father Thomas and Jimmy begin their bus ride to the monastery on the northern tip of England just below the Scottish border. "Father, I have been thinking of Stevie my old friend. I keep seeing his face smiling at me in the car. I know everyone thinks that I was hallucinating but I could swear he was there. Can it be possible that he was killed in another dimension but still lives in this dimension? I know it sounds crazy but I can't get it out of my mind." "Even if that was possible why would he want to hurt you? You were his friend?" "Yeah that is true but I was with Jennifer and he was crazy about her. Maybe some nutty jealousy thing? I ended up with her? I know it's crazy but I am so confused." "Jimmy, all of this is extremely difficult to comprehend. That being said I do believe it's possible for someone to be caught between two realms. Your friend Stevie could be in such a situation. In one reality he had a good soul and was killed. In another he was not killed and had an evil soul. He can be caught between evil and good. Part of the eternal battle between good and evil. He can be struggling between them. An evil spirit pushing him to the dark side and a good spirit to the other. This letter I received from Brother Aiden was in fact about this very thing. He believes there is some type of plan or uprising of the evil ones on earth and from the underworld uniting to begin the final battle. He sees these serial killings as a sign. The words carved in Latin, *Nunc tempus est*, meaning the time is now. You must know about the belief in The Apocalypse, or Revelation. Brother Aiden believes there are so many signs pointing too that beginning. Your friend Stevie could be caught in that scenario. I am going to see Brother Aiden to find out what he knows and possibly be some kind of help. He is not on the best of terms with the Vatican and he knows that. I have had a good relationship with many Cardinals and I could be a good mediator between the two. I chose a simple life here in the U.S. and turned down a few opportunities with the powers that be. I don't regret that decision. I always was gifted as a good peacemaker. Brother Aiden did what he felt was right and did not take well to authority. He pushed the boundaries of rational beliefs with his own. He has continued his pursuit of alternate realities. Calling on good messengers and challenging the dark ones. Trying to save souls his way. Highly respected in some circles and in others as the devil himself. He has been waiting a lifetime to prove he is right. There will be a final battle not just in mythology but reality. There are demons underground and demons here on earth. Waiting for the time to destroy God's work and begin their reign of evil. I am hoping that someday he will be able to help you find peace. We shall see. Until then please try to take this journey one day at a time. Your only hope lies with Brother Aiden. At any time, you change your mind and want to return home I would understand." "No Father, like I said before, I have no home to return to. If Brother Aiden can help me, then I will do what it takes to see him." "It won't be easy; we will need some good luck along the way. I for one hope he is still at the monastery and didn't decide to go to the Vatican. He hasn't left the monastery in many years but the letter was urgent. He is very head strong and I never know what he is capable of." "You said the Vatican cut him off. Would they let him in?" "Not unless they believe in what is happening is some type of sign. Although they mostly think Brother Aiden is irrational there are many that believe he is special. I know he had a number of believers that thought he was gifted. They were afraid to let that be known. As any entity the Vatican is very political. For one to be accepted it is in their best interest not to rock the boat. His radical and progressive views were way too dangerous to acknowledge." "Yeah, that makes a lot of sense. This is some beautiful country we are going through. I wish I could have taken Jen and the boys here." Jimmy sits back and closes his eyes.

Back on Long Island:

"Lisa, Lisa, I'm so excited. Come sit down. I have some unbelievable news. I just got off the phone with my mother and you will never guess what's happening?" "What, I have no idea?" "You will die. It's hard to believe. I can hardly believe it myself." "Believe what Charlie, what's going on?" Hold your breath, I'm moving to Long Island." "What?" I know, it's crazy. I can't stop shaking, I'm so excited. I spoke with my mother and she is fine with it. She actually sounded very excited for me. She said she is packing all my stuff and will have it sent here. I don't even have to go back there. I know she must be upset but she thinks it is the best for me. Now for some more great news she has a close friend that lives on Long Island and she says they can get me in their company right away. Isn't this unbelievable? "Yeah unbelievable. Would you be staying here? In this apartment? With me?" "Of course, silly, where else would I go. That you have a spare bedroom its perfect. It's just like we said how great it would be to spend more time together. It will be just like when we were kids." "What kind of work would you be doing? Where is the company located?" The company is Estee Lauder they sell perfume all over the world. I will be starting in the packing and shipping department. It's eight to four five days a week. Mother says they probably will give me some free samples for you. This so exciting." "Yes, it is exciting but what about the Moose Lodge and your friends?" "Oh, no problem mother said there are a few Moose lodges around the Island. My friends well, Lisa, I have to be honest, I don't have many. You are more important to me then friends anyway. We are besties. It's crazy my mother has thought of everything. I will go visit for the holidays of course but I really think it's time for me to leave the nest." Lisa was caught off guard and really didn't know what to say. "You sure you don't want to think this over? This is a big decision maybe you should sleep on it?" "Oh my God, I'm sorry I never asked you if it was okay. I just assumed you would be thrilled but maybe I was wrong. If you don't want me please tell me. I will understand. It was rude of me to make all these arrangements and I didn't ask if it was okay with you. You might not want me here." "Lisa felt horrible, she hated to hurt Charlie. "No Charlie, of course I want you here. I just want to make sure that is what you really want. I think it will be fun." "Are you sure?" "Yes, I think it's a great idea. I will clear some room in the closets and you will have plenty of room." "Of course, I will pay you some rent to help out. Plus, I am a neat freak, I'll do the cleaning, vacuuming, I can do the shopping. I can also cook. I took some cooking classes up in Buffalo. I do most of the cooking for mother and she says I'm very talented. You know, I might take more cooking classes down here. It's possible I can be a chef someday. We also could go to Karaoke night at the Moose Lodge. I'm sure they must have one here. I'm a regular every Wednesday night up there. I do some Neil Diamond and Barry Manilow that will knock your socks off. Wow, the more I think about all this I want to bust. You know I will really try to make new friends here. I think Stevie will be my first. We get along great. I can see us becoming very good friends. Then we will be like the three amigos. I have an idea why don't you call Stevie and tell him the news. No wait how about inviting him over for dinner. I will make a fabulous dinner and surprise him with the news. I'll take care of everything. I have the whole week before I'm supposed to go to work for training." "I'm not sure Charlie, maybe we should wait on that. It's a lot of work and you will have so much to do with settling in." Don't be silly, all you have to do is call him and I will take care of all the rest."

CHAPTER 14

After a long bus ride, we pull into Edinburgh Scotland. We drive into the heart of Edinburgh I can't help but be impressed with the architecture. There are so many churches with high steeples. I am looking at one now that looks like its ten stories high with multiple peaks. There is this big clock in the center of the peak. The background beyond the church is a high sky overlooking the North Sea. The architecture is heavy gothic to me. As we continue driving Father Thomas tells me, "See that statue of the dog on the pedestal? See it? As he spoke the bus came to a stop for the traffic light. I looked across the road and I did see it. A bronze statue of a mid-size dog looks like a Scottish terrier I would guess. "That's Greyfriars Bobby. I read all about him. He was the constable's dog. They were inseparable but unfortunately the constable died. The dog followed the casket from the funeral home to the cemetery. The dog would lay on the grave and wouldn't move. The town's people tried to get him away but he wouldn't leave. They gave up and they took turns feeding him at the cemetery. The dog stayed there until he finally died lying on his masters grave." As he finished his story he was crying and so was I. "We had a dog and I miss him." I wiped the tears from my eyes. "I know how you feel. I love dogs too and that is a sad story." Father Thomas reached over and comforted me. The bus pulled into the depot and I followed Father Thomas off the bus. We gathered our luggage and the bus driver says, "Have a wonderful trip. I hope your meeting is successful and you are able to return home safely to your wife and children." I was a little startled by his comments. I turned to Father Thomas, "Did you hear what he said to me?" "What did he say?" "He said for me to have a safe trip home back to my wife and kids. I never told him that I had a wife and kids." "I guess he assumed you did Daniel." "I guess your right but it was the way he said it. It was like he knew." Just another bit of strangeness to add to this journey. We walked over to a restaurant a block away. It was a traditional Scottish pub. All dark wood tables and a long shiny mahogany bar. We took a small table by the window. The walls were decorated with all kinds of framed pictures of the area through the years. The pub was over one hundred years old. We ordered a couple of pints of the local beer and two servings of shepherd's pie. After we ate, Father Thomas said there's a car service not too far from where we are. I followed him down a winding walkway farther into the small town. The walkway was cobblestone bordered by deep green hedges. We came to a small glass building. Father Thomas went in and spoke to a man at a small desk. Our driver will be here in ten minutes and he will take us to the monastery. After about ten minutes the driver pulled up in front and we went out to meet him. The driver was a middle-aged stocky Scot with a heavy Scottish accent. He smiled at Father Thomas and took our luggage and put them in the trunk. "Good to see you again Father. You will be staying awhile?" "Good to see you again, Shaun. I am not sure how long we will be staying. This is Jimmy, and this is my dear friend Shaun." "First time in Scotland?" "Yes, it's a beautiful country." "Indeed, it is." The road was rough and definitely not a main route. We were the only car on the road. There were many spots where we drove through carved out in mountains that were only passable by one car at a time. We continued to drive by streams along the narrow winding road. After an hour of silence and a bone jarring ride we came to a stop in the middle of nowhere. The driver gets out and opens the trunk takes out our luggage and places them on the ground. We get out of the car and I look around and see nothing but deep dark forest. Shaun shakes Father Thomas's hand and they embrace. He turns to me, "I hope you find what you are looking for. I wish you the best of luck." He gets back in his car and drives off. I turn to Father Thomas with a look of confusion, "Father I didn't pay him?" "No need, He is an old friend of mine and he would never charge me. It's a long story and maybe another time I will tell you." Father Thomas picks up his bag and starts to walk straight to the middle of the forest.

"Father there is nothing here. Are you sure you have the right location? "Quite sure, just follow me, we do not have far to go." I shook my head and followed him into the middle of a dense forest. We made our way through a deep setting of very tall trees and an eerie silence. I didn't seem to hear any wildlife just a still quiet that engulfed the area. There was no real path we were following. We just walked around the trees in what seemed to be a pretty straight line. After a while of following Father Thomas, we came to a brightness in front of us. The walk through the forest was dark and it was clear that we were coming to an opening. We walked out of the forest and there was an open field of green grass and shrubs. As my eyes readjusted to the daylight. I could see a large stone wall not too far in the distance. Beyond the wall was a mountain covered with green grass. At the top of the mountain was the monastery. As we walked closer, the wall was massive. It must have been sixty or seventy feet high or more. It was all stone blocks more like a fort then a monastery. There didn't seem to be any way to enter it but Father Thomas did not hesitate and continued to walk. We walked along the wall for a few hundred feet and then turned to the left. I didn't know what to say so I just followed in silence. We continued to walk around the bend of the wall and then suddenly Father Thomas stopped. I looked to see if there was any door but there was nothing. "There's no door, now what Father?" "Be patient Jimmy, you will see." What a mess I have gotten into. I'm standing here in the middle of nowhere waiting for I don't know what? Is he thinking the wall is just magically going to open? I have doubts about everything that I am doing. I am just about ready to go off on the good Father Thomas when from the top of the wall, I see this thing coming down. "What the hell is that?" Father Thomas smiles, "That is our elevator up to the monastery." "What?" I watch this basket come down lowered by some kind of pulley system. It descends and slowly lands a few feet from where we are standing. Father Thomas opens this little half door and says, "Come now, we are going up." I look at this basket that looks like something from Eighty Days around the World movie. A wicker basket attached to a rope with rollers attached. "You're kidding, right Father?" "No, this is the only way in or out. Don't worry, I have done it many times, it is perfectly safe." Well I don't have too many options so I step into the basket. Father Thomas shuts the door and upward we go. First it bucks up and I have to hold on to the side to keep my balance. The basket slowly continues to rise. It takes a few minutes and then we reach the top of the wall. At the top there are two monks waiting for us. They reach out to give us a hand and we step onto the monastery stone floor. "Quite the modern lift you have here." The two monks look right past me and greet Father Thomas with some kind of silent head bob. They pick up our luggage and we follow them. As I looked out to the west the castle sat at the tip of the North Sea. We followed the monks around the perimeter of the monastery and then down a steep stairway. We entered a very large wooden door that opened into a large room. The room was enclosed with white stone or cement like walls. The floor was wood planks. There was a stone fireplace against the far wall. Many long dark wood tables with wooden benches for seating. On the tables there were mettle pitchers filled with red wine. The monks left and Father Thomas and I sat at one of the tables. Father Thomas took a tin cup and poured some wine. "Would you like some. "Yes", I could use something a little stronger but the wine will do thank you." We sat and drank the wine which was not bad at all. One of the monks came back a short time after and approached Father Thomas. "Brother William will see you." "Brother William, I thought we were to meet with Brother Aiden?" "Patience Jimmy, Let's see Brother William, I'm sure he will explain." "Do you know Brother William?" "No." We went through a few narrow corridors and then down a small wooden stairway. We continued to walk through dark cold stone corridors to a small thin wooden door. The monk led us through the doorway one by one. It was very narrow and you had to turn sideways to fit through. It's a good thing we were all on the thin side or else we wouldn't fit through the opening. Once through we went down a stairway that descended for what seemed forever. It was dark and lit only with candle globes attached to the walls. We followed the monk all the way down and then onto a walkway that led into a larger cavernous room. We continued to walk down a narrow hallway. As we bent around the hallway, we entered a small room. There was a wooden desk and behind the desk a wall of very old looking books. The books were on wooden shelves that wrapped around most of the walls. Once again, the only lighting was candles and torches all around. There was no religious art or statues of any kind. There was a large stone fire place that simmered with what looked like coal. There were a few high back wooden chairs that faced the desk. There was one high back chair behind the desk. The monk pointed to the chairs and I followed Father Thomas's lead and we both sat down. The monk then turned and left the room. After a few minutes Brother William came in. He was much younger than I expected. I would guess around forty. He was about six feet tall blond hair on the thin side. He looked like a basketball coach I had once in a church league. "Sorry to keep you waiting. I know you were expecting Brother Aiden but unfortunately, he was called away on some urgent matters. I know all about you Father Thomas. Brother Aiden has told me many stories of your work and friendship with him. He speaks very highly of you. I'm sure you are wondering about me. I have been working with Brother Aiden for the last ten years. He kind of recruited me because he heard of my work in quantum mechanics. I have done research in physics and string theory. I have been told my work is anywhere from blaspheme, foolish, science fiction to insanity. Brother Aiden viewed my work very differently. He saw a type of connection between his beliefs and mine. He wanted to combine the two and work side by side. Of course, the Vatican sent word that I was not welcomed. I was going to follow an academic course before I was approached by Brother Aiden. I will not bore you with the details of my work but in simple terms how we have combined our views. Using my science and Brother Aiden's we have experimented successfully in applying our works. As you know Father your work with Brother Aiden in calling upon good messengers to help one enter a different reality. You have experienced this first hand. My work says that there are alternate realities/parallel universe. There is the one we are in right now. From our reality there are two alternate paths connected. From those there are more connections let me show you what I mean." Brother William takes out a pad and draws a diagram with circles. One that has two branches and from those two they have two more branches and so on. "You see there are many different worlds where we can be here in one and yet in another at the same time. My theory is based on physics. Brother Aiden is religious. He sees these worlds as Gods plan. We live in different dimensions and are being tested with trials and tribulations. As we die in one, we can be alive in another. As we continue in these Realms, we will eventually rise to the ultimate Realm which can be Heaven or the lowest Realm which would be hell. All the ones in the middle will be say Purgatory. There is a constant battle of good and evil in all Realms. There will be a final battle between Gods Angels and the Devils dark Angels as we know would be Armageddon. I can see that all this is quite confusing and maybe not believable. The bottom line is we believe we have been successful in crossing over to alternate universes." Jimmy looks at Father Thomas and then back at Brother William. "In this other universe or reality can my wife and boys be alive?" "In theory, I would say yes. The problem is there is no way we can be sure. Try to understand that there are crossroads in our lives that lead to different paths on how our lives turn out. In another universe you might have made different decisions or someone else made different decisions that could change your reality dramatically. In another reality you might not have ever met or married your wife. If you did enter into another universe your life can be quite different. For example, what was the most traumatic moment in your life?" "That's easy, when I was young a few of my friends, we went to a club. My good friend Stevie got into a fight with this guy over a girl. That girl was Jennifer who I met again years later. I was in a VA Hospital recovering from injuries I got in Viet Nam. She was a nurse there and we became friends. Later we fell in love and married. That night in the club Stevie liked Jennifer but this guy Carlo had gone out with her a few times and he said some things to Stevie. Make a long story short they fought in the club. Carlo takes out a gun and it goes off killing Stevie. We tried to break it up but it was too late. It happened so fast I couldn't stop it." "That was a very traumatic experience. Let's say that you acted sooner and stopped the fight before it went bad. Stevie could have lived, maybe he dated Jennifer and they fell in love. Your life would turn out very different. What if you decided to go to a different place that night? Once again who knows if you would ever have met Jennifer. There are so many scenarios that could have changed your life. In another universe one of these scenarios could have happened. In that universe you can be living a totally different life. These are things we do not know." "Well I see what you mean but if there is any chance, I could get my wife and sons back, I would be willing to do it. Can you do it? Can you help me crossover into that alternate universe? I have no life here. I missed them too much. Please help me." "Oh no, I cannot do it. Only Brother Aiden has the knowledge and the gift on making that happen. My work is theory only. He has had experiences in doing this. Once again even if it was possible Brother Aiden could not know what will happen." "Then help me go to Brother Aiden, please." "I am leaving to meet with him tomorrow. He is in Florence Italy. He is on a special mission for the Vatican. If you like you can come with me. I cannot guarantee he will help you." "The Vatican? I thought you said he was not recognized by the church, Father?" "Yes, Father Thomas is correct but there has been a series of murders that the Vatican is very concerned about. They called on Brother Aiden for his expertise in some very dark areas." "What do you think, Father?" "I have no problem with you accompanying us to see him. That is the reason I asked you to come. I can speak with Brother Aiden on your behalf and I believe if it is at all possible, he will help you." "Then I will go with you, thank you."

CHAPTER 15

Jamie comes over to Gulli, "I think we caught a break. I have a woman who says she was on the train the night that conductor was pushed off the train. She just walked in and said she wanted to speak with someone about it." "She's here now?" "Yes, she is in room two." "Great, let's go." They walk into room two and see the women. She is around thirty years old slim and attractive. "Hi, I'm Detective Gulli and this is my partner Detective Collins. You said you were on the train the night the conductor was pushed. Please tell us what you remember." "Well, I worked late that night. I was coming back home from Manhattan. I noticed a dark hair man sitting a few rows in front of me. To be honest he was around my age and he was very good looking. I looked at him but he didn't respond. I just went back to checking some of my work notes. When the conductor announced tickets, he got up and walked out the back. I didn't think much of it at the time. I have been so busy at work I totally forgot about it. Just last night on the same train when the conductor said tickets it hit me. That's when I decided to come in. I read about what happened but I just didn't think it could have been connected. He was like I said good looking and seemed very normal. He would be the last person I would think would do something like that. After thinking about it maybe he could have seen something or I don't know. I just thought I should come in." "I'm sorry, what was your name?" "Linda." "Linda I'm very happy you did. Was there anything else that you might have noticed. Any tattoos, facial hair, any scars, his clothing, his race." He was white with dark wavy hair. He was dressed casual but no nothing that stands out." "Do you think you can help a sketch artist do a work up on him?" "Yeah, but it was late and I was tired but I think I could help. We will need some more information like time, dates you know basic information." "Sure, no problem." "This case is very high priority, so I would like to get started right away, is that okay?"

"Yes, no problem. I will be happy to help. I read the man who died had a wife and three young daughters, it's horrible." "Thanks Linda, Jamie is going to help you through some forms we need. I'm going to set things up right away."

"Boss, we caught a break in the train case. We have a witness that was there the night of. She saw what looks like a POI that acted strange. I want to sit on this awhile before we bring the dogs in. She is on the shaky side and I don't want to spook her. She won't remember some important details if she becomes too nervous." "Do you think this has any relation to the other murders we are working on." "It's a totally different MO but I won't rule anything out you never know." "Okay, keep me updated" "You got it, thanks."

After a restless night Stevie dries his hair after showering. He starts to shave, "I want you to take that razor and cut your own throat. If you cannot do what you were brought back to do then you are of no use to me. You have waited long enough now you must act. We have plans and they are in operation now. Don't think for one second you are going to live out this fantasy of yours that maybe you can have a life with this woman. You were dead, I let you return to follow my direction. You have an easy set up with those two. I want you to kill them and leave my markings. You must do what I say. You have no free will you belong to me. I have warned you and now you must act. Kill or die. I cannot wait any longer. Time is now. You are part of a movement that will change the world. The end is near for your friends one way or another. They are a tiny piece that must be sacrificed to pave the way for the beginning of the end. You have been chosen and you have no choice. There is a new world order that is coming and if you want to be a part of it, then do what I say. There will be no room for feelings or doubters. There are rewards you will receive. You will be pleased that you are part of the new world. I will be watching you. Your time is running out." Stevie pushed back and slowly fell to the floor. He held his head and cried. He wished he could talk to someone who could help but he knew that was impossible. He was alone living in a world he didn't belong. He always thought he was a good person. "I don't know what to do. The reality is I am what I am. I have already killed so this is who I am. I'm here to kill to be part of this plan. What choice do I have? I will do what I have to do."

Stevie walks along route 110 in Huntington towards the water. He is in a daze. His mind is preoccupied with what has happened. It's a cloudy night with very little moonlight. It's late and the area is quiet. He sees a woman leaving a local pub heading towards the parking lot. She is in no hurry and seems to be staggering. He follows her to the car. The parking lot is dark and empty. He watches her struggle for her car keys. He waits as she eventually unlocks the car. As she starts to enter the car Stevie rushes at her. He pushed her to the side. She starts to scream and Stevie punches her in the head. She collapses and he pushers her into the passenger seat. He takes the keys and drives off. He drives about a half hour. The woman is out cold. Most likely a combination of the blow and alcohol. He makes a right off of route 110 and heads west. The road is dark and winds through a hilly part of the Island. He turns onto an isolated road which leads to a deserted area. He stops the car and shuts the lights. He stares at the woman. She looks around forty years old. He studies her face. She has dark hair long and wavy. She actually is attractive. He reaches in her purse and pulls out her wallet. He pulls out some cash and is surprised to see she had so much. He looks at her license, she is forty-six years old. He strokes her hair and looks over her body. Once again, he is surprised, she has a sexy body. She starts to moan and slowly tries to open her eyes. Stevie hits her again across her chin knocking her out. He feels aroused by her appearance and softly feels her lower neck. He moves his hands over the top of her chest. Then he takes both his hands and grips them around her throat and squeezes. She begins to struggle but he applies more and more pressure until she stops breathing. He takes his knife and carves into her chest. He takes her out of the car and drags her into the woods and covers her with some branches. He gets back in the car and drives back to the parking lot He locks the car and throws the keys in a dumpster. He walks back to the motel. He gets to his room, takes his shirt off and goes into the bathroom. He washes up. He lays down in the bed and shuts his eyes. A vision of a spirit rises in front of him. "I am pleased with your work. A very scratchy deep voice repeats, I am pleased. Now you must continue. Your new friends must be next. This is what you were chosen for. This is your calling. Do not disappoint me. I will be watching. Nunc tempus est." Stevie closes his eyes and falls asleep.

The next day Stevie calls Lisa." "Hi, I'm glad you called. I was going to call you and then I realized I didn't have your number. I was hoping you can come to dinner on Friday. I have some news. Nothing earth shattering but I thought you would like to hear it. "Sounds good, yeah I'd like that. Hope you're not moving?" "No, just a little surprise. How about seven." "Sounds perfect, I'll see you Friday." "Great." Lisa turns to Charlie; He's coming Friday." "Wonderful, I will do the shopping tomorrow. I'm going to make a superb dinner. Then I can tell him the good news. I think this is going to be fantastic".

CHAPTER 16

Jimmy picks up his suitcase after a pleasant flight on British Airways to Pisa Airport, Italy. He turns to Father Thomas, "How long a bus ride to Florence?" "It takes about an hour and a half. You will like the scenic road. We will go through wine country it's beautiful. It's one of my favorite bus rides." "Brother William, where are we going to meet with Brother Aiden?" "He should be at Santa Maria Novella on the western side of Florence. It's a beautiful church built in the fourteenth century by Dominican monks. It's stunning to see. I last spoke with him and he was there. I have not been able to reach him these last few days." "He will be there, when we get there?" "Yes, he should be, although he sounded quite upset when I spoke to him last. Try to relax Jimmy, we will find him." The bus ride was uneventful as they drove through the beautiful country side. As they pulled into Florence, Jimmy was in awe with the beauty of the city. They pulled up to a small hotel in the middle of the city. Jimmy could see the famous Duomo Cathedral standing high above the city. Father Thomas, Brother William and Jimmy walked through the city. They walked through the cobblestone walkway by the Uffizi Gallery, lined with street artists heading to the Ponte Vecchio or 'Old Bridge', that joins the center of the city with the district of Oltrarno, on the south bank of the river Arno, it's one of the most famous bridges in the world. Jimmy had to admit he was thrilled seeing this beautiful city but also saddened he is not with his wife to really enjoy it. He turned to Brother William," When are we meeting with Brother Aiden?" "Tomorrow we are meeting at the church." "You spoke with him? Did you tell him about me?" "Not really, but I was able to get a message and it was returned that he would see us." Jimmy nodded his head as they continued to walk. As they walked by the street artists Jimmy stopped cold. There was a street artist with about forty large sketches of tourists. There was one that was buried in the back row that caught Jimmy's eye. He walked over to get a better look and was stunned. "My God how could this be?" Father Thomas looked at Jimmy? "What is it?" "That drawing of four people that looks like my wife and me. The other looks just like my old friend Danny who was killed. The women with him I don't recognize. Father Thomas looked closely at the drawing, "Yes, it does have a resemblance to you, very much so." No Father that is me and my wife. Danny looks older but it defiantly is him. It's impossible, I never have been here. Danny died young along with Stevie; this is crazy. Jimmy goes over to the artist and asks him if he drew that picture. The artist shook his head saying he didn't speak English. Father Thomas bent over to the artist and asked him in Italian. He replied no. Father Thomas asked him if he knew who did? He snapped back no. Jimmy didn't know what to do. He was so confused," How could this be? This makes no sense." He asked Father to ask how much to buy the sketch? Father spoke back and forth before they settled on a price. Jimmy took the sketch and stared at it before putting it back in the envelope. Brother William looked at Father Thomas and they both shook their head. They started walking towards the bridge. As they approached the bridge Father Thomas tried to take Jimmy's mind off the sketch and said, "The bridge crosses the river at its narrowest point within the city, and a series of bridges. There is a total of five bridges. People have stood on or around this spot since the days of the Ancient Romans. The current bridge was finished by 1350, built after a catastrophic flood in 1333 carried away the original bridge. It is best known today for the wooden-shuttered goldsmiths' shops that line both sides of it, and for the Vasari Corridor that runs over it a private aerial walkway built in 1561 so the Medici family could move between the Palazzo Pitti and the Palazzo Vecchio, safe from risk of assassination in the streets below. Much has been written about the Ponte Vecchio. The Ponte Vecchio was designed in part as a defensive structure. In Medieval Italy the use of rivers to launch attacks was a well-established element of the art of war, and although

Florence was surrounded by walls, an enemy might attack in boats along the Arno itself. Following the practice of the previous bridge here, the Ponte Vecchio had four towers two at each end, and walls with battlements running down both sides, broken only by the observation area in the very center of the bridge. The Mannelli tower at the south end is the only obvious survivor of these fortifications, which can be seen in the famous 15th Century 'Chain View' of Florence. A document of 1346 lists regulations that include fines for shopkeepers breaking the exterior walls facing the river." Jimmy was listening but he was having a hard time concentrating. Father Thomas was very interesting and his knowledge was impressive. Father continued his tour guide dialogue, "The horizontal proportions used in the plan of the bridge and the blocks of shops built upon it, which can be reduced to 1:2:4, and correspond to the first progression of Platonic numeric theory. lateral proportions of 1:2 form a musical octave, also the sacred concord in Pythagorean Mysticism. All this suggests the sort of sophisticated thinking which believed that mathematics and geometry were fundamental to the divine order of the universe." "Now you are really losing me here Father." "Jimmy this is a very special place and I think this is an area where a portal to other dimensions exist. When I heard we were coming here, I thought this would be the perfect area for you. Brother William agreed." Brother William looked at Jimmy, "I do agree, I believe we can help you here. That sketch you have could be no coincidence. It is possible that in another dimension you, your wife and your friend did come here." "Brother my friend Danny is dead." "Yes, here in this realty but in another dimension he might not be." "Are you saying that in another dimension my wife is alive and so is Danny?" Yes, it is possible in theory. That drawing you have might show it is more than a theory." Jimmy softly leans back on the wall and tears up. "My God, if this is possible, I will do anything to go there, anything at all." "I know you will. Now let's take the evening, enjoy and see what tomorrow brings." "Yes Brother, thank you." They walk over the bridge and Jimmy can't help but notice all the gold jewelry in each store. "Damn, Jen would love this place. All the gold it's all eighteen carat and higher?" "Yes Jimmy, there is so much history here even Benito Mussolini wanted his guest of honor Adolf Hitler to enjoy a good view of Florence from the corridor during his State Visit on May 9, 1938. Accordingly, Mussolini had the original three windows in the center of the bridge on the west side knocked into one large viewing gallery for the benefit of Hitler and his party. It may be just as well he did, because when the retreating German forces blew up all the other bridges in 1944 to slow down the advancing Allies, they left the Ponte Vecchio intact, instead of reducing the buildings at both ends of the bridge to rubble, in order to block the streets. When a catastrophic flood hit the city in November 1966, there were real fears the bridge would collapse. It was repeatedly struck by large debris carried by the raging waters of the Arno and whole tree-trunks pierced right through the shops on the upstream side. The pressure of the water on the bridge set up vibrations that made the whole structure actually hum like a musical instrument. Well I don't know about you but I am starving. I know of a wonderful restaurant not too far from here. I assume you are of Italian origin Jimmy?" "Oh yeah, love Italian food." "Then you are in for a special treat. They started to walk back towards the Uffizi Gallery. "What also makes this city special is everything you want to do and see is in walking distance. All the restaurants are excellent but some are for tourists. The one we are going to is a little of both because some returning tourists know it and the locals are always there." They walk about ten minutes through the cobblestone streets. A brisk cool air makes the walk rather easy. They enter the restaurant and are greeted at the door. Jimmy looks up at the ceiling which is decorated with beautiful hand painted dinner plates. He has never seen anything like it. The walls, covered in murals. The place was like a museum. Father Thomas explains, "All the restaurants serve homemade pasta. There are at least three courses. First the pasta then the meat or fish and then deserts. The wine is local and the bread freshly baked. All the vegetables and fruit are local and fresh. Jimmy, I wish we had some more time to spend here. The City has so much to see. The Galleria Dell 'Accademia is incredible. Every time I see Michelangelo's David, I cry." "All sounds great Father but I'm just not into any of it. I'm concerned with how this all going to work out." "I understand, Jimmy let's eat and then get some rest and we will see Brother Aiden tomorrow.' "Sure Father, sounds good." They enjoy a delicious dinner and go back to the hotel. The room is small but clean and comfortable. Jimmy lays on the bed his head whirling with all that has happened. That doesn't stop him from falling asleep. The next morning, "Where are we meeting him?" Brother William sips a cup of coffee, "San Lorenzo church, It's the oldest church in Florence." After breakfast they head over to the church. As they approach the church, Jimmy stops, "My God, this is a church? Looks like a fortress and museum. It's breath taking, how old is it?" Just as he said that he realized Father Thomas would give him another history lesson. Even Brother William smiled, "It was consecrated in 393. The church was rebuilt twice; first in 1059 in Romanic style and second thanks to the Medici family who wanted to make a personal temple of it around 1421. There are so many stories about this church. It has a mystery to it. Let's go in." The church is huge with brilliant design and columns. Michelangelo and Donatello have worked their magic in here. The tombs below are filled with stories." "What kind of stories?" "Let's go, that is where we will meet Brother Aiden. The three walk around the back of the church they are met by a sister who points to them where to go. They enter a dark hallway to steps that wind and descend. After many steps they reach another hallway and it winds around to a columned room with an archway. A priest is waiting there. He welcomes them in Italian and explains that Brother Aiden had to leave early this morning. He was upset but he had to go to Rome. He wants you to come there as soon as possible. He left directions on where to meet him. The priest offered his apologies for Brother Aiden and explained this was unexpected. He nodded his head and walked away. Brother William looked at the note and put it in his pocket. He looked at Father Thomas and then at Jimmy, "I'm sorry, I know you must be disappointed." "I don't understand why did he want to meet us here to begin with?" "I am sure he wanted to help you, that is why he chose this church. He has been a part of the investigations on these multiple murders that have occurred. This church I'm sure had something to do with that but also this is where he wanted to help you. There are what he believes a few portals in different locations and this is one of them. I know he said that with the help of a good messenger he could use this location to enter a portal to another dimension in time and or an alternate reality. I mentioned that this was the oldest church and has many stories about it. Many are considered myths and legend. It has been said time travelers have come through this portal. Some say people have left from here and never returned. Of course, the church and the Vatican say that this is all silly stories and none of it is true. Brother Aiden used this location many times until the church sent him away." "Jimmy stared at Father Thomas, "Maybe you can help me cross over here?" "Oh no, Jimmy impossible. I have never done such a thing. I have worked with Brother Aiden in the past but I never have done what you are asking. If I could, I would help you. I am sorry Jimmy." "Jimmy turned to Brother William, "You Brother you can help me?" "No Jimmy, I think we need to find Brother Aiden." "Please Brother, I am begging you. I have nothing to lose, I have no life. We could be chasing Brother Aiden forever. Who knows if he will be able to help me when we do meet up with him? For some reason I have faith in you. I know you can do it." "Jimmy, to be honest Brother Aiden has been instructing me how to perform what you are asking. The problem is that I have never done it. Yes, I have witnessed some type of success right here watching and assisting him. I know the process but I have no idea what will happen. Possibly nothing or you could end up gone forever. I don't know what the outcome would be." "I don't care if it is a million to one,

I'm willing to take that chance. Whatever happens is fine with me. If I die trying or I end up somewhere unknown that's okay. Please Brother help me. I'm desperate, I will risk anything, if I have a chance to be with my family again. I'm begging you." Brother William shook his head and looked at Father Thomas. "If you think you can do it Brother, I will assist you." Brother William reluctantly nodded, "May the lord help me, I will do my best. Come it's not far." They walked through another corridor and then another. More stairs led them to a small room. There was a rock formation with water trickling down. A steady flow of water and a haze. Brother William told Jimmy to come close to the wall. "Jimmy, I hope to help you enter a paroral dimension where you will be in the same time frame but another reality. I will call on a good messenger to guide you. I hope there is no interference with you crossing over but I do not know. You must trust the messenger and follow them, if all goes well you will enter into a different reality. I cannot explain anymore because most of what happens I don't know. Do you understand?" "Yes, I'm good. I walked through the valley of death in Viet Nam so I am okay with whatever happens. Thank you, Brother." Jimmy looked at Father Thomas and smiled," I'm ready."

Brother William walked over to the wall where the sunken waterfall and the carvings were. Jimmy looked at the carvings and asked what did they mean? "They are different languages and some type of symbols. Most of it I don't understand. The one I do is in Latin. It translates that this is a passage way, back and forth to a destination to be unknown. Some are warnings and some are saying it's a sacred passage. Some of these symbols and carvings seem to be of a dark and a bright entity. Brother Aiden knows them well. He has shown me the way to use these instructions on entering the passage with the help of a good messenger. The process takes some time and it is in stages. All the stages must be completed to be successful. Once I begin, I cannot stop. It is possible if not completed you can end up in some limbo or returned. Honestly, I am not sure, this is unknown territory. If you are ready, we will begin." "I'm as ready as I ever will be." Jimmy stands by the sunken waterfall as Brother William begins. He starts with uttering some Latin words and sprinkles water onto Jimmy. He repeats this a few times. Jimmy closes his eyes and tries to concentrate and pray at the same time. After a few more minutes Jimmy starts to feel a weird sensation. His head feels pressure and vibration. The sensation starts to radiate down his body. He feels a cold wave enter his surroundings. He feels a presence and a message to reach out. It's not a voice but more in his mind. He reaches out with his hand and in seconds he feels a warm hand hold on to his. He then drifts into a tunnel. He can't keep from opening his eyes and when he does, he sees a swirling tunnel with black and white blasts of lights. The pressure builds and he feels his head will explode but then calmness. Now he feels like he is alone and floating weightless. Then he just goes blank and then nothing. He hears a voice, "Come on, sleepy head, let's go. We are going to be late. When we get home, you can sleep all day." Jimmy slowly opens his eyes and looks around. He is in bed in a hotel room. One like he has been staying in Italy. He looks across the room and sees a woman coming out of the bathroom. She is wearing a white robe, "Jen, is that you?" "Of course, it's me. Who else would be here with you? Come on, rise and shine, buddy." Jimmy reaches out and grabs her hand. He jumps up and hugs her. He can't speak as he starts to cry. He squeezes her so hard she could hardly breath. "Hey, what's going on? Are you okay? Come on talk to me, your scaring me." "I'm good, I just can't believe I'm here with you. I love you so much. I've missed you so much. "What are you talking about? We haven't been apart since we got here. You must have had too much wine last night." Jimmy couldn't stop holding her. He was confused, disorientated but over joyed to be with her. "The boys, where are they? Are they okay?" "Yes, they're with my parents. We dropped them off before we went to the airport. What's going on Jimmy?" Jimmy didn't know what to say. He couldn't tell her she would think he is crazy. "I'm sorry, I had these crazy dreams and they seemed so real. They freaked me out. You're right, must have been the wine. I even forgot where we are." "Italy, maybe we should see a doctor?" "No, I'm good. Just a bad night and I woke up in a fog. "Okay, now get ready we have to meet Danny and Maria down stairs and we are late." "Danny and Maria?" "Yes, our best friends. Danny who you grew up with and have been friends for forty years. That's it, I'm calling a doctor." No please don't, I'm okay. Let me go and get washed up." "Okay but hurry." Jimmy went into the bathroom and turned on the shower. He stared into the mirror and shook his head. He thought, can this be real? Can I be back with Jen and the boys? Did the accident really happen? Was I with Father Thomas and Brother William or was that a dream? Is this a dream now? The last thing I remember I was in the church with them. Did I cross over to some alternate reality? Is that possible? I'm in Italy with Jen and Danny, Danny, how is that possible. Danny was killed at the club. I was there. I held him in my arms and watched him die. How could he be here? How could he be alive?

Back in the tombs Father Thomas watches as Brother William continues chanting. Behind Father Thomas is a dark figure silently approaching him. A man in a black turtle neck sweater and black pants lifts a wooden mallet and strikes Father Thomas in the head' He goes down immediately and falls into Brother William. Brother William is startled and turns to face his attacker. The attacker lifts a large black handle knife and lunges at Brother William.

Jimmy washes his face and instantly falls to the floor. He is helpless as he begins to black out. Jimmy picks himself up and holds his head. He has a massive headache. He struggles to open his eyes and eventually does. He looks around and sees the waterfall and the rock wall. He screams out, "No, No please God no." As he realizes he is back in the tombs and in a world, he doesn't want to be in. As he looks around, he is startled as he sees Father Thomas and Brother William laying on the ground. He sees a puddle of blood.

He reaches down and turns Brother William over and checks his pulse. There is none as he realizes he is dead. He goes over to Father Thomas as he holds his head upward and the Father moans, "What happened?" Jimmy, looks at him, "I was going to ask you that. One minute I'm back with my wife and the next I'm back here." Father Thomas slowly sits up, "I was hit in the head from behind and blacked out. Of my God, Brother William is he okay?" "Sorry Father, he's gone. Who could have done this?" "There are so many evil things happening and this must be part of it."

"What do we do now?" "First we call the authorities and then I will call my contact in Rome. If Brother Aiden is in Rome, then we will go to him." "Do you think we can get to see him?" "I believe so. The problem is we are going to be tied up here for a while. I'm sure we will have to be part of this investigation. Plus, we will have some explaining to do on where you were at the time?" "Yeah Father, that is a problem. I'm not sure telling them I was in a different dimension will be acceptable." "No, it will not go over well. You don't have a scratch on you. I have this bump to show where I was, knocked out." "Damn, I can be a suspect in this. What am I going to tell them?" "Come with me. There is a room around this corridor with a small office. Here there are a few books here pick one. We will say you were in here reading while Brother William was showing me the wall with the carvings and explaining its meaning. You came to see us after a while and found us just the way you really did. I will explain you are here with me doing some research for a book you are writing about different religious beliefs. Good messengers and dark messengers, Just the way we have been explaining it to you. You will be fine. They will not suspect you because you are with me. After some statements we will be able to leave. I will call Brother Williams next of kin. I will notify Rome of the details just the way I explained it to you. Of course, we will tell Brother Aiden the truth. Once the police file a report, Rome will know. We should be able to leave in a day or so." "Okay Father, I will do what you say. A few weeks ago, I was happy, with a great wife and two boys, living on Long Island. Now they are gone, I am in Italy. Brother William who was trying to help me is dead and I have to lie to the Italian Police." "You have been through a lot. Things change quickly but all is not lost. I will help you and I believe Brother Aiden will to.

CHAPTER 17

Long Island NY:

Gulli bends down looking at the body of the victim. "There seemed to be not much of a struggle. This doesn't look like any rape or sexual attack. This fits the MO of our killer. The carvings are the same, looks like money was taken but this is no robbery. To me the killer does his thing but he can use the money. I would say he needs the cash and takes it as a bonus to his deeds." Jamie leans over and whispers, "Looks like we got company." Coming through the yellow tape is Detective 111, Carver. He is well over six feet and very well built. He is an Afro-American with thick black hair. He is very well dressed and has a reputation of a no nonsense by the book cop. He has been on a fast track up the ranks. "Okay Gulli, what do we have?" Gulli brings him up to date. Carver stares at him carefully. "I have been told you sat on a witness before bringing the task force up to date?" "She was scared and I didn't want her to freak out. I made a judgement call to let her relax a bit and then be able to give the best description possible." Carver stared at Jamie. Gulli jumped in, "It' was my call it's all on me." "This case is starting to leak. There is a lot of pressure to find this killer. We don't want a full panic on our hands. From now on you keep the task force up to speed as soon as it's possible. Any information I want you to call me directly. Do you understand? "Yes, no problem." "Good." Carver walks away. Jamie looks at Gulli, "Yeah, he is a sweetie." "He's all business but he is fair. He cuts through the BS and tells you like it is. I really don't have a problem with that. Let's circulate the sketch and see what video we have."

Later that afternoon. Gulli leans over Lori's shoulder, Anything good?" "Not really. I have the victim coming out of the bar but the camera distance is limited and the she is out of range." "What about anyone else show up?" "Nope, that's it, sorry Gulli." Gulli walks away and sits at his desk. Jamie comes up to him, "It was late the lot was empty and nobody in the bar saw anyone fitting the description. He must have been outside waiting. The street video shows her car heading off west and then nothing. He must have hijacked her car and took her somewhere. Then drove the car back to the lot. There no prints so far except hers. They are checking for DNA it's pretty new and takes a while to get results. He left her car so he might be local or he had a car and drove off." "Let's have a total net around the area knocking on doors with the sketch. I agree he could be local."

Stevie finishes packing. He has but a few clothes he stuffs in a carry bag. He is on his way to have dinner at Lisa's and then he will leave. He is deep in thought thinking over his options, "I need to get out of here. I need to see Lisa one more time and put that behind me. It is a dead end and I know it. Maybe in another life another time who knows. I need to find somewhere where I can start over. I'll head west and see what happens. Maybe south Florida sounds good. It's warm and I won't need much clothes. Yeah why not. After I'm done with Lisa, I'll drive to Florida." As Stevie drives off, he feels a hot sensation running through his body. He tries hard to control it but he can't. He hears a voice piecing through his head. "You have to do what I tell you to do. This little friend of yours must be terminated. She must be sacrificed for our mission. You have no choice. You must understand you have been brought back to do our bidding. You are not here to have a life. You are part of a battle that has just begun. The world will be reborn under the rule of our master. If you do as you are told you will be rewarded. If you do not you will be punished for all eternity. Do you understand." Stevie reluctantly nods his head and whispers, "Yes, I understand." Stevie starts to come down and continues to drive. He pulls up to Lisa's house and parks. He holds his head and cries. He slowly gets himself back together and wipes his face. He then heads to her door. "Stevie, welcome come in. Lisa, Stevie's

here. You don't have a coat, you must be freezing, get in here."
"Charlie, I thought you would be back in Buffalo?" "No, I'm not.
I'll tell you all about it." Lisa smiles and kisses Stevie and gives
him a big hug. "So happy you could make it. Sit down and I'll
get you some wine." Lisa goes into the kitchen. "Stevie, what have
you been up to, anything exciting?" "No not really, same old shit."
"Well, I have some exciting news, are you ready? Stevie nods his
head. "I am staying here. I moved out and I have a job here on
Long Island. I'm working at Estee Lauder in Melville and I will be
staying here with Lisa. Isn't that exciting?" "Stevie slowly shakes
his head," Wow, I didn't expect that. How's Lisa feel about that?"
"You kidding, she loves it. It's just like when we were kids." "What
about your mom? Your friends?" "No problem my mom was really
great about it. She packed all my stuff and shipped them already.
Friends to be honest I don't have that many. Plus, I can visit any
time but I'm looking forward to making new friends here. Plus, I
have you and Lisa that is a great start. What do like doing in your
spare time?" "Not much." "What about your work, what do you
do?" "I'm going to check on Lisa, if she needs any help." "Hey is
he making you crazy with all his questions? He can do that some
times. He means well but he can get a little annoying." "What
about you are you okay with him living here?" "Yeah, it's okay, I
guess. I'm sure once he gets settled, he will want his own place. He
is a lot of fun most of the time. To be honest I was kind of surprised
by him asking to stay here. I just couldn't say no. It will work out.
I'm just going to see how it goes. What about you, do you have
plans for the immediate future?" "Yeah, I have a job offer out of
state that I'm thinking about. I really don't have much around here.
I'm kind of a loner so it might be best to go somewhere I can
make some money and then I'll see what I want to do." As Stevie
is talking, he feels a wave of heat running through his body. "Can
I use the bathroom?" "Sure, it's right around the hallway to your
left." "Thanks, be right back." "What's going on in there, you guys
forgot about me? I better check on the roast in the oven." Stevie

goes into the bathroom "What are you doing with all this bullshit. You are here to sacrifice those two pathetic beings and move on. All your little talk is pathetic. You are here for the mission what don't you understand about that. Stop wasting time and finish what you came here for." "I didn't know he would be here that complicates things." "What that piece of talking meat, stop the stalling. Help in the kitchen grab a knife and do it. Him first and then your little girlfriend. Just do it, I'm losing patience with you." Stevie holds his head with both hands, "Alright leave me alone. Stevie rubs his temples and rubs his hands through his hair. "My head is killing me." He shuts the water off and dries his hands and face. He opens the door and walks back in the kitchen. Charlie has an apron on and is leaning over the oven. Stevie slowly comes behind him. He sees a large carving knife on the counter. He slowly moves towards it. He looks at Charlie, "Where's Lisa?" Without stopping what he was doing Charlie answers, "She just went to her room to get something. She'll be right back I'm just basting the roast; I'll be done in a second." Stevie slowly picks up the carving knife and holds it by the handle looking at the blade and then at Charlie. He begins to raise the knife, "How you guys doing in there? I'll be right in just finishing setting the table." Stevie stares at Charlie and puts the knife down. He turns and runs past Lisa and out the door. He goes right to the car. "What just happened? Lisa looks at Charlie, "I don't know. He just ran past me and out the door. Did he say anything to you?" "No, I was basting the roast and he asked where you were. Next thing I hear him running out. Do you thing he was sick?" "I haven't a clue. He was kind of strange tonight since he got here but this is crazy." "How much do you know about him?" "Not much at all. He never spoke much about anything personal. Just he moved here from Arizona and that's about it. He said he was a loner and didn't have much here, I am stunned." "Lisa sit down let me get you some wine."

Stevie drove off heading west on the Long Island Expressway. As he was driving the voice was pounding in his head, "You fool what did you do that for. They were all set up for the slaughter and you run away?" Stevie screams in the car, "Leave me alone. I couldn't do it okay. Leave me alone. Just go away, leave me the hell alone." Stevie then blasts the radio to drown out the voice. Sweet Child of mine by Guns and Roses blasts through the car. Stevie continues to drive and finally decides to get off at the next exit and heads north. He turns on to Jericho Turnpike and heads west. After a few miles he pulls into a motel. Parks the car. He sees a McDonalds down the road. He gets out of the car desperately needing a black coffee. He starts to walk towards the McDonalds. Officer Jack Walker on the force just over one year sits in his patrol car. He is thinking about asking his girlfriend Danielle to marry him. They have been dating for over two years and he is in love with her since the day he met her. He keeps on rehearsing the way and the words he will use to propose to her. He steps out of his car and starts walking to the McDonalds, it's late and the parking lot is empty and dark. He spots Stevie walking his way. Stevie has his head down and does not notice the officer. Officer Walker looks at Stevie and he seems to recognize his face. He had a composite of a person of interest in the train killing and he felt there was enough resemblance that he should investigate and stop Stevie. As Stevie continued to walk with his head down, he came up to a high bush divider entering the parking lot. Officer Walker approached Stevie, "Excuse me, can I ask you something?" Stevie is startled but quickly reacts. He kicks the officer in the groin and punches him in the throat. The officer goes down gasping for air. Stevie pulls the officer's gun and hits the officer repeatedly over the head. He drags the officer into the bushes. He takes his wallet and takes the cash. He walks slowly back to his car. Gets in and drives westward.

CHAPTER 18

After a few days of questioning and trying to help in the investigation Father Thomas and Jimmy are headed to Rome. They roll their luggage over the cobblestone streets of Florence towards the rail station. "I am happy that is over with. I didn't think they were buying our story. I was getting nervous they might have thought I was the killer. They seemed to take your word and that seem to sway them." "Well, I spent many years in Florence and I have some good friends. Plus, they know my reputation and I am a priest. They have been aware of what has been happening with the killings. I am sure they have been in contact with Rome. Nothing happens here without Rome being involved somehow in these matters. They also had evidence showing there was someone else there."

They enter the station and Jimmy looks up at the schedules, "I am lost in here Father, everything is in Italian and I don't understand a word." "I thought your parents were Italian. Didn't they speak it?" "Yeah but when they didn't want us to understand what they were saying they spoke it. They wanted us to speak English. My Aunt taught me some words but I never pursued it. Now I wish I did. To tell the truth I never thought I would be going to Italy. I used to talk to Danny about going to Italy someday. Both our grandparents were born in Italy. Danny's dad's side came from Calabria and his moms from Naples. My dad's side from Sicily and my mom's from Salerno. What about you Father what is your background. My parents too were born here. My father was born in Rome and my mother was from Sorrento. You know they would go back and forth on that. My father said my mother's family were peasants. My mother said that my father's side were snobs, they were special because they came from Rome, Alti Italiani, meaning high Italians. They would go back and forth and I would laugh. It was funny to hear them go at each other. My Father did admit my mother's family made the best food. Peasant food was the best." "I'm surprised, I didn't think you were Italian. I know your fluent in the language but your name, for some reason I didn't think Italian." "Jimmy, my real name is Tommaso Giardelli. I was born on Mullberry street in little Italy." "That's crazy Danny's mom was born on Mullberry street, small world." Father Thomas smiled, I think this our train but I'm not sure." Father Thomas asked the conducter on the platform," "Mi scusi è questo il treno per Roma. This is it grab your luggage and follow me." They boarded the train and walked to take their seats. The train car was immaculate. They were seated face to face and had these fold up tables between them. After the train took off a very pretty lady in a uniform came around with assorted packaged cookies and sodas. Jimmy looked at Father Thomas, "Now this beats the Long Island Railroad." "They take there railway system serious in all of Europe. The trains are hi-speed and are very well maintained."

"Where do we meet with Brother Aiden?" "I left word at the hotel we are staying at. He will be in contact, don't worry." Jimmy and Father Thomas pick up their luggage and walk towards the exits. There is a driver with a sign waiting for them. The driver spoke english and was very friendly. "Welcome to Roma, I"m Giuseppe Lacobucci let me take your luggage the car is right outside." They got in the car and drove off, "This is like New York, very crowded and busy." "Yes in many ways." "Giuseppe was very animated as he drove and swayed through the maze of traffic. "This is some crazy roads, there are no lanes, it's like go carts flying all over the place." "The Romans are notorious for their driving. It's quite different here. We don't have far to go. I think we will get there safely." Giuseppe pulls in front of the hotel. The entrance is small but very pleasent. Giuseppe refuses to take any money and says it has all been taken care of. "If you need anything at all please call me anytime." Giuseppe hands Father a card and takes off. Jimmy and Father Thomas check in and a bellman helps them with their luggage. Jimmy looks at the elevator," We're going to fit in here?" Father smiles, "Everything is smaller then we are used too. The bellman helps them into the room and he too does not accept a tip. He just smiles and leaves. After a few minutes in the room, "Jimmy looks at two twin beds divided by a large dresser. He walks a few feet to the bathroom and looks in, "Yeah, much smaller and I stayed in some small rooms in the city but this makes them look large." The phone rings and Father Thomas answers, "Yes, I understand that will be fine. We will be there tommorow. Yes, thank you. That was our contact we are going to meet Brother Aiden tommorow at the Spanish Steps. It is a big tourist attraction and is always very crowded." "Why there? I thought it would be in some church or at the Vatican." "I think they feel it will be safer in a public place." "Safer, seriously this is like some kind of spy novel thing." "I know Jimmy, but look what has happened already. Brother William, all these murders, it is best to be carefull. Are you hungry?" "Always." "We are walking distance from the resturant district on Via Veneto. Many resturants but I know this small resturant only a few streets from here and the food is fantastic." "Sounds good to me." After an excellent dinner, Jimmy and Father Thomas are walking back to the hotel."You know Jimmy the original Rome is really beneath what you see now. The ruins are well below us.

As they walk down the dark street, they are the only two people around. As they are walking a man in a hooded sweat shirt quickly approaches them he unexpectedly pushes into Father Thomas and seems to grab at Father Thomas's pocket. He continues to walk past them and slowly vanishes. "Father are you alright?" "Yes, I'm fine, what about you?" "Yeah I'm okay. What was that all about and where the hell did, he go. He just seemed to disappear." Father Thomas reaches in his pocket, "He put a note or something in my pocket." "What does it say?" "Be careful they know you are here. They are watching you. Go to the city where the spirits roam free.

Follow the past to save the future." "What does that mean? Who's watching and the city where souls run free? What is that all about?" "I believe I know but we will meet with Brother Aiden tomorrow, I'm sure he will shed some light on all this. Jimmy, this is not your fight or what you came here for. If you want to go back home, I will completely understand." "No Father I have no desire to go anywhere. I want to stay with you and if I can be of help, I'm all in. Plus, I came for a reason to see if Brother Aiden can help me. I'm not leaving until I see this through." "I have to admit I'm happy you are staying. I'm getting kind of old for all this. I feel better with you here. I think things could get intense and dangerous. There is great danger ahead. That note is a warning and I can feel the evil that is among us. Now we go back have some rest and meet with Brother Aiden tomorrow. Did you enjoy your dinner?" "Are you kidding the food here is unbelievable. I can eat all day and night. You know father when I was in Viet Nam, I had that experience of my buddy saving me. I told you about that. He was a vision, a spirit, I'm not sure what he was but he saved me. Maybe there was a reason for that and maybe I was meant to be here." "You could be right and time will tell."

Next day Jimmy and Father Thomas walk down the streets towards the Spanish steps. "Where do we meet him?" "The fountains in front of the steps." As they approach the fountain the area is crowded with tourists Many are sitting on the steps just watching the beauty of the city. There are many sitting around the short wall of the fountain. As they walk closer to the fountain Father Thomas points, "There he is." They approach the priest, Father this is Jimmy and I'm Father Thomas." "Yes, I know who you are. Please follow me." Jimmy looks at Father Thomas and they both follow the priest up the steps. When they get to the top, they face the magnificent church." "It's beautiful. "It is Jimmy, the church of Trinity Dei Mont it was built in 1502 by Louie X11 of France. He built it in French Gothic style. They continue to follow the priest. He stops and looks around and then continues to walk. "Does he think we might be followed?" "Yes, I'm sure." They enter the church and walk towards the back. They go around and then they follow the priest down many steps deep into the catacombs. The priest stops every so often to make sure they are not followed. Once at the bottom in a dark corner Brother Aiden awaits. "Brother how good to see you." Both men hug, "So good to see you Father. Its' been too long. Are you in good health?" "Yes, as good as could be expected at my age. Brother this is my good friend Jimmy, he has come here for your help." "Good to meet you Jimmy. This is Father Regis who is my close confidant" Father Regis just nods. "Can I speak freely, Father?" "Yes, Jimmy knows pretty much all that I know. He is here to help and be helped. He is to be trusted and counted on." "Good. Oliver Wilhelm is one of the richest men in the world. No one knows how he gained his fortune. Nobody knows hardly anything about him. He has been a recluse for many years. Interpol has nothing on him. The Vatican has been aware of him for a very long time. He is believed to be the most important man in a very secret society. This society has no name that we are aware of. We do not know when they meet or who the members are. Oliver Wilhelm for the first time in many years has been active and has been in public. He has been seen with one man but this man has not been identified. They have no records of birth, nationality or anything. It's like he just appeared and is extremely rich. We at the monastery were advised of him many years ago. I have been researching and keeping tabs on him. Like I said before with nothing to show for it, Until now. I have been contacted by a messenger warning me of him. He has been orchestrating many evil doings. I have been warned that he and his society are responsible for these murders happening. I am not sure how he is doing it but he is a conduit to this evil. Some of my colleagues believe he represents the devil himself."

"When we were walking back to the hotel last night we were bumped into by a man in a hooded sweatshirt. He stuffed this note in my pocket and walked away only to vanish." "What did the note say?" "Be careful they know you are here. They are watching you. Go to the city where the spirits roam free. Follow the past to save the future."

"Yes of course, we are on the same page. Where the souls of the dead inhabit the dogs that roam free are in Pompeii. We believe that Wilhelm has a meeting set there. We believe they will be setting forth an army of evil. This is the beginning of the final battle as prophesized in the book of revelations. Wilhelm and his society are the pawns in this war. What they will be unleashing is way beyond their knowledge and their control. Once this evil is allowed to surface the world will be in a war like they have never seen before. We do not know how this will happen but we know it must be stopped before they can open the gateway to hell. This is why they are in Pompeii we believe this is where the gateway is. The armies of the dead will rise through this gateway and spread like locust. They have no allegiance to any country just the devil himself. This will force God's hand to bring his army of angels to destroy this evil in the final battle. We have no idea when this will be but it is foretold it will happen." "Jimmy looked at Brother Aiden, "How can we stop them?" "It must be done before their ritual to open the gateway. These murders were just a smoke screen to send authorities in different directions so they go about their business. I will be able to call upon the good messengers to stop this gateway from opening. This must be done in the center spirit world. The one that is in between earth and the under earth. There are an army of messengers that can protect this opening. As Wilhelm calls upon the evil ones, we will call upon the good ones to protect this evil from rising. We believe that Mount Vesuvius is that opening." "You mean the volcano?" "Yes, it will explode and break the opening of the gateway and the evil will come pouring out." "What about the police or the government to step in and do something?" "Jimmy, they would laugh at us if we even tried. Most of the Vatican doesn't believe this. Only a few of us do. Wilhelm knows nobody believes this which gives him a free reign to work his plan." "How do we stop him just the four of us?" "We have to gain access to where their final meeting is. There will be many that gather but only Wilhelm has the power to call upon the evil. The rest will be performing some kind of ritual that will allow Wilhelm to be successful." "Who are these people and why do they want to do this?" "These are a group that have sold their souls for earthly riches and power. They believe that evil is just a way for them to get what they wanted. Power, riches and who knows what they were promised. The devil works in many different ways and creates his puppets to do his task. They could be world leader's, business moguls, we really do not know. If you look at what has happened in the world all the suffering and divide between the rich and the poor. Most of the world lives in poverty and a small percentage live like kings. Look at the atrocities through the years. Leaders of countries killing millions of their own people. Because they were a different race, religion or didn't follow their orders. Men like Hitler, Stalin and countless of others that committed such evil upon their own. This is the work of the evil one himself. I believe all of them were his puppets. I am working up a plan to be part of this gathering. I need to be close enough to what I have to do. There is a meeting set up in Sorrento and Positano. I and Father Regis will go to Positano and Father Thomas you and Jimmy will go to Sorrento. I will get information to you once you are in Sorrento on what you must do. I promise it will not be too dangerous and your mission will be very important. Father Regis and I will do what we have to in Positano and then we all will meet again in Pompeii." "Brother, what about my personal reason for coming.?" "Jimmy, I promise as soon as our mission is done, I will help you." "What if we fail?" "Father Regis has something for you. I must leave now." Father Regis opens his coat pocket and hands Jimmy a gun, this might come in handy. Here are your papers allowing you to carry a concealed weapon. Do you know how to use it?" "Thirteen months in Viet Nam, I would say yes." "Brother you didn't answer my question. What if we fail?" "Then God help us all." Brother Aiden and Father Regis walk away. Jimmy turns to Father Thomas, "Did you know what we were getting into?" "Honestly, not really. Brother never involved me in anything like this before. I have faith in him so he must know what he is doing." "What now?" We go back to the hotel and then in the morning we go to Sorrento. You will love Sorrento; it is my favorite city in Italy." "Whatever you say, Father." Jimmy shakes his head and follows Father Thomas out.

Positano Italy:

Winding Roads with houses and restaurants leading down to the Mediterranean. One of the most beautiful places in the world. A calm warm sunny day finds Oliver Wilhelm, Jacob and one other sitting at an outdoor restaurant.

"I spoke to our contacts in Sorrento and all is set. They will be in Pompeii for our meeting. Also, I have our associates here in Positano all set, everything is in order." "There can be no setbacks, we need all members present. We have to have all twelve of the high counsel there will be no exceptions. They must all be present. The ceremony will be at midnight. All the other members must all wear their given attire. We will call on the chosen ones and they will all rise. These chosen ones will spread throughout the world. They will be brilliant scientists, Academics, Politicians, Biologists, Chemists, Artists of all kinds. They will penetrate every powerful country in the world. They will lead to the destruction of all the Governments. They will start revolutions from within and will decay all religions and eliminate all that stand in their way. This will happen quickly. All their fame and fortune will be handed to them. There will be uncontrollable disease which will lead to mass fear. Their leaders and their culture will be destroyed. There will be rioting and dissension in all phases. We will turn countries against countries, turn races against races, brother against brother. Then the chosen ones will rise and take control of the world. They will pave the way for the Master who will rise and take his throne. He will then wait for the Lamb to come with the word of God. He will raise his armies to meet us. Then as it has been told the final battle will begin. You will see a new world order led by our Master and he shall rule for all eternity. We will be rewarded with all the worlds treasures and power. The Master has been waiting for this time since the beginning and he says that the time is now. He is pleased so far all has gone on as planned. Now we are ready for the final ceremony. Have all the society there and we will all witness the resurrection of the chosen evil." "Oliver did you speak about this Brother Aiden?" "Yes, I can't believe he is still alive and here. I thought the Vatican was done with him many years ago. He has been a problem forever. He has interfered before many times. His ability to call on his good messengers has been a major problem." "Why don't we just kill him?" "No, the Master forbids it. For some reason he wants this to happen. He wants him involved and he wants him to attend the ceremony. He wants him to witness the coming of all the chosen ones. He wants him to see it with his own eyes and then he will have him taken care of. He wants us to make it easy for him to be there without him knowing. This is like a game to the Master and he enjoys it. I have made arrangements that he will be there and his little helper can come with him?" "Then they will be eliminated?" "This is the Masters decision."

CHAPTER 19

Stevie after driving for eleven hours sits in the motel room in Dillion South Carolina. Laying on the bed after dinner he thinks, "What do I do now and where should I go? As he unwinds, he starts to drift off, he sees a burst of light. Then he sees a life-like movie played out in front of him. He has the feeling that he can change what he is seeing.

Come on Stevie it's seven o'clock, let's go." He looks around the room, it's his mom's house. "Danny, Jimmy, what's going on? "What's going on, what are you nuts, it's Friday and we're going out like we always do. Come on Sal and Ray are in the car waiting. Come on get dressed. You should have been ready by now." "Where are we going?" "What's up with you? We're going to Lido Beach, where we always go. Come on move your ass, we got some partying to do." "Okay, I'm coming." Stevie goes into the bathroom and looks in the mirror. He does seem to look a lot younger than the last time he saw himself. He is confused but he has no memory of anything else. His friends, his bedroom, his house is all normal. The problem is something doesn't feel right. He is not sure but it's like this is not who he really is. He washes his face and combs his hair. I look good, my friends, I guess it's all good. He calls out, "Let me get dressed in peace and I will be right out." "Okay, but hurry up." Stevie goes to his closet and pulls out a clean shirt and pants. Everything fits perfect. He opens up his dresser drawer and takes out his wallet. He opens it and pulls out his driving license. Steven Bracken born June 6, 1948. He walks to his night stand and sees Newsday dated, July 15, 1967. Everything seems normal but he can't shake the feeling he doesn't belong here. "It's crazy it's my house, my friends, come on let's have some fun." He walks out to the kitchen and sees his mom wiping down the counters. "Mom" "Yeah, Stevie what's up, you going out with your friends?" "Yeah,

I am." He walks over and hugs her and starts to cry. "I love you Mom, I missed you." "Stevie, are you, all right? We just had dinner an hour ago. What's wrong, honey?" "Nothing Mom, I just wanted you to know how much I love you and always will." "I Love you too and you will always be my baby boy. Now go out and have a good time with your friends but don't stay out to late. Be careful and don't drink too much. I'll see you in the morning." "Okay Mom, love you." Stevie picks up his keys and starts out the door. His mind is racing, "What the hell is wrong with me. I must be cracking up. Come on get it together, it's Friday and it's fun night." He walks out to the car. Danny yells out, "There he is, finally, what the hell took you so long?" "Sorry guys but here I am." Stevie gives a big smile and they all laugh. They pull out and head to southwest to the club. After an hour of hanging out in the parking lot, they decided it was time to make a grand entrance into the club. They managed to kill most of the shitty vodka with Stevie doing most of the heavy damage. They all tried to look as cool as possible as they walked into the club. The entrance into the club was a big deal, this would be the first time all the good-looking girls would see us and hopefully like what they see. Well that was their thought process back then. Look cool and hope for the best. As Stevie entered the club it was a typical dark smoky, noisy scene. It was a rush to be young having my buddies all around me and the excitement of maybe meeting that one special beautiful girl who would take one look at me and fall in love right then. As much as Stevie liked hanging out with the guys, He felt different this time. He was still buzzed from the vodka but something was off. He could never tell his friends what was on his mind, that would be very difficult because he didn't know exactly what it was. They made their way to the bar and Stevie ordered Dewar's and water. They parked themselves across from the lady's room, which was Ray's idea. Ray said it's the best spot because all the girls would come this way one time at least as the night went on. To be honest he was right. They hung out there and drank, smoked their Marlboros looked cool and tried their luck with the girls as they passed by to the lady's room.

Later that night Jimmy had hooked up with a cute blond and Stevie was dancing up a storm with a very attractive brown-haired girl in a very short dress. Ray, Sal and Danny were not as lucky but they were still having a great time. As the night flew by, they were making plans to meet at late morning and were going to Jones beach to spend Saturday. Where else would you go on Saturday in the summer on Long Island? It was getting late and the place had really thinned out. There were about three or four couples on the dance floor. It was getting to that time when they would hit the closest diner, stuff their face with some burgers and head home.

Stevie was so into the girl, he almost felt normal. As he held her in his arms his head began to burn. He really liked her but something was boiling inside of him. He had these weird feelings that he should pull away from her. He tried to shake the feeling off and kissed her gently. As he kissed her, he felt excited for a moment and then a rage building in him. She smiled as she seemed to sense something, "Everything okay Stevie?" "Yeah, I guess maybe I drank a little too much." "You want to sit?" "No Jennifer, I'm good." Danny was thinking it was nice to have a night out with no problems, all is good. Jimmy came over to him, his girl left with her friends but he scored her number and he was happy. Now they were waiting on Stevie. He was still slow dancing to what was the last song of the night. They decided as soon as it was over, they would grab him and hit the road. As the music stopped Stevie walked over to them, arm and arm with Jennifer. Danny pulled Stevie over and told him to get her number because they were ready to go. Stevie took Jennifer by the hand to a corner they spoke a while and she was writing down her number, Stevie's head started vibrating. He was back in the bed in the motel. Everything was blinking, sounds were going on and off. The room was breaking apart. A split second later he was standing in front of Jennifer. She had just written her number, "Stevie, what's up? You seem to go off into some kind of daze." "Man, I'm sorry. I mixed vodka and scotch and I'll never do that again." Two guys came from the back door. One of them pulled Jennifer by the arm and away from Stevie.

Danny saw what was happening and he told Jimmy to get the car and get ready to pick them up so they could get the hell out of here real fast. Jimmy grabbed Sal and they went to get the car. Danny was watching Stevie waiting for him to do something stupid but he didn't move. He just watched as Jennifer and this guy were in heavy conversation. Danny told Ray to come with him and they would get Stevie out of here. Ray and Danny went over to Stevie and told him to be cool and let's get out now. Stevie smiled and said he was good he just wanted to wait to make sure Jennifer was okay with this guy. Stevie seemed calm so they all started to relax a bit. Ray went to the door to see if they were ready with the car. Jennifer waved at Stevie and mouthed to call her. Stevie smiled nodded his head. They both turned and started for the door, Danny thanked God, no problem. He thought this was going to get ugly but it was just another Friday night out with the guys. As Danny and Stevie walked away and were a few feet from the door this jerk yells out, "You better get the hell out of here, you asshole." Stevie stops short he starts to walk towards this guy. Danny sees where this is going so, he gets in front of Stevie and tells him, "No, don't be stupid just forget it and let's go." Stevie stops looks at him and smiles with that angelic look on his face and says, "You're right let's go home." As they start walking out Stevie feels strange once again like he is watching a movie. It's like he's seen this before. He starts thinking, "Don't go back, just leave." He hears a voice in his head, "Go back Stevie, you been here before and you will always do the same thing. You must go back your fate is waiting for you. You can't change anything. You are what you are. Your face is the mirror of your mind and your eyes without speaking confess the secrets of who you are. Do what you have to do. This is your destiny and you can live it over and over but it will never change." Stevie is frozen as he sees pictures of life flash before him. His mom smiling and his brothers all playing together when they were kids. He sees his Dad punching him and beating him because he was protecting his mom. He sees himself laughing with his friends. He sees Jennifer kissing him and then he sees her dying in front of him as he smiles watching her die. He hears his mom say I love you Stevie and you will always be my baby boy. Stevie hears the guy holding Jennifer, "What are you waiting for asshole." The rest happened so fast it was surreal. "Stevie cry's out, no don't, just leave." Stevie instead of leaving turns back at the guy and goes right at him. Danny goes after Stevie and he tries to get to Stevie to stop him. Stevie punches the guy in the stomach and they both fall to the floor. Danny gets in between to break it up and a second later, Pop, pop, pop, the guy gets up and runs out the door. Jimmy sees blood pouring from Stevie's chest and Danny is lying right next to him. It all happened in seconds, Jimmy fell to his knees, grabbed Stevie and Danny and screamed out call an ambulance. He cradled them in his arms pleading with them to hold on. About fifteen minutes later the ambulance showed up but it was too late; Stevie bled out and Danny died in Jimmy's arms. They had no chance the bullets tore them apart.

Stevie jumps up in bed he is sweating profusely. He runs to the bathroom and is sick to his stomach. He washes his face and gets back into bed. His body is shaking as he tries to hold himself together. "He hears a voice speak out, "Stevie you poor stupid boy. I told you what to do but you run off to do what? Start a new life? Maybe you can get married, raise a family. Buy a house and grow old with your loving wife. No, you fool that is not what's going to happen, your soul is mine. You were brought back to do what I want. You can go back a million times but it will not change. You cannot change anything. If you want to continue to exist you will do what I direct you to do from now on." Stevie buries his head in his pillow and screams.

CHAPTER 20

Charlie looks at Lisa, "Thank you, it's going to be fun. I know you don't know them but Mr. Sherman is a great guy. He asked me over to get to know me a little better. Being that I work in his department. He is also a friend of my mom's friend that recommended me. I think he is just doing me a favor trying to make me more comfortable. He knows I just moved here from Buffalo." "It's fine Charlie, I'll be okay. Just one night it won't kill me. Come on let's go so we're not late. Don't want to upset your boss." Charlie and Lisa drive to Charlie's boss's house. A nice split-level brick house in Plainview. They are greeted and sit around the living room making small talk. "This is a beautiful house Mr. Sherman." "Please call me Bill, I'm just a supervisor, Charlie. "Well Bill, I love your home." "Thanks Charlie the house has been in my family for years. My Dad retired and him and my mom relocated to Florida. I was able to get a family discount. The housing here in Plainview has definitely gone way up in costs. I don't think we could afford it unless I got a great deal. The decorations are all my wife's doing. She is the decorator and in complete charge." Lisa smiles, "Well then you've done a beautiful job Mrs. Sherman." "Thanks Lisa but please call me Emma."" Do you come from this area?" "Yes, matter of fact me and Bill both grew up here in Plainview. We were high school sweethearts and were married a few years after graduating. It's funny we were reminiscing just before you came. Our twenty-fifth reunion is coming up soon and we were going through our year book." "Is that your yearbook right there?" "Yes, it is." "Can we see your pictures?" "I don't think you want to be bored with our high school pictures." "No, I'd love to see them, please." "Okay." Emma opens the book and pages through to Bills picture. "There's my handsome husband." "Oh wow, Bill you hardly changed." "I don't know about that Charlie." "Let's see your picture Emma, I love this." Emma smiles and flips a few pages back from Bills page. "There I am, oh not sure I want to show you, it's embarrassing." "You were and still are beautiful. You know Emma was a cheerleader." "Let's see, oh you are gorgeous" "Charlie stop." "That was your maiden name Brockovich, Did I say that right?" "Yes, close enough but some teachers really messed it up. Much easier now with Sherman." "I love looking at these pictures. Oh my God, Lisa look at this boy here. This is crazy look Lisa at this guy." "Wow, I see what you mean. That is amazing." "What is it, do you know him?" "Well no, can't be but Lisa has a friend she is been seeing and that is exactly what he looks like. I mean I would swear that is him and his name is Stevie." Who are you looking at? "That boy Steven Bracken." "Oh Stevie, no it can't be the same. He and another boy from school Danny Amendola were killed in a fight, in a night club. It was about two or three years after we graduated. Both were sweet boys and very good looking. It was tragic the whole graduating class showed up at their funeral, it was so sad. It must be some one that looked like him." "It's incredible and I know it's impossible but I could swear that he is a duplicate. The same hair and eyes it's crazy. Don't you think so, Lisa. "Yeah, it's remarkable how they look alike. Could he have had a son?" "No, defiantly not. This is a tight community everybody knows everything that goes on. I'm sure it's just a coincidence. You know they say everyone has a double somewhere." "That's true." After coffee and cake Lisa and Charlie head home. They are silent in the car and then Charlie can't be quiet anymore, "Lisa it is Stevie. I know I'm going to sound crazy but that was his picture. I have a photo memory and it was him." "Charlie, your crazy. You heard he was killed over twenty years ago. Not only that he would be a lot older and wouldn't look like that anymore. Emma was right, just a coincidence." "You know that Stevie is mysterious. We knew nothing about him. He shows up then disappears. The way he stormed out the other night was freaky." "What are you saying, Charlie he is a ghost or something?" "I don't know what I am saying but I got the heebie-jeebies when I saw that picture." "Stop please Charlie your freaking me out. Let's go home, please!" "Sorry Lisa."

Charlie is in the lunch room eating with a few of his co-workers. Above them is a small TV. There is a lot of noise so he couldn't hear the sound," So Charlie how did your visit go with the boss last night?" "Well it was very nice he has a lovely wife and home." "Don't feel to special we all went through the same tour when we started." "I don't feel special it was nice of him to do it." "Okay, just kidding with you." "Sorry for the tone just had a bad night sleep. When I don't sleep, I get a little grouchy." As Charlie bites into his sandwich he gazes up at the TV. It is the local news channel 12 showing a drawing of someone. Charlie gets up and goes close to the TV. He looks at the drawing and he hears the audio that this is a person of interest in the railroad murder. Charlie almost chokes as he can't believe his eyes. He quickly goes to his co-workers, "Oh my God, I think I know that guy." "What guy?" "The one on the news they are looking for." "You're kidding?" "No, I wish I was. I need to see that picture closer." "I saw that poster up at the community board in the lobby." Charlie storms off and goes to the lobby. He comes close to the poster and gasps, "Oh my God, this can't be." He looks around and takes the picture off the board. He goes into the office and makes a copy of it. He puts the other back on the board. He looks at the copy in his hand and shakes his head, "I have to show Lisa." That evening after work Charlie comes in to their apartment and yells," Lisa, Lisa, are you home?" He realizes she is not and sits down on the couch and just stares at the picture. After a half hour passes Lisa comes in and sees Charlie just sitting there, "Charlie, you okay?" "Lisa, please sit I have to show you this. I might be losing my mind so I need you to tell me what you think." Lisa sits down, "What is it?" "Look at this." Lisa looks at the picture and stares, "No Charlie, I know what you're thinking but no it has to be a resemblance but I don't know." "Yes, you do it's him. I might be nuts but last night we see him in a yearbook from over twenty years ago and now this. If he is a murderer and he was in a yearbook over twenty years ago, my God." "Charlie, there has to be some rational explanation. I mean this picture does look like him but the picture last night, I don't know what I'm saying. This is crazy, this can't be the same guy in both, can it? "I know Lisa it is way too weird and quite impossible but I know what we saw. I know you couldn't talk about it last night but we can't just forget it either." "Well what can we do? Who would believe us? we go to the police and say we think this is Stevie who has been here and who I dated. Then we tell them we saw the same Stevie in a yearbook that's over twenty years old they will send us both to the psychiatric ward." "I agree but what do we do?" "Let's slow down and think about this. After dinner we will go over our options." What options? We don't have any. We can't just sit on this I will go crazy." "Your right Charlie we have to get this over with. I say we go to the police and tell them the truth." "Everything, even last night?" "I don't know but we will cross that bridge when we're there." "Okay,"

Next day Lisa and Charlie sitting in their car at the Police Station:

"You think we are doing the right thing?" "Yes Lisa, we have no choice. We have no idea if Stevie did anything wrong. He might just have witnessed something and he might be able to help the police in finding the murderer." "I know you're right. It's just that I really liked Stevie and I feel I'm betraying him somehow." "Well you're not. He is a witness that's all." "What about the yearbook?" "I have no idea what to say or if we should say anything about that." "Yeah, I agree. They might think we are two nuts." "Come on, let's get this over with."

They walk into the station house to the front desk:

"Excuse me officer we might have some information on a police flyer of that man wanted concerning the rail road incident." The Sargent looks at them and says to wait here he will be right back. The Sargent approaches Jamie, "Jamie, I got two citizens at the desk saying they have some information on the rail road case." "Really?

okay bring them into room two." Lisa and Charlie are escorted into room two and have a seat by the table. "Lisa, this is so exciting. I feel like I'm on Hills Street Blues TV show. I've never been in a police station before. Do you think they have someone watching us right now?" "Just be calm Charlie we are just here helping not suspects."

The door opens and Jamie walks in, "I'm detective Jamie Collins you have some information that might be helpful? So why don't you start with your names and let's hear what you got." "Hi, my name is Charlie and I have never been interviewed by a real detective before. To be honest I'm a little nervous but also excited. Is there someone behind that glass watching us?" "No Charlie just me. So just relax and tell me why you came in." "I don't know where to start." "Anywhere you want." "Okay, well Lisa is my cousin and I have just moved here from Buffalo. We are sharing her apartment which she was so nice to let me move in. I just love her we have been close since we were kids." "Excuse me Charlie but I'm really swamped with cases so can you just tell me what you have on the railroad case." "Sorry, I know sometimes I do talk too much. Well Lisa has been seeing this nice boy Stevie and I must say he seems really nice." "Charlie, get to the information please." Sorry, I was eating lunch at my job when this news station was showing a picture of a person wanted for information on the railroad incident. I couldn't believe my eyes when I saw it. It looked a lot like Lisa's friend Stevie. I went out in the lobby and they had a picture of him up on the bulletin board. I made a copy and brought it home for Lisa to see. She looked at it and agreed it looks just like Stevie. So, we felt we should come in and tell you." "Lisa, Does the picture look like your friend?" "Yes, it does. I can't be sure it is definitely him but it does look a lot like him." "when was the last time you saw him?" "A few days ago." "Detective can I speak?" "Yes Charlie." "The last time we saw Stevie he came to dinner at our place. I made a special dinner just for him and tell him the good news that I was staying with Lisa and moved from Buffalo. Well I must say he was very strange that evening and for some unknown reason he just ran out of the house without even saying anything. No thank you no good night nothing. Just ran out the door." "Lisa, did you have a fight?" "No, nothing, he hardly talked he was kind of strange." "You know detective I spent hours preparing a wonderful meal specially for him. He could've said something, don't you think that was very rude?" Jamie just shakes her head and slightly rolls her eyes, "Lisa, do you have an address for him?" "No, he said he just relocated from Arizona and was staying in a motel until he found something." "Phone number?" "No, sorry he really was kind of mysterious about his life. I know it sounds strange but we just kind of met and just started seeing each other. He has been a gentleman and very nice to me." "Would you have any idea how we can find him or where he might hang out, anything?" "No, again I'm sorry." "Do you think he lives around where you live?" "I'm not sure but he was familiar with the Huntington area." "I tell you what, why don't you take my card and if he contacts you try to get some information on how we could find him. If you should think of anything else that you might think is helpful please call me anytime." "Detective, do you think he was involved in this murder or maybe just witnessed something?" "I can't really say., it's a going investigation. For now, he is what we say a person of interest and that's all at this point. Do you think he is dangerous?" "No, not at all. Not from anything I've seen. Like I said he has been nothing but nice to me." "Okay, if that's it I want to thank you for coming in. Please call me if anything pops up." Lisa and Charlie stand and start to walk out. Charlie stops and looks at Lisa, do you think we should say something about you know what?" Jamie looks at Charlie, "Is there something you are not telling me?"

Lisa looks at Charlie, "No not really." "Please, if you have any information no matter how small it might be of help. We really need to find this guy he can be very important in this investigation."

Charlie stares at Lisa and then looks at Jamie, "It's really nothing and it is just some crazy coincidence." "Charlie tell me what is it?" "Me and Lisa went to my bosses house the other night. He and his wife are the nicest people. They have a lovely home in Plainview. It was my boss's parents' house." "Charlie tell me what is the information, please!" "Sorry, I know I talk too much. Anyhow, he had a year book from when they graduated Plainview High School in 1965. His wife was a cheerleader and very pretty." Jamie was about to scream and gave Charlie a scary look. "Okay, we were looking at the pictures and then we see this picture of a student that, I don't think you are going to believe this." "Just say it." Well, the student looked like our friend Stevie. To be honest more then looked like him, it was definitely him. I will swear that was his picture." "Was he a teacher or something?" "No, he was a graduating senior. Mrs. Sherman said he was killed in a fight at a night club a couple of years later." Lisa jumps in, "Detective, we know this sounds stupid and we don't want to waste your time. That is why we were not going to mention it. It must be a coincidence that they look alike." "Tell me Lisa, do you think it is the same guy?" "I don't know for sure but it looks exactly like him. It's nuts I mean it was so many years ago and he was killed. Look we're sorry. Maybe we should leave?" "Charlie do you think you can get the year book from your boss. I'd like to see it." "Should I make a copy of the picture?" "No, I would like the book if you can get it." "Okay, I could do that, I think." "Anything else you can remember?" "No, That's it. Detective, we're not crazy what we told you is what we believe to be true." "Thanks Lisa, you both have been helpful. If there is anything else you remember please call me. Charlie as soon as you get the book let me know?" "Yes, I will. Detective, can I ask you something?" "Sure." "Do ever watch the TV show Hill Street Blues? It's my favorite show. I was wondering if you think it is realistic of how you guys really work?" Jamie shakes her head, "Thank you for coming in and Charlie be careful out there." Charlie smiles, you do watch the show, they say that every episode. I knew it." Jamie smiles and walks away.

Jamie sits at her desk and watches Gulli walk across the room to her." Hey, anything new?" "No, just another dead end. Anything happen here?" "You better sit down for this one." "Okay, something good, I hope." "I had two seemingly normal people come in. They had some info on our P.O.I. Her name is Lisa, has been seeing this guy Stevie. Both of them say that our P.O.I. could be the guy she is seeing. Her cousin, Charlie saw the picture on a work bulletin board. He made a copy and they both agreed that it could be him." "Well, that's good news." "Wait, that is just the good news. They have no contact info on him. No phone, no address and no last name. Seems he said he just moved here from Arizona and is living in some motel. They have no idea but they said he seemed familiar with the Huntington area." "Well, that's a fit." Yeah, I agree but we have no way to locate him." "Do you think they are covering for him?" No, I think they are telling the truth. Here's where it really gets strange. They were at Charlie's bosses house and they were going through their high school year book from 1965. Both of them swear that there was a student picture in there that they said was this same guy Stevie. His name was Steven Bracken. His boss's wife said this Steven Bracken was killed a few years later in a night club." "Okay, so two weirdo's that get off on making up this bull shit stories. What else is new." "Gulli, I'm telling you I believe them.

Look, I'm not saying it's the same guy in the year book has come back to life, but I believe they believe what they are saying. I asked for him to bring in the year book and he said he would." "Jamie, it's not that I don't believe you it's sometimes people are not what they seem. The two walk in and say their friend is the one we are looking for but they have no information on him. They don't know nothing about him. No phone, no address, no nothing but yet she has been dating him. Then they say they see his picture in a year book from 1965. Just to make it more interesting this guy was killed over twenty years ago. Maybe their playing out some game or bet or something. If I told you this story what would you believe?"

"I'd think the same but I have to go with my gut. I do believe their story. I looked up this Stevie Bracken and he did graduate in 1965 from Plainview High School. He was killed in a club a couple years later. How would they even know about this guy? What did they do just randomly pick out this guy's picture and make this bull shit story up? Sorry, I'm not buying it. They believe it and if you met with them, I believe you would too." "Okay, let's say their story is true, so what then? We have a guy who came back from the dead dated this Lisa as he went around killing people? That's what you're saying?" "I don't know. I agree it's ridiculous." "You know we have no leads except this sketch of him to go on. I say you follow up on this Steve Bracken maybe he had a twin or had a kid that resembled him. Who knows but it's all we got right now? How's that sound?" Jamie smiles, Thanks Gulli, and you know there has been no prints and no DNA no nothing. Maybe we are chasing some ghost." "You're watching too much TV Jamie or reading those Stephen King novels."

CHAPTER 21

Pompeii, Italy:

"Oliver, I have been told that Brother Aiden's friends this Father Thomas and his American traveling companion are headed to Sorrento." "For what purpose?" "I'm not sure. They have been with Brother Aiden and must be helping him with finding out about our meeting. It's possible they have some plan to stop some of our associates from completing their tasks. Shall we stop them or does the Master want them there along with Aiden?" "No, he never mentioned them. If they are of some concern then have them eliminated." "I will take care of it. Do we have any idea how many we will be rising at our ceremony?" "No, he has told me very little. I'm assuming this will be the complete rising as we have talked about. The Master has told me many times that the time is now. We must be ready for the final battle."

Sorrento, Italy:

The bus winds through the narrow streets of Sorrento barely avoiding the concrete side walls to its side. "Father these streets are so narrow it's amazing that this bus fits." "It is amazing how they drive through these streets. Jimmy, look at those lemon trees, they grow all over Sorrento." "Some of them are the size of grapefruits, amazing." After they leave the bus they continue to walk to their hotel. On a corner they stop as a parade of children march down the main street. They are all wearing large chef hats and blue and white printed aprons. Other children had Christmas hats on. They had banners and were led by teachers. The children were all happy and it was a marvelous sight. Hundreds of people smiling and cheering them on. The day was picture perfect and Sorrento was beautiful. They walked by shop after shop selling everything from leather goods to Limoncello. Stands of lemon ices all over. They continued to walk until they reached the hotel. The hotel lobby was small and right off the main street. They checked into their room. "Jimmy, come with me, I have to show you something." They walked out of the hotel and a few streets away they were overlooking the ocean. "Look that is the hotel Vittoria it is majestic. Look at the way it projects over the ocean. Look at the roof top balconies overlooking the ocean. I never have stayed there way too much money for a priest. It is some place I always admired. Look straight out and you can see clearly see Mount Vesuvius. That is where the volcano erupted in 79 A D. By the time the Vesuvius eruption sputtered to an end the next day, Pompeii was buried under millions of tons of volcanic ash. About 2,000 Pompeiians were dead, but the eruption killed as many as 16,000 people overall. It's getting to that time are you hungry? "Always, especially here in Italy." "Come, I know a small delightful restaurant just a few streets from here. As they walked, "Father, look at all those motor scooters lined up." "Yes, because of all those narrow streets and nowhere to park they are the most favorable way to travel."

Sitting in the Italian restaurant, "The food here is unbelievable." "They make all the pasta fresh every day. The vegetables are all local and same with the cheese. The tomatoes are perfect. No additives everything home- made. You can taste the difference." Just as they are finishing their veal the sounds of Italian songs surround the room. A four piece strolling band with a mandolin, a guitar and an accordion player approach the table. One man asks something in Italian. Jimmy looks at Father Thomas, "What's he saying?" "He is asking you to request a song." Jimmy smiles, "I'm not sure of any Italian songs but how about That's Amore?" "The band immediately starts to play That's Amore in Italian. In seconds all the patrons start to sing along. Many standing with their glasses of wine swinging in the air. Jimmy couldn't stop from feeling, "If only my Jennifer was here to see this. There is not a better place on earth I would rather be then here with her sharing this with me. As he thought this, tears rolled down his eyes. Father Thomas could read his mind, "It's okay Jimmy, I know what you're thinking." He raises his glass of wine, "To all the ones we love that can't be here with us, salute." With that a hat is passed around and all the patrons tip generously.

After dinner they sit back and enjoy a glass of Limoncello. "God bless the Italians they know how to enjoy life." "They do Jimmy, we should learn from them." Just after speaking a man comes over to Father Thomas and speaks in Italian and slips a note in his hand. He then quickly walks away. Jimmy looks at Father Thomas, "What was that?" "He said good to see you Father, God bless you and stay safe and handed me this note. "What does it say." "It says to meet at the ferry to Capri. I know where that is. It's a short walk and down the steps to the water." "You have any idea who we are meeting and why so secretly? "I don't, the instructions I normally get at the desk or by phone." "What should we do?" "I say we go and see what is this all about." "Okay Father, let's go." Jimmy and Father Thomas walk a few streets and come to a cement wall. Steps lighted with glass round globes leading down to the water. Normally a busy area with tourists walking, sightseeing and waiting for the ferry to Capri. Now it was quiet and they were the only two there. They descended down many steps to the bottom walkway. As they walked to the ferry Jimmy stops, "Father this is kind of creepy down here maybe we should rethink this." "Let's wait a few minutes and if no one shows we will leave." As they waited and looked out at the water a man slowly comes from behind them, "Mi Scusi Father Thomas." He speaks in Italian for about five minutes. After he is done, he nods and leaves. "Okay Father, what's happening?" "He says there is a meeting in Pompeii that we are to attend. We will meet with Brother Aiden and Father Regis there. He told me the meeting place but the day will be sent to me when it is finalized. He said to be careful that the society is aware of our presence here in Sorrento. They are not sure if we are in danger but that cannot be ruled out." "What exactly are we to do at this meeting?" "Brother Aiden is here for one purpose and that is to stop the society from completing its ritual in summoning the evil from the underworld. Brother knows I can help him succeed in stopping them. You Jimmy are here for your own reasons but they cannot be filled until this task is done. Also, I admit you are here to help me get there." "Like your body guard?" "Yes, and as my friend." "No problem Father, like I said there is no place for me so I am with you one hundred percent." "Thanks Jimmy." They turn around and start to walk back to the steps. From behind a stranger approached, he is dressed in black with a hood covering most of his face. They walk on, unaware of the danger. The attacker closes in on them and pulls a large knife out of his side belt. As they come close to the steps the stranger lunges at Jimmy. His instincts kick in as he senses the attacker. He turns and the attacker misses stabbing him. Jimmy grabs the attacker's arm and snaps it on his knee knocking the knife loose. The attacker kicks Jimmy in the stomach and Jimmy falls in pain. The attacker reaches for his knife but Father Thomas steps hard on his out stretched hand. The attacker looks at Father Thomas and then he grabs him around the throat with both hands. Father Thomas begins to gasp for air. Jimmy rises and grabs the attacker pulling him away from Father Thomas. The attacker hits Jimmy in the head and he goes down. He then reaches for his knife once more. Jimmy takes his gun from behind his back and screams at the attacker to freeze. The attacker turns towards Jimmy seeing the gun. He turns and runs away. Jimmy points the gun but doesn't shoot. He turns to father Thomas, "Are you okay?" "Yes, I'm fine, thanks to you. One question why didn't you take out the gun sooner?" "I forgot I had it." Jimmy smiles and shakes his head. "Looks like someone doesn't want us around." "Yes, it seems that way. This is something I have not been involved with before. I'm a little too old for this. I know Brother Aiden wants me so I will follow through. Jimmy you have every right to leave now." "As I told you before I will see this through and hopefully Brother Aiden can repay me. Besides, it's obvious you need my help. Should we report this to the police?" "I don't think it would help at this point. There will be paper work, reports and to many questions. I think it is best we just keep a low profile and leave as soon as we know where and when. I do think it will be wise to stay in more safer areas from now on." "Yes, sounds good to me." "I think I have had enough excitement for one night. Let's go back to the hotel and gets some rest."

In a dark room Oliver sits by a fire place staring into the darkness. Jacob approaches, "Is everything all right?" "I am not sure. I have heard from the master and he confuses me. I am expecting an army to rise from the underworld. He says an army is not needed. He assures me the ceremony will produce the evil that will not disappoint. To be patient and do what we have been told to do. I am not sure what to expect from our calling. He does not answer many questions. He expects one hundred percent obedience and does not tolerate doubts. At this point we have no choice but to continue as planned and wait for the results. He says he is sending his flesh and blood that will transform the world. We will follow the dark ones who will lead the way. A Nation will rise against nations, and kingdom against kingdom. There will be great earthquakes, famines and pestilences in various places, and fearful events. He said the beast will be rising out of the earth. It will have two horns like a lamb and it will speak like a dragon. He opposes and exalts himself against every so-called god or object of worship, so that he takes his seat in the temple of God, proclaiming himself to be God. This is the words of the master." "This is what is coming, some kind of beast?" "I do not know what or who, all we can do is wait and see.

CHAPTER 22

Amityville Long Island NY:

Stevie checks the address and rings the bell. After a minute the door opens, "Can I help you?" "Otto?" "Yes." "I would like a session with you, can I come in?" "I only do sessions by appointment. If you call this number, I will be able to set up an appointment." "No, that won't work. I need to see you now. Can we please go inside?" "Absolutely not. I only go by appointments, no exceptions." Stevie pulls his gun from his pocket and points it at Otto's head, "Will you make an exception now?" Otto retreats and walks backwards into his house. "What is it you want. I have no real money here but I can give you what I have." "I don't want your money just go inside and let's talk." "Fine, please don't hurt me." "I just want to talk so just do what I say and you will not get hurt." They walk into Otto's den and sit. "Otto, I know it was you that brought me back on Halloween night. I want you to now return me to wherever I came from. Better yet if you can send me back to the night, I was killed maybe I can change that." Otto shakes his head, "I'm sorry but I do not know what you are talking about. Maybe you have the wrong man?" "Cut the bull shit, I know it was you. I read the papers, so don't waste my time. If you want to live just do what I ask you to do." Otto sits back, "I just cannot wave a magic wand and send you back. Yes, it was me that night but it was an accident. I had no idea what was going to happen. I do have a gift, I have spoken to the deceased and called upon them to answer some questions. Many times, I have faked it too. I can only do so much. That night was a pure accident. I never intended or thought it was possible to bring you back. You have to believe me." "Do you believe there are alternate realities? "I have had visions of being back when I was young. I can swear I was living the night I was killed over again. I want you to try to send me back to that time and that reality. I don't want to live this life anymore. I have done things that are not me. I can't take it anymore, please help me." "Believe me if I could I would but what you are asking is impossible." Stevie feels the anger building in him. The rage that comes and goes. He stands in front of Otto and puts the gun to his head, "I'm not going to ask again either you do what I ask or I'm going to blow your brains out." Otto was shaking so bad he could hardly speak, "Okay, please, I will do what you ask." "Good, that's better. See Otto, we can work this out. Now, do what you need to do." "I will need your total concentration. I will put you in a state like trance. I will summon a spirit to guide you to where you want to go. I Cannot do this with you pointing the gun at me. You must put it down and I will begin." "Okay but if you try anything your dead, understood?" "Yes, of course." Stevie puts the gun by the table near his side. Otto comes close and puts his hand on Stevie's head. "Try to relax and take a deep breath. Close your eyes and clear your mind completely. Try to silently hum as I begin to chant." Stevie does what Otto says. Otto begins to chant,

 "Adducere ad me, et spiritus ortus tui
 adducere ad me, et spiritus ortus tui, adducere ad me, et spiritus ortus tui"

Otto keeps on repeating the chant over and over. Stevie starts to drift into darkness. He sees flickering of white lights and bursts of pictures moving quickly by him. He hears sounds of voices that are flickering in and out. The pictures are now more like bits of movie film speeding by. He feels an energy pushing and pulling him in different directions. He sees a dark presence coming at him. As it comes closer and closer his body starts to vibrate. He feels like he is burning up and his heart rate is racing. Then in a second the dark presence disappears. His body cools and slows down. He has a feeling as if he was floating. A second later he feels nothing and everything goes black.

 "Stevie, hello, what do you think?" Stevie shakes his head and is confused. He looks around the room. He sees his friends Danny, Jimmy, Sal and Ray all just looking at him. "Stevie, what's up with you? You feeling okay? At least answer us?" "Sorry, I just feel weird. Like I was somewhere else. You ever get the feeling you are not what you are? Like you been somewhere or even someone else?" "What the hell are you talking about? If your trying to prove your nuts, you should wait till you go before the army doctor to try this act out. I will ask you one more time, where should we take Jimmy for his going away party. Ray said the Music Lounge but I'm kind of sick of that place. Besides what happened there a couple of weeks ago will cause a lot of girls to stay away." Stevie looks confused, "What happened?" "This act of yours sucks. Like you don't know that guy got shot and killed there. Who knows if we went there that night it could have been one of us that got killed? Sorry about what happened with your mom but in a way, it could have saved one of us. How's she doing? "Yeah, no she's okay but thanks for asking." Danny rolls his eyes, "Come on Stevie we are always here for each other, you know that." Stevie starts to remember everything that happened. "You know my dad, when he drinks, he becomes a jerk. He hit my mom and I went nuts. He is impossible to stop once he starts. I had no choice; he could have hurt her really bad. I did my best without trying to hurt him. He got me pretty good as you can tell. At least, he stopped and went away. He came back real late and went down the basement and slept it off. I couldn't sleep until I knew he was out for the night. The next day he was all sorry to my mom. Promised it won't happen again. Same bullshit story he says every time. He is not talking to me but that's okay. I have nothing to say to him. You know let's not talk about that shit anymore. You know you are right it could have been one of us. The girl that those guys fought over was hot. I know I would have gone after her too. With my charm she would have been all over me. Who knows what could have happened to me? It's funny but I get this feeling that I was that guy somehow, the one that got killed. I know that's crazy but I can't help this feeling. Like sometimes I'm two different people.

Like I'm living two different lives." Danny laughs, "You mean maybe there are two Stevie's? Believe me one is enough." Every one laughs and so does Stevie. Danny stands, Okay, now that we know that there are two Stevie's let's decide where we are taking Jimmy tomorrow night. I say we go to dinner and then to Manhattan to some club. Ray, what do you say?" "Danny, I don't care, something to eat and then we go wild. We go to some club drink and pick up some girls and drive everybody crazy." Sal stands, "You guys got no class. Listen to me, we go to Little Italy, Mulberry Street a nice Italian restaurant. We start with a nice antipasto, you know Italians sausage, provolone, salami, those hot peppers, you know the works. Then we have the pasta, say ravioli or stuffed shells with tons of ricotta. Next we have veal or chicken cacciatore and then a juicy steak." "After all that Italian food you want a steak?" "Of course, Danny, what's wrong with you. "Then we have our dessert, assorted pastries with a lot of cannoli with a nice cup of demitasse. Then some assorted nuts and fruit with a glass of anisette." "My God Sal after eating like that all I would want to do is sleep." "Danny, stop I'm not finished. Then we go to a classy club where they play some Sinatra music, maybe some Tony Bennett and we meet some nice girls. Then on the way home we stop at the Syosset diner for a juicy hamburger deluxe with tons of French fries. How's that sound? Jimmy laughs, "Sal, do you think about anything else but food?" "Yeah, I just said Sinatra music and girls too, what's a matter with you? You know sometimes I think you guys have no class. Listen to me I know what I'm talking about." Jimmy looks at Sal, "Your right Sal, I'm good with that for my night out. You know I'm going to miss you guys. I wish I wasn't going but I have no choice. Uncle Sam calls, so we go. We do what we got to do. Maybe I get lucky and get sent to Hawaii instead of Viet Nam. What about you Stevie what are you going to do?" "I'm thinking of enlisting. I know it's only a matter of time. I don't want Jimmy coming home and I'm just beginning my tour. I guess I should get it over with. Look, we are like brothers no matter what happens we will always be there for each other." "You got that right Stevie. Come here let me give you a hug." "That's all right Sal, I'm good." "Come here." Sal grabs Stevie and gives him a big hug. Everybody joins in and laughs. Sal starts to tear up, "I love you guys." "We love you too Sal." Danny smiles, "Look this is not like we're saying goodbye, Jimmy will be home before you know it. Then we have the rest of our lives to live. We will always be together so let's stop this crap and plan our night. Let's have a great night and see Jimmy off the right way. We will get him so drunk he'll forget all about Viet Nam." Stevie feels good. He feels great being with his friends. This is the way it should always be. As good as he feels he still can't shake the feeling that this is not real. All he wants is to stay here with his friends. This is the life he wants to live. He knows his dad is an ass but he has his mom, his brothers and the greatest friends. He is happy in this world and he knows he is a good person. He would do anything to protect his mom. He would do anything for his brothers and his friends. He feels nothing but love for all of them. He knows he never wants to hurt anybody. Something inside of him he has done bad things but he knows deep inside of him says he is good. As he looks around the room his friends are all laughing and having a great time being together. As he tries to let go of that black cloud hanging over his head and enjoy just being here with them. He promises himself to stop and be happy. As he begins to accept that he is here and things are good, his body starts to tremble and his vision goes in and out. He feels a force pulling him away. He tries hard to hold steady but he is helpless, the force is pulling him in and out of the present. His head begins to spin and once again he hears sounds of voices fading in and out. Lights bursting around him. Scenes flashing quickly by him and then all goes black.

As he begins to waken, he sees flashes of the room he was in before he went black. His friends are no longer there. The room is where he came to see Otto. It all comes storming back to him. He is here where he held a gun to Otto's head. His friends were some kind of dream. He remembers telling Otto to send him back where he came from. He starts to cry realizing this is who and where he is. As he looks around, he sees a puddle of blood and then he sees Otto lying face down. Part of his head blown off. Stevie says out loud, "Oh shit, what happened, no way I did this. Stevie looks at the gun lying on the floor and he knows that is the gun he had with him. He bends down over the body, "How could this be, I didn't do this" He hears a voice loud and clear, "Oh but you did my friend. You must remember that you put the gun to the back of his head and shot twice blowing his head apart." "No that's bullshit I wasn't even here. Was I?" "Where Stevie, some other world or some other reality? Maybe you were dreaming after you blew his brains out. I don't think the police will believe you were somewhere else. Try explaining how you couldn't have done it. I could see their faces when you tell them you were back with your little friends having a good time twenty years ago. I'm sure they will believe you. You see Stevie you can't escape from me. I own you and your soul. You have no choice now or forever. You belong to me and you will do what I say. You were brought back by that idiot you just killed. Somehow the idiot without knowing what the hell he was doing managed to send you to an alternate reality. For reasons even I do not understand you have been able to crossover. The problem is I won't let you. Your one chance is dead. If I didn't come along the idiot might have succeeded in getting you there permanently. Sorry my friend I put a stop to it just in time. Lucky for me not so lucky for you. For some reason I cannot explain I have become fond of having you around. You were and are not of the Master's grand plan but you can amuse me with your little reign of terror you can spread. I enjoy watching you add to the world's misery, piece by piece. When the time comes and I have to move on to bigger and better things, I will be done with you. Then, I will send you back where you belong. Until then you are mine to do as I please." "I didn't kill him. I just wanted to scare him into doing what I ask." "Enough of your whining just pick up your gun and leave. I'm done wasting my time with you." Stevie is totally confused; he knows he did not kill Otto but no one would believe him. He picks up the gun and slowly walks out the door. He gets in his car and drives. He pictures himself back with his friends, he was happy. If Otto could have lived, maybe he could have stayed and had a chance to live his life over. He has no idea how Otto sent him back and how any of this could be possible. He knows it wasn't a dream, he was there. His friends were real, he was real, he was there. Now what does he have? He has no choice but to continue doing things he hates. He thinks, "Maybe I could get away from this entity that haunts me. I can go somewhere and live a normal life. Start over and screw this entity. First, I want to see Lisa, one more time. I need to try to explain why I left her that night. I left because I didn't want to hurt her or Charlie. That voice in my head telling me to kill them, well, I didn't do it. Maybe, I can do what I want. Either way, I have to try. I need to get a room and lay down, clear my head. Then I will get a plan on what to do."

A woman in her late seventies, knocks on the door pushing it slightly opened, "Hello, Otto it's Phyllis, anybody home? Otto, hello." She slowly walks into the house again calling out. She continues walking into the main living room and see's Otto lying face down in a pool of red. She lets out a piercing scream and runs out the door, 'Help! Someone call the police. Help, Help!" After a couple of minutes neighbors come out to see what is going on. Phyllis cries out, "Otto, is dead, please call the police." In a few minutes police car siren's blasting pulls up to the house. Two officers listen to Phyllis, telling them what she just saw. One officer takes her aside as the others walk in. They call it in and Gulli and Jamie are notified.

Looking over the crime scene, Jamie shakes her head, "This has to be related to our Halloween killer. I know there are no markings but he was there that night. He must of knew something more than he let on to us. The killer wanted to make sure he would not talk.

We should have given him some protection." "Jamie, I believed he knew nothing more than he told us. This one is on me. If there are no prints or any other leads, I'm going to lose it." "So far no one has seen anything. He was shot twice and no one heard anything?" "No, so far nothing." "Well, keep on canvassing the entire area. Jamie circulate that sketch we have and see if anyone recognizes him. Maybe we can get lucky for a change. What we have so far is that our victim summoned a ghost on Halloween. He then rises and kills four people. Then he continues on as a serial killer and now kills Otto who brought him back from the dead. What do you think, Jamie, sound about right?" "I know Gulli, sounds more like a Stephen King novel then a murder case." "look, Jamie, we just keep on grinding until we catch this son of bitch."

CHAPTER 23

Jimmy twisted and turned as he watched himself in the rain, it was another hot humid day. He sees himself marching through some heavy bush following single file over a narrow path and we come to a sudden stop. One of the guys on point must have heard or seen something and held us all up. We wait a few minutes and we start moving on again. I'm walking with Red in front of me, Maytag ahead of him and just in front of him was Moo. Behind me were Andy, Gulli, Sonny and Gordan. As we continued walking it was the same old crap, a little chatter a lot of bitching. We all enjoyed the complaining about being there and the Army in general. We were also talking about home and what we were going to do if we ever got back to the Real World. The Real world meant home and the real life not this nightmare that dragged on and on. As I'm walking, I stumble just a bit on a rock and almost go down. Andy holds me up from the back and as I turn to thank him, I hear popping sounds of bullets bouncing all around us. As I am turning towards Andy; he falls into my arms. We all go down on the ground. There was return fire from all around me but I am looking at Andy. He is motionless in my arms. "Andy are you okay? Andy, Andy!" I yell at him but there is no response. As I was holding him there is a stream of blood running down my arms. I look at his head and I could see he was hit through the neck. I scream for a medic for help. I just stared at Andy as I cradled him in my arms. I started to cry and curse, "Look what these bastards have done. Andy, Andy no not Andy." The medic came but there was no hope. Andy died instantly. I just stayed on the ground and I couldn't move. Moo comes running back a few minutes later saying they killed the two snipers that fired on us. All my buddies sat around me. They all felt the same about Andy. Rega said, "This can't be, not Andy, he didn't belong here. He shouldn't have been here. This was no place for Andy." Gulli looked at me, "Buddy, I'm so sorry. We all knew you looked after him but there was nothing you could have done. Rega is right, Andy didn't belong here. He wasn't a soldier; he was a Muppet. I don't mean that in a bad way. I learned to love the kid. The Army should have known that he didn't belong here. He was a soft, kind, lovable and an annoying beautiful kid." Wise ass Red couldn't help himself as he kneeled down by me. He held me and cried just as hard as I did. Sargent Willie hugged me and said, "I'm sorry kid, we loved the guy. We will miss him and we will never forget him. He has to be in a better place, God rest his soul." The days passed by as we continued on. I was mostly in a trance like state. A big part of me felt like giving up. In my head, I was almost hoping for a sniper bullet to put me out of my misery. I was sick of the smell, the heat, the rain, the blood, the pain and the death that was all around us. My stomach was sick. I hurt bad inside over Andy. In nine months, he became my brother and I loved him. He was so happy anytime I would spend time with him. The plane ride over to Nam when he never would shut up. I promised him when we got back, I was going to beat his ass in bowling. He wanted me over for all the holidays. He promised that his Grandmother would make me Italian food I would die for. He even said that I could come live with him. But he did make me promise not to touch his sisters. Every few steps I take I look around and it tears me up that he is not behind me anymore and never will be. I was always complaining to him, if I stop short, he would end up in my ass. He just laughed and said he was sorry. Now I would rip my arm off, to have behind me. It's crazy but in months you form a bond with your buddies that would take a lifetime to do in the real world. No one knows what it's like unless you were here. Only the few of us that have walked through this hell understands. We're not soldiers we are just kids. We can't even buy a drink in the States. We would be still in school if we weren't here. We are here for what reason. The Politicians send us here but for what? The VC are fighting for their country. This is their country and we are the invaders. The farmers want no part of us or any war. This hell is turning us all into mindless killing machines. We have no idea what we are doing here. All we want is to get it over with and go home. Andy's death was ripping me apart. He was a gentle soul and he should not have been forced into a war in a country that hates us. He shouldn't have been sent here. I couldn't sleep at night until I was exhausted. I kept waking up all the time because I heard Andy call out for me. I couldn't write home anymore. I started to just stash the few letters I did receive. I couldn't deal with the little everyday bullshit that was happening in the real world. More days and weeks went by. Jimmy kept on moaning and grunting. Father Thomas gently shook him, "Jimmy, it's all right, you've been dreaming. It's okay you're here with me." Jimmy rises in the bed and sits up, "Father, I'm sorry did I wake you?" "It's okay Jimmy, you were having a bad dream." "Yeah, it was like watching a movie of myself back in Viet Nam. It was the day my good friend Andy was killed. I saw all my old buddies. I heard the gun fire and the bombs exploding. I was watching my life there and I felt the pain. I felt the tears for Andy. I could smell the stink of death all around. I've had dreams before but they are getting more and more real. It was like I was back there. How I miss Andy even after all these years. He was so young. We all were so young. Andy was special, he wouldn't hurt a fly. He wasn't cut out to be a soldier. He should never have been there. It tears me up when I think about it. They pull this kid out from his family, from his home. They give him a gun and tell him to go kill these Vietnamese people. He was never away from home and now he is in this hell hole. He never had a chance to live his life. He was a sweet soul Father, a kind human being. He didn't deserve to die at nineteen years old. He's never been with a girl, never had a drink in a bar. I honestly think he never had been in a fight. Why does this happen? I wished it would have been me that took the bullet. Tell me Father, why does God allow a kid like Andy die for no reason, why? Jimmy put his head down and cried. Father Thomas spoke softly, Jimmy, I couldn't answer that question and I don't think anyone can. You have to believe God called his son Andy home to be with him, in a better place. A safe place where there is no pain and no suffering for all eternity. You have to have faith Jimmy. I know it's hard but we all lose our loved ones. We all suffer the loss of a friend, this is life. You went through a lot and these memories haunt you. When you get back home maybe you should talk with a professional to help you deal with all this." "Yeah, a shrink, I know. I'll be all right Father; it was just a dream. Thanks for consoling me, I will be fine. I know we have things to do so I'll let you get some sleep. I will be better in the morning."

The next morning there is a knock on the door. Jimmy answers, "I have a message for the Father." "Thanks, I'll give it to him. Father there is a message here for you." Jimmy hands the note over to Father Thomas. He reads the note and looks at Jimmy. "It's from Oliver, inviting us for lunch and a meeting in Positano." "What do you think he wants?" "I'm not sure, this is something I did not expect." "Could it be some type of trap, setting us up to be killed?" "No, I don't think so. I know the restaurant it is on the beach at the bottom of the mountain side. It's actually beautiful. It is a huge tourist spot and very popular with the locals that can afford it. There is a bus that goes there and it takes about an hour. I think we should go. I am very interested in what our friend Oliver has to say. I would imagine some type of warm warning to leave the country. From the information we have so far, his big meeting and some type of ceremony is to be in Pompeii. Maybe he is inviting us to attend so he can lure me to the dark side. I think we will go if that is okay with you?" "I'm good with whatever you think. I have never seen Positano and guess I never will so why not." Jimmy and Father leave the hotel and head over to the bus station. They buy tickets from one of the most unfriendly ticket agents, "Wow, he was a joy to deal with. Father I have to use the men's room before we get on the bus." "It's over in the corner." "Be right back." Jimmy walks over to the men's room and there are turnstiles by the entrance. Jimmy tries to push and open but they do not open. He stands there trying to figure this out. A man approaches gives Jimmy a strange look, puts a coin in the slot and walks into the men's room. "Damn, you got to pay to get in." He looks at the turnstile and shakes his head. He walks back to father Thomas, "This is embarrassing but I don't know how much money to put in the turnstiles to enter the bathroom." Father Thomas smiles, "Here put this in and you will be good." "Thanks." After a few minutes they board the bus. The bus is very crowded and Jimmy gets pushed to one side and Father Thomas to the opposite side. The bus takes off and really picks up speed. It is a rough ride as Jimmy tries to balance himself. After a very scenic ride they start up a huge mountain on the most narrows of roads. They start winding up around and down this winding road. As Jimmy looked out the window the bus was on the edge of the road overlooking the ocean. The bus does not slow down at all and actually picks up speed as it flies around the mountain. Jimmy looks down and just holds his breath as it's like the bus can go over the edge at any time. He looks at the other passengers and they are very calm. After fifteen minutes of terror the bus pulls to a stop. Father Thomas waves at Jimmy, "We get off here." They get off and Father Thomas smiles at Jimmy, "You enjoyed the ride?" "Father, that was scarier than the Cyclone roller coaster in Coney Island." They begin to walk down the rest of the mountain side. As it winds around with little shops and a mixture of homes. "This is quite a walk down." "Yes, the bus could never pass these roads. They can hardly fit a car." It was a beautiful walk with sun shining and the ocean a perfect light blue. They reached the bottom on the beach. They walked into the open dining area of the restaurant. A Maître Di approached them and smiled, "Welcome, your party is waiting for you." They follow him to a private table away from the other diners and overlooking the ocean. "Oliver stands, "Greetings Father, I'm happy you decided to come. This is my friend Jacob." "This is Jimmy." They shake hands and they sit down. "Would you like a drink before our lunch? I was ordering a fine wine to complement our lunch." "That sounds wonderful." "Jimmy smiles, "Sounds good to me." After the bottle of wine is opened and poured, "I sure you are wondering why I asked you here?" "Yes, you are right." "I know we are on opposite sides in our beliefs but we all respect your ability to work so well against us. You and Brother Aiden have been formidable opponents for many years." "I believe it is Brother Aiden who is the gifted one. I merely assist him. I do not respect your beliefs. I believe you and your society is evil and cause nothing but pain and suffering to mankind. I know your work is the bidding of your master. The bible has foreseen the destruction and the war that is coming. I warn you now I and Brother Aiden will do whatever it takes to stop your plans from becoming a reality. Sorry for my bluntness but I believe you know where we stand." Jimmy was taken back as he had never seen this side of Father Thomas before. "I appreciate your honesty. I will be just as honest I see you as our enemy. You and Brother Thomas have been a hinderance to our cause many times in the past. I will enjoy the day when my master rules all of this world. I will enjoy every moment of witnessing the destruction of your precious church fall to him. All the righteous leaders will fall in line and worship your new lord. The day is coming much sooner than you could imagine. The coming of the new world is almost here. He has promised his followers the richest rewards. We will have all our desires filled and then some. We will watch you and the few followers of your religion that will stay loyal suffer for all eternity. I know why you are here and why Brother Aiden is going to Pompeii. You still believe that your powers will somehow call upon your messengers to stop the coming. You both are fools to think you will have any success in doing so. I called you and your friend here to welcome you to Pompeii and join your Brother Aiden. You can be the first to witness the new world order rise before your eyes. You will be helpless in trying to stop it. Our master will be sure to have a very special welcoming for all of you. Maybe you should have tried to have me killed instead of your pitiful rituals. That would have made no difference to what is coming. I was indeed in favor of having you eliminated but our master requested you to be a witness instead. You can run to your Vatican and tell them what is coming. You are the master's entertainment not his foe anymore." Each word that Oliver spoke enraged Jimmy more and more. Father Thomas sat and listened without showing any emotion. Jimmy was ready to choke him at any given moment. Father Thomas sensing Jimmy's rage put his hand on Jimmy to calm him. A few minutes went by without anyone speaking. Father Thomas stared at Oliver, "Besides boasting about your new world order and the coming of your master, why have us here?" "I actually was being generous in seeing that you are warned on what was coming. I thought, I could spare you of all this and maybe you would choose to go back to America and enjoy your retirement years. I know Brother Aiden has been summoned by the Vatican but you possibly were not as involved. I now believe that was not my real motive. To once again being honest down deep, I wanted to give you the news face to face. I too enjoy this little game we play and wanted to witness your reaction. That being said be warned from now on this is no longer a game. The reality is what is about to happen you will not enjoy." Father Thomas stood, "I see no need to continue this charade. I will not go back to America. I will join with Brother Aiden and do everything in my power to stop you and your sick society from succeeding. You are the one who is warned that the true savior will come. When he does you, your society and all your followers, will be cast into an eternal fire. This has been written and the word will come through. I'm sure we shall meet again and your so-called new world order will be nothing more than your nightmare." Father Thomas turns and starts to walk away. Jimmy stands and goes into Oliver's face, "You are a piece of shit. You and your bullshit are a joke. All your treats mean shit to me. I hope we do meet again and I get the chance to send you to hell where you belong." Jimmy joins Father Thomas and walks away. Oliver stands, "You will receive an invitation to our meeting in Pompeii, see you there." He smiles and sits.

"Are you okay, Father?" "I'm fine, thank you. I should have known better than to let him bait me here. He is an evil man and I do believe a very dangerous one too. He is very confident and that is worrisome. I will let Brother Aiden know but this will not change anything. We will continue to Pompeii and meet with Brother Aiden. I believe Oliver will send us an invitation and I'm sure that Brother Aiden will certainly join up with us before this meeting. As I said before, Jimmy this is not your fight and you can leave, I will understand." "Father, now for sure it is my fight. That arrogant son of a bitch needs to be dealt with. I want to be there for this meeting and I will do whatever I can to bring this guy down." "Once again for selfish reasons I am happy that you are staying." "You know Father the one thing I regret from this meeting we didn't get a chance to try the food. Everything smelled delicious. I am starving is there some place to eat before we go back?" "Yes, just up the hill there are a few places, not to worry." "We have to walk all the way up there to get the bus?" "Yes, it is a long way up."

CHAPTER 24

Jamie rolls her chair over to Gulli's desk. She lays out the pictures on Gulli's desk. "Look at this year book picture and the sketch of the POI. They do look like a match. Charlie swears that this guy Stevie is the same guy in the yearbook picture. This Stevie runs out of their house and is acting strange. If rational thinking wasn't involved, I would say this could be the guy. Then the fact remains how could it be that the guy was in the yearbook twenty-three years ago. He doesn't age, oh of course let's not forget the small detail he was killed twenty years ago." "I been doing this a long time and seen a lot of strange shit but this one might just be the strangest of all. You know Jamie, I've been going over the same pictures over and over and I still come up with nothing. It just doesn't make sense. I agree one hundred percent this guy is the key and we have to find him. Let's assume he is the killer. He does these murders starting Halloween night. He is the same guy that pushes the ticket agent off the train, for some reason. He is the same guy that befriends Lisa and Charlie. The only catch is the yearbook and that just could be some type of coincidence. He could be a relative or just happens to be a look alike." "What about no DNA, no prints and Otto. We can't forget the gravestone was for Steven Bracken and the picture that Charlie said was the same guy was of Steven Bracken." On top of all this, he comes back to kill Otto because he witnessed the murders. This guy just happened to be in the cemetery the same night.?" He could have followed them to the cemetery and then made his move." "While Otto was there? Then why wouldn't he have killed Otto that night along with the others? How the hell does one guy kill four young people without a gun and Otto there too.? Plus, we have no motive and no weapon. No sexual activity but a possible robbery? I just don't get it. Somehow, it doesn't add up. Something is missing." "Yeah, I would say a coffee, a burger and some fries will help." "Okay Gulli, I hear you. Maybe we should pay a visit to Lisa and Charlie? We might have overlooked something or they might have something to add that could help." "What do we have on this Steven Bracken, that was killed. Did he have a twin or a son? Did we come up with anything?" "No, he was killed, had no kids. He has a couple of brothers; his mom and dad died a number of years ago. One of his brothers is in Colorado and the other lives in New Mexico." "Let's get something to eat and give it a rest. Dinner is on me" "Sounds good."

"I love Amato's, have you been here before?" "No but I heard it was really good." "It's a little pricey but it's worth it." They order their drinks, "Too catching this creep." "Gulli, I keep running these things through my mind. The train and Otto that's not the M.O of a serial killer. What Jimmy said that it was this Stevie he saw as plain as day smiling at him after the accident. Jimmy swears it was him and it was intentional. The way Otto said that Halloween night that this entity seemed to be coming to life. He was so scared he just ran. Otto's credentials were that he was rare, that he was gifted and not a con man. The fact that the murders were on this Stevie bracken's gravestone. The witness that the sketch looks just like the same guy. Then you throw in Charlie and Lisa saying it was the same Stevie Bracken in the sketch. The yearbook picture that Charlie swears that is Stevie that was at their house. If it was not so damn impossible, I would swear this is our guy. Otto brought him back from the dead and he went on a killing spree. The robberies were always about the cash to keep him going. The train conductor somehow pissed him off and Otto was covering his trail. The carvings I don't think is anything other than he is trying to play games. I don't think he is a serial killer but more like a psycho." "You mean a zombie psycho killer. Look Jamie I agree with you on everything you said but there has to be another rational explanation. I just don't buy into people rising from the dead. It could be just some nut who happens to look like this Stevie Bracken guy and is playing games. I do agree he doesn't fit a serial killer profile. I say we go visit Charlie and Lisa and see if we missed something. Then it's back to reviewing all the evidence till we get something. The answer is out there we just have to find it. There is always a clue or something that will come to light. We need patience and maybe some luck." "How about we visit a psychic or maybe a priest who specializes in this area?" "What area zombie rising? Let's put it to rest for a bit to enjoy a good meal." "Okay, let's change the subject. How come your not married?" "I tried it twice and both times a disaster. This job takes its toll. The lifestyle is just not good for marriage. You can't help to bring the job home most women don't get it. They want you to be a different person at home and not a cop. The problem is I can't do it. The drinking doesn't help either. What about you?" "Same story, I was engaged once and it just fell apart. Not much time for the dating scene. I think I'm waiting for that perfect guy to come along and sweep me off my feet. You know like in the movies, a special moment when you just fall in love. Your knight appears when you least expect it. Then boom, love at first sight. You get married have a few kids, a dog and a house. It's just a dream but not reality. Chances are I'll be doing this job and live alone for the rest of my life. I'm not complaining I do love my job. Your right it becomes an addiction you eat and sleep with it twenty-four seven." "What about family?" "My mom and dad retired to Florida. I have a sister that is married and lives in Rocky Point. I had a brother but he was killed in Afghanistan. He was in the Marines and it was his second tour. Don't like talking about that, it still hurts." "Sorry Jamie, I understand. I think another round is in order." "Sounds good. Changing the subject one more time. If our killer is a zombie do you think we can kill it with our normal rounds. Maybe we need some heavier shit?" "What about silver bullets don't they work.?" "That's for werewolf's, speaking of werewolf's, I loved those old horror movies. Dracula, Frankenstein, and The Wolfman they were great movies. Friday nights were great they had this guy Zacherle, who was a Dracula like guy. He came out of the coffin to tell you about the movie we were watching. Sounds goofy but when I was a kid, we loved it. We all gathered around the TV, with popcorn to laugh and be scared at the same time. The old Dracula movies when he would turn these people into vampires, they would give me nightmares." "Well, on that note, I think I'm done. I don't need nightmares about zombies keeping me up half the night. See you tomorrow."

Stevie follows Lisa as she leaves work. He has been watching her for a while now. He wants to talk with her but he doesn't want to hurt her. The problem is he doesn't trust this evil that is inside of him. This entity, spirit or sickness, whatever it is that tries to make him do these evil things. He keeps going over in his mind," If I can just talk to Lisa, try to explain why I left. I can't tell her the truth; she will think I am crazy for sure. I really should just leave her and disappear. I just feel I need to talk to someone and for some reason I think Lisa will be able to help me. I wish I could start all over again and have a chance to live a normal life. I could see me being happy with a girl like Lisa." He watches as she gets in her car and drives off. He follows her. She does not go towards her home, instead she gets on the Long Island Expressway. He continues to follow her. "What do you expect to do by following her? I don't know what I want to do. I just want to see if I can get her alone and talk. I'm not sure what I will say but I need to talk to her." Lisa gets off the Expressway and heads west. She gets off and turns into the Holiday Inn. Stevie follows her into the parking lot. She gets out of the car and she meets up with two other girls, they speak and then enter the lobby. Stevie waits a second and then follows. He watches as they enter and sit at the bar. They order some drinks and get into a conversation. Stevie exits the bar and goes back to the car. He sits in the car for what seems like hours. He closes his eyes and once again he hears a voice within him. "You think you will be able to control your own destiny. You're a fool. Sitting here for what, to talk to your little friend. That is not what is going to happen. Like our friend Otto, how did that turn out?" "I didn't kill Otto." "Of course not, it just seems to happen while you were visiting your friends in another reality. You are more foolish then I thought. You are my servant you will do what I say. You don't want to kill your friend Lisa? Well you will do what I say and as I wish." "No, screw you, I won't hurt her." "You will and you will do it when she comes out. You will grab her and choke her until she is dead. You will take out your knife and carve into her chest. Do as I say or you will suffer." Stevie feels his whole body burning and trembling. He shouts over and over again, "No, No I will not hurt her." Just as this is happening, he sees Lisa come out of the bar. It is beginning to rain. The voice, then screams in his head, "You will pay for this. You won't do what I say but that will not stop me from quenching my thirst for death. You are pathetic and you will suffer. I will have my way without you." Stevie's body starts to cool down as he watches Lisa. She seems to be waiting for the rain to let up. After a few minutes she begins to walk away from the building towards her car. The car is around the side of the hotel. Stevie notices an unmarked white van pull into the parking lot. The van pulls in front of Lisa. A man in a hooded top gets out and grabs Lisa. He puts a cloth over her face and forces her into the van. Stevie gets out and runs after the van. Just as he approaches the van it speeds off. Stevie jumps into his car and follows. He follows the van for a few miles. The van drives off the road into a desolate area. The driver of the van realizing he was followed, pulls sharply to the left and comes to a stop. Stevie pulls alongside of the van. The driver just sits there. The windows are darkened so Stevie cannot see in. There is no movement from the driver. Stevie walks slowly around the van with his gun drawn. He approaches the passenger side cautiously. As he waits by the door for some kind of response. He puts his hands slowly on the door handle and tries to open the door. He has the gun in front of him. Just as he was about to open the door it flies open and knocks Stevie down. The driver lunges at Stevie with a large hunting knife.

Stevie spins away but the blade cuts his arm. He rolls around and picks up the gun. The driver kicks Stevie's hand and the gun goes off. It misses the driver but he drops the knife and runs into the woods. Stevie watches him run but does not chase him. He rips the sleeve off his shirt and ties it around his arm. He goes over to the back door of the van and opens it. Lisa is lying down and slowly opens her eyes. She rubs her face and looks at Stevie and screams, "No please don't hurt me, please." "No Lisa it's me Stevie. I'm not going to hurt you I wanted to save you." Lisa looks around seeing where she is, "Save me, you knocked me out and kidnaped me. Is that the way you save me? Please Stevie let me go." "You don't understand. I was watching you at the hotel and then this van pulled up and some guy grabbed you. I tried to stop him but he got away. I followed the van to this place and I fought him off and he ran. It wasn't me that brought you here. I would never hurt you, please believe me." Lisa looked confused, "You were following me? So, you are stalking me and just happened to be there when this guy attacked me. Please Stevie, please let me call the police." "No, they won't believe me. Look at my arm, see I've been cut by your attacker. Come here look there is my car. How could I have driven the van and my car at the same time. I'm telling you the truth. I wasn't stalking you, I wanted to talk to you but I just couldn't find the right time to do it. I would never hurt you Lisa, believe me. I care about you. I wanted to explain why I left that night. My life is very complicated but I wanted you to know I really liked you." Lisa stood up and looked at his car and his arm. She started to calm down and sat at the back of the van. "I'm confused, you just followed me tonight to talk to me. You just happened to be there at the right time to save me. Why I was attacked is scary and you being there at the same time is just coincidence. I don't know what to believe. What if he comes back? I'm still scared." "Lisa, look I have a gun and he knows it. Believe me he is not coming back." "You have a gun? My God, your following me with a gun?" "No, the gun has nothing to do with you. Like I said my life is very complicated right now. I'm trying to straighten everything out. That's why I wanted to talk to you." "Stevie, I want to call the police and tell them what happened. I want to go home." "Okay let me drive you home." "No, I don't want to get in the car. I want to call the police. There's an attacker out there and I want to notify the police." "I get it but can we talk before you do that. He is long gone by now you're safe with me." "Talk, Stevie your face was on a poster for a person of interest in the railroad killing. Me and Charlie saw a Plainview yearbook over twenty years ago and there was a picture of you in there. How can all this be. You have told me nothing about yourself. I don't even know your real name or where you come from." "My real name is Steven. I was on the train that night but I had nothing to do with that killing. I didn't want to come forward because I didn't see anything. I could not have helped in the investigation. The picture in the yearbook, I have no idea. Must be some look alike thing. Look would it make any sense if I told you I was the guy in the yearbook? I'm a time traveler. No, I don't think so. I'm sorry for what happened to you tonight but you have to believe me it was good luck that I came looking for you tonight. If I wasn't there you could have been really hurt or maybe killed. I saved you and that's the truth. I think it's best if I drive you home. I'll give you a minute to think about what you want. I want to check the van and see who it belongs to. I will be right here in the front." "Okay Stevie." Lisa took a pager from her pocket that one of the detectives gave her. If she felt in any danger, he told her to page 911 they could rack the general area she was in. She looks at the pager hesitates and then presses 911. Stevie comes back, "You coming with me, Lisa?" "Stevie, I'm sorry. I want to believe you but I'm scared. I really did like you right away. I thought we could have something special between us. I have so many doubts about you that I am confused. I have to warn you I paged 911 and I think the police will be here in a short time. I don't want anything bad to happen to you but I can't go with you. I will tell the police you did save me. Please just leave before they come." Stevie walks in circles trying to deal with this. "I don't want to leave you here alone." He walks around the van and stops. He takes his gun and wipes it clean. He goes back to Lisa, "Here, take my gun. I will leave but I want you to be safe." Lisa hesitates, "No, I don't want the thing. I'll go in the car with you if you promise to take me to the nearest store. I will be able to call the police and you can leave." "Okay, let's go." They both get in Stevie's car and drive off. They drive a few miles in silence. Soon they see a gas station with a phone booth, "Is this okay?" "This is fine." They pull on the side of the station. Stevie looks at Lisa, "I'm so sorry if I scared you. I'm sorry my life is so screwed up. I've been thinking of you all the time. I wish I could do my life over again. I did some things I'm not proud of. I did some things that I know wasn't me doing them. It's too complicated to believe but just know I am not a bad person. I would want the chance to make you happy. Maybe in a different life we can meet again and I could get that chance." Lisa tears up, "I'm sorry to. I know now and I believe you would never have hurt me. I hope you get your life straightened out. Who knows maybe we can meet again and things will be different? Now Stevie I think you should go, be safe." Stevie starts the car and Lisa takes his hand and pulls Stevie close. She softly kisses Stevie, "Thank you for saving my life. I will never forget what you did tonight." She opens the door and goes to the phone booth. Stevie pulls away and heads west.

"Oh my God. Are you all right?" "I'm okay Charlie, just a little shaken up." "I'm confused was its Stevie who attacked you?" "No, he saved me." "Did you know he was coming to see you?" "No, I know it sounds crazy but he says he was coming to talk to me." "How did he know where you were?" "I don't know. He must have followed me from work, I guess." "Did they catch the guy who attacked you?" "No, not yet. I didn't really see him. He came from behind and put this rag over my face. The next thing I know I'm waking up in this van. Stevie is there and explained what happen." "Are you sure it wasn't Stevie?" "Yes, he was cut and he had his car there that he followed me in. Charlie believe me I know how freaky it all sounds but he saved me. If he wasn't there I could have been killed or God knows what else. I told the police the story over and over again. I'm kind of wiped out."

Jamie walks over to Lisa, "Can I get you some coffee?" "No thanks." "I just need to ask you a few more questions if that is okay?" "Okay." "Do you have any idea where Stevie would have been going? Any idea at all where we might be able to find him?" "No, I don't. When he left it seemed like I would never see him again. He said his life is very complicated and he couldn't explain why. He also said he did things that he was not proud of and it wasn't really him. He said that he is a good person." "You said he had a gun?" "Yes, he wanted to leave it with me if I didn't want to go with him to find a phone." "You seem to believe what he says and, in some ways, you trust him." That's right, I do trust him. He saved my life." "You said before that you questioned him on the yearbook and he said he was a time traveler?" "No, he said would I believe him if he said he was a time traveler. He said that it had to be a look alike in the yearbook." "Do you have anyway of contacting him?" "No, I told you I don't." "Sorry Lisa, I know we are going over the same things but we are trying to solve this. Sometimes you could have missed something that could help us find him. Look, I know you are beat I can Have a patrol car take you home. Try to get some sleep and maybe there is something you might remember that will help. You have my card call me anytime." "Charlie is here he will take me home." Charlie stands, "Detective do you think she is in any danger? Is it possible that this lunatic can come back?" "I don't think you have to worry but we will place a car at your apartment to make you feel better." "Thank you. You know I watch all the police shows so I know about these things. You can't be too safe as far as I'm concerned." "I know Charlie, you know your police stories." Charlie and Lisa walk out to the car. "Lisa, I'm so sorry that this happened. I should have been there for you." "Charlie I'm a big girl I don't need a baby sitter. This was just a freak thing. It happens but I'm safe now." "Of course, I'll get you home and make you a nice hot chocolate that will help you unwind. I'll stay up all night to make sure your safe." "That won't be necessary, there is a police car in front of the house."

After driving over four hours Stevie gets off route 17 and drives through a small town. At the end of main street, he sees a sign, vacancy at the Deposit Motel. "This looks like a good place to crash. I need to rest and clean up this arm." He checks in and pays cash. He got some strange looks but everything seemed to be okay.

CHAPTER 25

Pompeii, Italy:

Father Thomas and Jimmy walking through the ruins of Pompeii. "These bodies have been lying here since the volcano erupted?" "They are plaster casts of bodies. Plaster was pumped into the space left behind in the hardened ash after the biological material decomposed. It was thought that the facial expressions revealed in the plaster were the victims' gasps for air. This is exactly where they were buried by ash." "Couldn't they run or get away somehow?" "Jimmy, they had no time. You can't run away from a current of pulverized rock and volcanic gasses flowing at speeds of up to 150 miles per hour. The people of Pompeii had no chance when that flow hit them full-force. They barely would have had time to see it coming. Its leading edge filled the air with ash, dust and gas." As they walked through the ruins Jimmy noticed the dogs roaming and sleeping, "These dogs just seem like they own this place." "In a way they do. They are free to roam and are fed all the time by locals and visitors. They are said to have the souls of the ones that were killed here. They soak up the sun and seem to enjoy the attention." "Where are we to meet Brother Aiden?" "At Our Lady of Pompeii. It is a beautiful church with a long history. You cannot miss it; the architecture is dramatic and breath taking. The story of this shrine is that of a man named Bartolo Longo, a lawyer from the area and, although he was baptized a Catholic, had fallen away from the faith and fell under the influence of two radical former priests while attending University who had very strong anti-Christian doctrines. Does that sound a bit familiar? He became quite an enemy of the Catholic Church, and actually became a Satanic priest. Then, through the efforts and the example of his friends, a professor and a Dominican Priest. By 1865 he came back to the Faith with a renewed zeal. By 1871, he had turned full circle and became a Third Order Dominican, taking the name of Brother Rosario in honor of the Rosary. He received his law degree in Naples in 1864 but later gave up his legal career and devoted himself to charitable activities. In that time, Countess Marianna de Fusco entrusted to him the administration of her property. On a visit to Pompeii on her behalf, Bartolo was distressed to see that the church building in the town was practically falling down. Worse yet most of the local population did not practice their faith and chose to work or play on Sundays rather than attend Mass. Having a great devotion to the Rosary, he placed an image of Our Lady of the Rosary in the church and soon there were reports of miracles from those who visited there. Bartolo Longo took this as a sign that Our Lady wanted a shrine built here and began to seek contributions from the local populace. The Church was begun in 1876 and also included a school, workshop, orphanage and social center. Brother Aiden spent many years here when he was younger. His work in alternate realities took place here. His battles with demons became known and caused a stir in the Vatican. Soon after he fell out of favor with the Vatican. They knew he had unique gifts but he would not bend to the warnings from the Vatican. A few years later he was exiled and ended up in North Umbria. He continued his work without answering to anyone. The Vatican secretly has called on him when they need him. He always responds to their requests and in his way is loyal to them. We will get something to eat and then head over to the church." "Eating always sounds good to me. I am looking forward to meeting with Brother Aiden.

After dinner they head over to the church for the meeting. Jimmy follows Father Thomas as they walk around the side of the church. They enter a door and walk down a flight of steps. There are carvings and drawings on the walls. They continue to walk through deep walls that lead to two large pillows of carved stone. Looks like they are going into a dead end. The hallway is lit with a golden reflection of light. As they come to the end Father Thomas moves his hand slowly along the top of one of the square pillows. Jimmy watches as Father Thomas pulls a large stone sideways and the pillows open. They enter another hallway that bends and goes downward. They follow this hallway until the come to an opening. There is a stone pathway that runs through more ruins. The area then widens into an entrance to a large square room. There are statues carved into the walls. There are rounded archways that lead to other rooms. In the middle a large sunken square opening. "Jimmy, these are remains of the old Roman bath house." "This is where we're meeting Brother Aiden?" "Yes, he should be here any minute." A few minutes pass by and Brother Aiden enters. "Thomas it's been too long." Both men hug. "Brother it is always good to see you. This is my friend Jimmy." "Nice to meet you Brother." "I heard good things about you. Father Thomas has kept me informed of your travels. You have had quite the interesting journey. I hope you enjoyed the good parts of Italy." "Yes, it is a beautiful country." "I also heard of the encounters you had to deal with. I know Father Thomas is grateful that you were with him. I also heard of your meeting with our adversary Oliver and company." "Yes, it was an interesting meeting. I have to admit he did get under my skin." "Yes, he can do that. He also is a very dangerous man. He somehow is responsible for many evil happenings. This ceremony he has graciously invited us too, I'm sure is also a very dangerous event. I am very grateful for what you have done in helping getting Father Thomas here safely. I feel we owe you and I would like to repay you for what you have done. Father has told me of your great loss and I'm so sorry for what happened to your family. As Father has told you I have worked in this field of alternate realities for many years. I have had different results in doing this. As you know the Vatican has not been happy with my work. I call upon good messengers to help in crossing over to these other realities. There are dark messengers that interfere. If successful and the crossing does happen the results are not always what you desire. These realities can be different every time. Every crossroad in our lives sets a different course. There are many dimensions and I cannot assure you if we are successful the path that you desire will be there. Sometimes one can get caught between realities. I have seen one being pulled in and out of these realities. I have no answers for this. I have no control of what happens. What I'm trying to do is warn you there is no guarantee on what will happen." "I understand. You don't owe me anything. Father Thomas has helped me get through this painful time. I am more than happy to be of help. I also would want to come with you to this meeting. I am worried of what will take place and maybe I could help. There is nothing more important to me than to try and return to a reality of where my family are. If that is at all possible, I am willing to take the chance." "Jimmy, the problem is that this might be your last chance to try. I'm not sure what will happen at this ceremony. I don't know if the opportunity will be available so I suggest that we try now." "Okay Brother I'm good with that." Father Thomas comes over to Jimmy. My prayers are with you. I hope you will find the life you want. In the short time we have known each other I have become very fond of you my son. God be with you and hopefully if this does work, we will meet again. I want you to have this. It was a gift from my Father but I want you to have it. It has no real monetary value but think of me wherever you are." Father Thomas hands Jimmy an old pocket watch. On the inside is inscribed, **multas vitas, sed unum Deum aeternum novit omnia.** "What does it say?" "When we meet again, I'll tell you, I promise." "Thank you, Father, I hope you stay safe and we do someday meet again." "Are you ready?" "Yes." Brother Aiden sits Jimmy down on the stone wall. "Clear your mind and don't be afraid. You might encounter some strange interference but I will have a good messenger to guide and protect you." Father, join me in our prayers." Both men begin to pray in Latin. Then they chant in Latin. They continue chanting and Jimmy begins to drift. He seems to start to float and there is a total calm. He feels himself drifting and floating into darkness. He sees a bright light and bursting flashes coming towards him. A soft voice penetrates inside his head. "Don't be afraid, come with me." Jimmy reaches out and feels a warm touch surround his hand. He floats through the darkness being led by this light. After a few minutes a cold wave comes in front of him. A loud voice surrounds him, "Go back while you can. This will not end well for you. You don't belong here, go back." The white light and bright figure begin to glow and get larger. An arm swings at the black cold figure. "Silence and begone." The black cold figure bursts and disappears. Jimmy feels calm and at peace.

Father Thomas looks at Brother Aiden, "What happened?" "I am not sure but I believe he has crossed over." "Is he safe? Do you think he went where He wanted?" "I set the path to where he would go before the accident. You know Thomas, I can't be sure of the final result." "I know, I hope it went well for him." "Now we must prepare for this ceremony.

CHAPTER 26

Gulli turns to Jamie, "If Stevie saved Lisa what does that mean? He wasn't the attacker. So, there is another POI. Is this guy the real serial killer.? "He could be a copycat or the attack on her was just a single random coincidence." "Again, the coincidence. Stevie just happens to follow her that night. Just happens to be there to save her. The attack is on Lisa of all the women he attacks her. Somehow this is no coincidence. They have to be connected. Stevie is telling her he was on the train but didn't see anything. This guy keeps popping up, on the train killing, the gravesite, The attack on Lisa. No this is no coincidence." "I agree, plus the yearbook that just happened to look like him. Otto's death, we have to connect the dots." "Lisa is the key. It's obvious Stevie has feelings for her. Maybe we get lucky and sometime down the road he gets in contact with her. We have to go see her and try to get something from her. She has to have some information for us. We just need to keep pushing her to see if there's something there." "You want to hear my crazy theory?" "Sure, Jamie why not." "It's like beauty and the beast. Otto brings this Stevie back from the dead. This Stevie is pure evil. He kills the four people there. He then continues on this killing spree carving his satanic words into the victims. Then he's on the train and for some reason this conductor gets in his way and he pushes him off the train. He then realizes Otto can be a problem so he goes back and kills Otto. In the meantime, he meets this Lisa and falls for her. Even beasts have soft spots. He then stalks her deciding if he should kill her or romance her. He is there that night stalking her and sees this creep attacking her and comes to her defense and saves her. Now he is off on the run trying to figure out what is next. The good news is that he will need some type of closure with Lisa. Kill her or take her for himself. And so, there you go, beauty and the beast. What do you think?" "I like it all except the fact he comes back from the dead. That's the one that stumps me." "Yeah, that's a problem.

Next day Gulli and Jamie visit Lisa and Charlie:

"Lisa, thank you for seeing us. Now that you have had some time is there anything you remember about your attacker that can help us find him?" "I'm sorry but I told you everything. It happened so fast. I was walking and from behind I felt this rag placed over my face. There was an awful smell and then I blacked out. The next thing I know there is Stevie looking at me in this van." "You sure it wasn't Stevie that attacked you?" "Yes, I told you he saved me." "You did say you blacked out and then the only one there was Stevie." "Yes, but he was wounded and bleeding. Plus, his car was there. I don't think he could drive both his car and the van. I totally believe he saved me." "Why was he stalking you?" "He wasn't, he wanted to talk to me and explain a few things. I told you all of this." "Can I say something?" "Yes, Charlie go ahead." "Well if Lisa says he saved her then I for one believe her. I know you're playing good cop, bad cop. I watch a lot of police shows so I know what's going on." "Charlie, I'm asking all the questions so am I the good cop and the bad cop." Gulli and Jamie both smile." "Okay, make fun of me but I know my police shows. "Let me ask you Charlie how would Detective Andy Sipowicz handle this?" "You know him?" "No but I have seen the show. Look guys nobody is playing good cop bad cop. We are trying to find out who attacked you. One of the ways is to eliminate any possibilities. The van was stolen before he attacked you so that is a dead end so far. Lisa are you involved with anybody else even in the smallest way? Maybe someone at work that has befriended you?" "No, I can't think of anyone. I have a couple of friends but they are all girls." "No secret admirer or someone that seems to want to get to know you?" "No, I can't think of anyone like that." Jamie steps in, "What about at the bar anyone talk to you or offer to buy you a drink?" "No, it was just my girlfriends. The only guy I've dated at all recently was

Stevie." "What about you Charlie where were you that night?" "Oh my God, you think I could have attacked my cousin? How dare you? I love Lisa we grew up together. I wouldn't harm a fly and steal a van; I never drove a van. This is disgusting that you would even ask me such a question. I think I'm going to be sick." Charlie gets up walking in circles. "Ow, ow, ow how can you ask me that?" "Calm down Charlie it's just routine questions. We're just doing our job. I'm sure Sipowicz would ask you that same question." "Okay, I will tell you exactly what I was doing Thursday night. It's my favorite TV night I watch, The Cosby Show, A Different World, Cheers, Dear John and L.A. Law. Would you like a recap of each show" "No Charlie that won't be necessary." "Lisa anything you can think of on how we can find Stevie?" "I told you no. He always contacted me and he never said where he lived or where he worked. He was very mysterious and private about his life. I know it sounds strange but at the time, I just didn't think much of it. You have to understand we just dated a few times it wasn't like we were in a long relationship. He was different and he was fun. I liked being with him. We had a chemistry or something and I was attracted to him." "Okay, sorry to bother you with these same questions but it is part of the process. It can get pretty intense but we are looking for a possible killer and we want to find him. It's possible he will attack someone else. Charlie, who's your favorite character on Cheers?" "Oh, that's simple, Sam Malone he is gorgeous. I love Sam." Gulli smiles and says, "Well if you think of anything please call me or Jamie anytime. We will keep the patrol car around but I'm sure you guys are safe." "Thanks detective and I'm sorry I couldn't be more of a help." "No problem." "Keep on watching NYPD Blue, Charlie and you can help us out in the investigation." "The show ended this year Mr. Smarty." "Sorry to hear that Charlie but I'm sure there will be reruns."

Stevie walks around the town looking for somewhere to eat. He stops into the Big M Supermarket. He asks at the front desk a middle-aged woman. "Not much in town but if you go a couple of miles there is Scotts Hotel. They have a nice restaurant in the hotel. You can get a great meal and the prices are very reasonable." "Thanks, I appreciate your help. I will give it a try. Stevie drives to the hotel. An old large rustic hotel on the lake. He goes into the restaurant and is met by an attractive hostess. "Hi are you alone?" "Yes, just me." He follows her and sits by the window overlooking the lake. Can I get you something to drink while you are waiting?" "Yeah, a house wine will be great, thanks." She returns with the wine and a large menu. "You here on business or visiting?" "Just passing through." "Not too many handsome strangers eat here this time of year or any time of year to be honest." "You work here year-round?" "Yes, for now. My Aunt and Uncle own this place." "Well that sounds good." "I don't want to be pushy but this town is pretty boring. Not much to do here. I get off in an hour would you like to have a drink with me?" "I don't even know your name?' "Mandy, what's yours?" "Stevie, but you really don't know anything about me. I could be dangerous. You never know who you're dealing with. Didn't your parents teach you not to talk to strangers?" "You don't look dangerous to me. I can take care of myself. So, is that a yes?" "Well, if you want to take a chance, then yes." "Great, I'll come back when my shift ends. Don't leave without me." "I'll be here." As Stevie drinks his wine, he hears a voice inside his head, "I hope you appreciate the gift I just sent you. You now can pay me back for all the opportunities you have had to do my biding. I handed you a lamb for slaughter. Now do what I want and I just might forgive you for interfering with that Lisa friend of yours. You couldn't do her so I sent someone else to do your job. Now after you fill your stomach you will give what I want." Stevie puts his hands to his head and wants to scream. He controls himself and waits for his dinner.

CHAPTER 27

Pompeii, Italy:

"Brother, have you heard from Father Regis?" "No, he was called back to Rome. He has an urgent message for us but he had to receive it in person. He should be back later tonight. He will call us when he returns." "Do you know what it is about?" "The meeting and ceremony that our friend Oliver is about to have. I'm sure it must be of great importance for Father Regis to have to get it in person." "I have a bad feeling about this meeting, Brother." "I have that same feeling. We have no choice we have been sent here for a reason and we must see it through." "I understand."

Father Regis looks at the sealed envelope with the Vatican seal on it. "This must be very important. After this meeting I have to return immediately to Rome. I'm sure an hour or two won't matter." As he thinks to himself as the rail speeds towards Naples. "I haven't seen my mom in over a year. I can take the Circumvesuviana and be in Pompeii in forty minutes. My mom is only a couple of minutes from the station." Father Regis walks up to the apartment building and up three flights of stairs. He comes to the door and knocks. "The door opens, "Enzo, oh my God I didn't know you were coming. Come in here." She gives him a big hug and yells out, "Sofia, look who's hear. Father Regis's sister comes running to him, "Enzo, so glad to see you." "Come sit are you hungry?" I have a nice pot of spaghetti and sausage, I just made." "I can't stay long Momma I have to go to Pompeii for a very important meeting." "What do mean you can't stay. That's crazy, I haven't seen you in a year. Since last Christmas, what's a matter with you. I know you're a priest but still you can spend time with your family." "I'm so sorry Momma, I would love to stay believe me. I have a very important message here with me and I have to bring it to this meeting. Look here see it even has the Vatican seal on it." "Oh, the seal, Italian excelsis, look Sofia, how important your brother is?" "Momma, I promise soon as I'm done with all this, I will take some time off and come stay here for a nice vacation. Is that okay? I promise." "That's good, now you eat. "How have you been, Sofia?" "Good Enzo, I'm still working at the department store. Not the greatest but it's a job. I'm taking some courses in book keeping and accounting. I want to work in an office someday." "Good for you. I know you can do it. You are a very smart girl, Sofia." "You know Enzo, Me and Momma are very proud of you. I have to be honest, I never thought you would become a priest. I mean you were very handsome and knew a lot of the girls always liked you." "I never thought I was going to be a priest either. The only one that did was Momma. She always would say, Enzo, you're a good boy. You serve God and make me proud. One day I was in church and I felt this wave of emotion and from that minute on, I knew I wanted to be a priest." "Enzo, come on your dinner is nice and hot." "You know Momma, Christmas is not that far off. I could come that week and stay. I have the time coming and I'm sure they will let me." "Good, that would be wonderful. We will have the whole family come. They are all so proud of you Enzo. You know you're the only priest in the family. You made me so happy and I will never forget the day you told me. That made me cry with happiness." "Stop crying Momma, you're going to make me cry." "Yes, your right, that's enough. Now eat before your spaghetti gets cold. You want some vino with dinner?" "Thanks Momma, that will be great." After dinner they sit around the dinner table and drink some black coffee. "More coffee, Enzo?" "Sorry Momma but I really must get going. It's getting late and I have to get to Pompeii." "I understand but can you stay a little longer." "Sorry Momma, I have to go." They all rise and exchange hugs and kisses." "You be careful Enzo." "Momma, I'm a priest, who wants to hurt a priest?" "All right, then go and be safe." "Love you, God bless." Father Regis leaves the building and walks to the rail station. He waits about five minutes and boards the train. He sits and smiles. He loves going home and he does miss his family.

Christmas is coming and he promises himself he will go home for the week. After about forty minutes the train pulls into the station. It's kind of late and the station is empty. He walks around the corner and up the street. He hasn't noticed but since Naples a man is following him. He knows there is a bus not too far which he takes to meet up with Brother Aiden. He continues to walk down the dark street. From behind the man reaches for Father Regis's briefcase where he has the letter. He is taken by surprise as the man pulls on his briefcase. He reacts quickly and squeeze's his hand tightening his grip on it. The man pulls a knife from his pocket and stabs Father Regis in the side of the chest. Father Regis still refuses to let go of the case. The man again stabs Father Regis in the chest. This time Father Regis falls to his knees. The man grabs the case and walks quickly down the street. Father Regis falls over in pain and the blood seeps onto the street.

"Jimmy, how are you feeling?" "I'm not sure. It's like I've been dreaming or having nightmares. First, I think I was in some cave or old church with drawings on the wall. I'm talking to two priests and they are telling me to be careful. One of them starts chanting in Latin, I think. Next thing I know I'm like floating away and then nothing. I get these flashes like bits and pieces of a car accident. I'm trapped in the car and my wife and two kids are bleeding and lifeless. My old friend Stevie is laughing at me in the window. A moment later, I wake up and I'm out on patrol in Viet Nam. I started to feel sick. I mean really sick. The next thing I knew I was burning up with a fever. I was totally out of it when they choppered me back to Pleiku. They started to give me these ice baths to bring my fever down. I would reach for a blanket because I was freezing and they would pull it over me. More ice baths the bastards were trying to kill me. They tested me but they found nothing. They then shipped me to Cam Ranh Bay, a larger and better equipped hospital. I was mostly out of it and I was hallucinating from the high fever. All crazy things, I was seeing bodies, explosions, weird colors and all sorts of nightmares. The Doctors at Cam Ranh Bay finally found that I had malaria and started to treat me with Quinine. Sorry Doc, am I talking too much?" "No not at all, Jimmy. Please go on tell me everything." "Then I had a very weird dream, I think. I was kind of in a twilight like sleep when I heard a voice whispering in my ear, "It's no big thing Jimmy you are going to be fine. I miss you buddy but you can't come to me, not yet. You will get out of here don't worry. Thanks for being there for me. You were and always will be my brother. Getting shot was no big thing I am good. I have been watching you. You're a great soldier and a better person. Take care of your self be careful out there when you go back. Be really careful in the village. I love you Jimmy please be safe." I opened my eyes and I saw Andy my buddy. He was killed on patrol. He was smiling and backing away. Then it was like he just floated and slowly disappeared. It was freaky but I had been hallucinating so many times that I just thought it was just another bad night. The next morning the Quinine slowly started to kick in. I dismissed the visit from Andy as a dream but there was something different about it. It was so real it stayed with me. I found out that my buddy Red was in the same hospital with Malaria. We both caught it at the same time. While we were recovering the guys had come in from the field and they visited with us. Me and Red pulled some favors and they put us in beds next to each other. After the fever finally broke both of us were feeling a lot better. The nurses were great and the doctors took good care of us. The only problem was that we knew that as soon as we were recovered, they would send us back into the field. I said to Red, "Hey I have to be honest I don't want to go back. I miss the guys and I want to be there for them but I don't want to go out there anymore." Red smiled, "Damn right. I don't want to go back either. I am spoiled now for sure. Pretty nurses, warm beds, good food, no way do I want to go back. We have to think of something to stay. We could say we are still sick. We can fake it." "No way will that work." We started to count the days we had left because now we were short timers. Two months and we are out of here. Just as they were ready to release us we started to wander around the bases. There were Army, Navy and a large Air Force presence there. We spotted a poster for a painting detail and we volunteered for that. We were painting a few days. Our names were being called to be assigned back into the field. We ignored the calls and wandered around the base. We wandered into an Air Force Base and made friends with a couple of guys there. They said there was no room in the barracks but we could sleep on the floor and no one would say anything. That's what we did. We would have stayed anywhere to keep from going back out. We didn't have any leave but we hitched a ride into, Cam Ranh Bay sin city. We were like wild men on the loose. We drank ourselves to the limits and were totally wasted. As we were sobering up a bit, we were just walking the streets when two MP'S stopped us. They asked for our passes. Unfortunately, we didn't have any. Red tells the MP's, we lost them. When that didn't work, we tried everything to talk our way out. We told them what we had been through but nothing worked. They put us in the jeep and escorted us back to Cam Ranh Bay Base. The next day they put us on a plane and escorted us back to our base in Pleiku. The MP's writes us up on Article 15 and they bring us to our C O (Commanding Officer.) The big mouth all gung-ho MP starts telling the C O that we are AWOL. The C O yells at the MP to slow down. "I'm a Captain and you're a Sargent so stop right now. I will deal with this matter. You both are excused, so leave my office now!" We smile at the MP's and gave a little finger wave as they slowly walk out the door. The Captain looks at us and says, "Wipe that smile off your faces and get the hell out of here. I don't want to see either of you again. Do you understand?" We both reply, "Yes Sir" He then rips up the paper work, smiles as he tosses it in the garbage. The next day Red finds out his Father is very sick. The Army is letting him go home right away. We hug and I wish him the best. He says he's sorry to leave me but his dad needs him. I understand but I wish I was going home with him. After Red leaves, I bounce around doing everything I can to not let them find me. That doesn't work out for too long. They send me back to the field and my unit. I rejoin the guys and it was good seeing them. We all hugged and caught up on everything that happened. I told them about me and Red's adventures at Cam Ranh Bay and Red going home. There were a lot of new greenies in our Company. Just a few of us were left from when we started. We were short timers and we just wanted to stay safe and get the hell out of this place. After seeing Red leave and be reunited with my buddies I was in a daze. I still couldn't get Andy out of my head. That night in the hospital still was bothering me. I know I had the fever but I saw him and I heard him. It was different then the dreams and the hallucinating, it was somehow very real. I tried to block it out and concentrate on my time left. I thought of going back to the real world, all my old buddies. I had mixed emotions on what it would be like but I knew it was a million times better than being here. The next thing my old buddy Sargent Willie tells me that Army Intelligence is saying there are VC held up in a village not too far from where we are. This is normally a search and destroy mission but this one is search and capture. This was going to be a night mission of twelve men and an interpreter. Sargent Willie says that because of my expertise as a forward observer and in reading maps I would be one of the twelve. We all hated night patrols you couldn't see shit. I had to read the map with a red lens. That night the rain was coming down very hard as we moved out. I was with five of my buddies and a few other grunts. The squad leader, Sargent Lambeau was a GI Joe type of guy from the boonies in Louisiana plus an interpreter. I was towards the back with a grunt who was carrying the radio hidden in a sand bag. The radio would be a target for a sniper so we hid it as best we could. We tried to be as quit as possible as we went towards the village. The rain hitting our ponchos would intensify the sound. As we slopped through the mud, I couldn't help think about that night back at Cam Ranh Bay hospital and the whispering of Andy. He said "Be careful at the village." At that time, it made no sense but now we are headed for a village with VC there, it sent a shiver through my whole body. As we approached the village, I felt very tense. I was always tense, scared on any patrol but this time it was worse. Look we had a few weeks left and we all can get out of here in one piece. If we are lucky this could be our last patrol. Red is back home; my other buddy Moo was sent back after being shot. The rest of us our time was almost up. Now is not the time to get shot. We approached the first hut and Sonny, Sargent Lambeau, Vogel, me and the interpreter enter it. There are two women there alone and we see no one else. The Interpreter asks the women where are the VC. They keep on repeating, "No VC. No VC. They left." The Sargent loses his patience and puts his weapon directly to their heads saying, "Show me where the VC went, now!" The two women make a sign to follow them. They lead us out of the hut and a short way down the road. They approach an entrance to the jungle and point that way. The Sargent tells the Interpreter to tell them to lead the way. They say, "No, you go." Again, the Sargent loses his patience and points his rifle, for them to lead the way. The two women then jump over a group of rocks and begin to run, the Sargent opens fire and the bullets rip them both apart. He pushes us back and shows us the mines they wanted to lead us into and blow the shit out of us. It was sickening to watch. Kill or be killed, simple as that. Shoot first take no chances they were all VC, women, kids, young men, you could never tell. We returned to the village the squad had a male villager in the second hut. We came over to the hut and entered. We were all getting antsy now after the gun fire. We knew the VC could be closing in on us at any time. We entered the hut and the interpreter started to interrogate the villager. He kept on denying he was VC. We told the Sargent to bring him back to camp to interrogate him. The Sargent agreed and told the Interrogator to tell the VC to come with us. He refused to move. The Sargent went over to him and grabbed him by the arm and pushed him towards the front. The VC stopped, reached behind his back and pulled a pistol out. He fired point blank at the Sargent hitting him twice in the chest before any of us could react. He fired again hitting Sonny in the stomach. I returned the fire and shot the VC twice in the chest. He fell to the ground. We checked the Sargent but he was gone. Sonny was wounded pretty badly so we wrapped him up and carried him out. I dragged the VC out of the hut. We rushed as fast as we could but dragging the VC was a slow go. As we were making our way as far from the village as possible the VC starts to scream out. I tried to shut him up but he wouldn't stop. We dragged him into the jungle and we hear all kinds of sounds coming from the village. There was no question, it was VC coming after us. I grab the radio and call in our status. The Captain says, "Shut him up, the hell with bringing him back." I went down on top of the VC and I grabbed his throat with both my hands and squeezed as hard as I could. I looked into his eyes as he was dying and I felt nothing. I just watched him kill the Sargent and put two holes in Sonny. I was following my orders and I did what a soldier should do. I pushed him away and barked out to move out. We started to move out as fast as possible but there were bullets flying all around us. We returned fire and moved out. After we moved quite a distance from the village the jungle got deeper and darker. We could hardly see anything. The good news was even the VC couldn't see us. We waited for a long time and it seemed they gave up. I was the highest rank so I was now the squad leader. I ordered them to slowly move out and don't make a sound. We made our way through the jungle as I checked the map and plotted our course to get back to our camp. It was difficult carrying Sargent Lambeau and Sonny, it took two men each to carry them. As we approached an opening in the jungle I hesitated. We had to cross an open field. I thought that this would be a good place to call in a chopper, to evacuate our wounded and dead. As the chopper got close, I called in for illumination, so they can find us. The chopper spots us and lands. It was a dangerous decision because the VC in the area would now know where we were but I was afraid Sonny wouldn't make it. We get Sonny and Lambeau on it and it takes off. As I lead the squad out, we get to the middle a blast of fire comes at us. I turn to my left and I see the flashes and the tracers of light leaving the VC rifles. I scream and open fire. I take out at least three of them. Then I feel a burst like someone kicked me in the face. I hit the ground and everything goes black. I'm sorry Doc, I'm going on and on. The crazy thing is that I know this really happened. I mean all of it. Like I said before there is this other dream or something that I get flashes of. Almost as if another life. I have a wife and two kids. I'm really happy. Then they are gone. Then I'm back in the army in Viet Nam. I must be going crazy or I am crazy. Well that's why I'm here right? I mean you are a shrink." "You're not crazy Jimmy, you've been through a lot. You saw your buddies killed. You have seen so many deaths and horrible acts. They take a toll. That's why you're here. Yes, you need some help and someone to talk too. Also, your wounds were significant. The head injury is still a problem we need to address. They have more tests to run. When they are finished, we will evaluate where we go from here. In the mean time I here to talk to. At this time the best thing is to get some rest.

"Jimmy, we have the test results and there is a problem. You have some swelling on your brain that we need to operate to correct. The operation is going to be difficult and we are transferring you to New York Presbyterian in Lower Manhattan there you will get the finest care possible." "Fine, I had a feeling something is wrong in there. All these crazy dreams and nightmares. These flashes of different lives popping in and out. I feel like I'm watching a few different TV stations at the same time. Whatever it takes I'm good with. I just want to get back to normal."

Jimmy is transported to Manhattan. After being set up in the room the nurse comes in to prepare him for surgery. "I'm going to give you something to relax you. Then we will be wheeling you down to the operating room." "Whatever you say, I don't think I have any choices here." "Afraid not but you're in great hands. Before you know it, you will be in recovery and it will be all over with." "Sounds good, I'm ready." Jimmy there is someone here to see you, can I let him in?" "Sure." "Hello Jimmy, I'm Father Thomas. I was here visiting a friend and I heard of your operation. I just wanted to see you and maybe say a prayer for a successful operation." "Father Thomas, do I know you?" "I don't believe so but there is something." "Yes, this might sound crazy but I think you have been in one of my dreams." "That is strange and quite a coincidence. I heard of these types of occurrences before. I do work in exploring multiple realities, so you never know. That in some way it is possible we have met before. If it is okay with you, I would like to pray for you." "Definitely Father, I could use all the prayers I can get, thank you." "Sorry to interrupt but it's time." "Okay, I'm ready, hope to see you again, Father." "Of course, I'm sure you will."

As he lays on the operating table, he hears the doctor say, "Jimmy, can you start counting backwards from one hundred." "Sure Doc, ninety-nine, ninety-eight, ninety-seven." A few seconds later Jimmy drifts off.

Pompeii, Italy:

Father something is wrong. I spoke to the Vatican and Father Regis left yesterday with the document. No one has heard from him since he left Rome. I called his mother she lives in Naples. She said he was there for dinner and left later in the evening. I didn't want to worry her so I said I'm sure he was on his way. This is not like him at all. He would have notified me someway if he was detained." "Do you think that something has happened to him?" "I'm afraid so. I don't know of how anyone could have known he was bringing me this message and the document but anything is possible. I'm sure Oliver has spies everywhere, even in the Vatican." "Do you think they could have hurt him?" "I don't know. I do feel they are capable of anything. Especially anything that can interfere with their plans." As they are speaking the hotel phone in their room rings. "Hello, yes, oh my God, no, this is horrible." Brother Aiden puts down the phone and sits down. "Brother, what is it." "Father Regis was killed last night. They found his body late last night. The cause of death was multiple stab wounds. He died in the street." "My God, I can't believe it. It must be Oliver and his sick society behind this." "Yes, and the document he was carrying is gone. These are very sick and evil people and they are capable of anything. We must be very careful. I will call the Vatican and see what happens next."

CHAPTER 28

Jimmy opens his eyes and looks around. He is not in the operating room or a hospital room. He is laying in a corner in the back of a cement one story building. He hears sirens wailing and voices over a loud speaker. "Remain inside until the fugitive is in custody. He looks over a garbage disposal to see what is going on. There is a black armored truck slowly driving down the road. It has an insignia with NWO on it. Jimmy knows he has never seen that before. For some strange reason he gets the feeling they are looking for him. This makes no sense. He has no idea where he is or what he could have done. He sees two men dressed all in black with body armor on carrying large automatic weapons. They have black helmets that have a blackened shield covering their faces, they have red armbands with that same insignia NWO. He is not sure where to hide or where he would go. He just stays in the same spot waiting for a way out. As the two men pass him by, he watches them continue down the street. He hears a voice, "Come in here. Come in here I will help you." "He looks and sees a young woman staring at him from a hole in the wall. "Now before it's too late. They will be back any second." He crawls over to her as she helps him through the opening. She then slides a large cement piece of wall back over the hole. "Follow me." She crawls along the floor with a very low ceiling. This is some type of crawl space. She then leads him to a trap door and steps that goes down to a dark hallway. They are able to stand but he could hardly see. She continues and opens another door into a large room. "You will be safe here. Jimmy looks around and there are multiple monitors around the room. She sits down on an office chair with wheels. "Sit down, you are safe, trust me." "Who are you? Where the hell am I? "You're in zone H15. My name is Nicky, what's yours?" "Jimmy, what is H15, never heard of it." "All the quadrants are broken up into zones have been for five years. Where did you come from?" "I don't know. The only thing I remember is I was in a hospital then in a church with two priests and I was in the army in Viet Nam. I'm not sure which is real. It's all very confusing. My memory is all messed up." "Well the last one would be why they are looking for you." "The army, why?" "Yeah, you must have amnesia for sure. Under the law instituted by the supreme leader Oliver Wilhelm all military present and past are incarcerated while awaiting extermination." "What are you talking about, that's insane." "Of course, it's crazy but that's what the psycho Wilhelm ordered." "I'm totally confused. Who is Wilhelm?" "Okay, it's obvious you have had a bigtime memory loss. I'll give you a history lesson. Over five years ago the nut job Wilhelm took over as the leader of the New World Order. The evil sister and brother, Lilith and Aaron, came from hell and took control of all the world. They put Wilhelm in control of all the countries. "Okay, this is all insane. You must be crazy this makes no sense at all. These two took over the world. Two people?" "Well they were not really people but more like kids. Maybe Fourteen and thirteen and can't forget their two headed pet dog, Cerberus. If I didn't live through this, I wouldn't believe it myself. They came from nowhere and issued these ultimatums to surrender to them or else. One by one they visited each country and when they refused to obey them, they were destroyed." "Destroyed, how?" "Just in a heartbeat, all that would not yield they said a few words and they would burn in flames. They couldn't be stopped. They are somehow indestructible. After a few months of seeing all these world leaders destroyed all the countries gave up. They formed what they call the NWO meaning the New World Order. They put Oliver Wilhelm in charge. He decreed that all military, religious leaders, politicians, professors, and any objectors be eliminated." "I don't know what to say. I'm so confused." "Yeah, I don't blame you. This is a living nightmare for all of us. There are a few cells of us left that have basically gone underground to stay safe. The few religious leaders that are left say God will send his army of angels to destroy this evil.

Others just try to figure out how to stay alive. There are some military that survived trying to find a way to fight back. This seems impossible." "Why are you hiding? are you any of those that will be eliminated?" "I ran into hiding with my dad. He was a minister and would have been killed." "Did he die?" "Yes, he had a heart attack about a year ago." "I'm sorry." "He's better off, it was torturing him to see this evil rule the world. Are you hungry, I have some food." "Coffee?" "Sure, I'll get you a cup." "What's with all the monitors?" "We have a few tech nerds who keep this network going. We can monitor what's happening all around. They tapped into the NWO cameras they have set all over. They have millions of cameras they watch everything." "How do you get supplies?" There's an underground network that has help from the outside." "How is the outside? Do people work?" "Oh yeah, they all have conformed to the new world. The NWO employs almost ninety-percent of all the people. There are a few small independent businesses that are in operation. There are gambling machines all over. Houses of prostitution are on every corner. All the religious houses of worship have been turned into prostitution and gambling parlors. They have banned marriage, funerals, charities, single family homes and anything that resembles suburbia. They are building hi-rise apartments all through the country. Plus, anyone over sixty years old seemed to disappear." "Incredible, there is no way of stopping them?" "None, that anyone can think of. They now have armies of police, cameras everywhere, and they show no mercy. If you break a rule your dead. They have killed people in the streets for no reason. If you wear a medal of any kind, religion or military your carted off to work camps, if you're lucky. There is nothing left of our history. Every statue, monument, any book, film, picture, library, personal scrapbook is destroyed. This is their new world, like it or not no choice. They appoint their own brain washed puppets in every country. Anyone dares to criticize or resist is a goner." "Where are your friends?" "We have underground tunnels connecting many parts of the area. They are always looking to save people like yourself. Anyone that wants out they try to bring them down to safety." "Their police don't know of all this?" "They kind of do, I'm sure. So far, we've been able to stay safe but I think it's only a matter of time until they locate us. In the mean time we keep doing our thing. Praying for a miracle is all we really have." "What if you can kill the leader, this Wilhelm?" "Yeah, love to but it's impossible to get to him. Even if we could do it the devil kids would just appoint a new leader. There are cells planning to kill him all over our system. So far no one has come up with a plan that will work." "What about a bomb?" "Tried it about a year ago. A team of six hijacked a truck carrying food into the compound where he resides. The old Whitehouse was leveled and they built a new ultra-modern complex. They were able to get into the complex but they have a bomb protection system that uncovered them before they had a chance. They were captured and beheaded at the front of the complex for all to see." "Does he ever come out in the public?" "Very rare but he has a few times. He rides in a special armored vehicle and has an army around him." "Does he ever leave the country?" "Yes, he has visited a few countries every so often." "What about his plane, can you get a bomb on it?" "Can't get anywhere near it but that could work. We have discussed it many times. Haven't found a way yet. Come look at the monitors and I'll give you a tour of the country." Jimmy followed Nicky to the monitors. He watched in shock. "where we are now before it was H15 what was it?" This area was Huntington. Are you familiar with it?" "Yeah, I know the area well. I grew up a few miles from here." "So, you have some memories?" "I do but they are all mixed up. I remember being young and then things get mixed up. It's like I was in many different places at the same time. It's all scrambled. Very hard to explain." "Well you just seemed to pop up here from nowhere?" "Yeah, I guess.?" "Maybe you're our savior, sent from heaven to save us." "I don't think so." "Well that's our only chance. Either that or we get lifted up into heaven away from this hell. You know the rapture. My dad was a minister so I have a lifetime of the bible." "That would be great but I have the feeling I would be left here." "You did say that you have a memory of being with two priests?" "Yeah, I do have that memory but it's not clear. I'm not sure what I was doing or even who I was." "I still don't understand how they could have taken over all these Governments. Just doesn't make any sense." "The way it happens the devil kids visit the leaders and after a short meeting they somehow brain wash them into bowing to their command. Some are burnt up in seconds and others just become their puppets. I know it sounds crazy but that's the word. Of course, no one witnessed it and there is no real news anymore. Come with me, I want to show you something. They walk through to another room. Nicky slides open a large metal door." "That's an impressive amount of fire power." "Yeah, we have enough to supply a small army but we're not sure where and when to use them. Come in here we have our veggie supply. We grow carrots, potatoes, spinach, tomatoes, lettuce, kale, strawberries and even lemons for our tea. As you can see these tunnels run for miles. We have our own medical facility and we have quite a few doctors and nurses." "You have a city under the city." "Yeah, pretty much." "Where is everyone else?" "Most are in meetings. We have a number of cells throughout. First, they meet in cells and they meet in a larger quadrant. We do have some people outside in the upper world. They have been able to convince the powers that be that they are one of them. They bring us supplies, meds, and many other necessities. Our General or the one that we believe in, doesn't have a title, is out there too. They also bring us vital information that we hope will someday give us a way to defeat them. It's late and you must be drained. Why don't you get some sleep and we will talk more in the morning? I'll set you up in a bed and a little space of your own. In here there is a makeshift bathroom facility. Here's a blanket and a pillow. I'll see you in the morning." "Thanks Nicky." Jimmy lies down he is trying to make sense of everything that has happened. He keeps seeing different lives that he thinks he was in. At this point he has no idea what was or is real. Now he finds himself in a world that has been taken over by total evil. He thought Viet Nam was hell but this tops that. How he ended up here and where he came from is a total mystery to him. The last memory he had was lying on an operating table and then he wakes up in another world. After a while he drifts off and sleeps. "Good morning, some coffee?" "Please." "Did you sleep okay?" "Yeah, I did." Nicky hands Jimmy a cup of coffee. He takes a few sips, "Just what I needed." "I want to show you something." They walk over to a cabinet. "This look familiar?" "Yeah, a bible." "Good, have you ever read revelations?" "I think when I was a kid but not sure if I read it completely." "In revelations there are seven seals. They state a leader will arise he will have the power to take away all the peace on earth. There will be deaths kingdom where people will be killed with swords, famines, diseases and wild animals. In the last years there have been riots, senseless murders, disease, famine, earthquakes, storms, flooding, and now this state of control. They have destroyed all our history, our religions our traditions and our basic freedom. They round up people all the time and send them to work camps or death. This to me is the bible prophecies coming true and more. Our only hope is that we can kill and destroy the leaders. Wilhelm, Lilith and Aaron the devil kids. That is what we live for. There has to be a way to destroy them." Jimmy watched Nicky closely. He realized that she was passionate and very beautiful. She had dark skin, long brown thick hair. Jimmy also couldn't help to staring at her perfect body. Nicky went on for quite a long time explaining in detail the dire situation. Jimmy listened intently to every word. She was compelling and he felt his passion for her and the cause to be growing. "Nicky, I don't know how I got here or what happens next but I want to help." "I'm not sure how you ended up here but I'm glad you're here. I'm sure we will find a way for you to help. You are unknown and that might be to our advantage. Like I told you before they have millions of cameras all around. They monitor everything twenty-four seven. They have this facial recognition system. They can identify you in seconds. Every person is in their system. You might not be. Of course, we would have no way of knowing." "What about a hood and dark glasses, something like that." "No good. Any coverings like that are illegal. If you're seen wearing any kind of cover ups, hats, hoods, sun glasses, they will pick you up in minutes. How you didn't get caught is baffling." "Luck, I guess. Maybe because I'm not in their system and didn't put up any red flags. If that's the case I can go out for some supplies or information or anything that could help." "That might be possible. One other thing all of their approved citizens have to be marked. They scan that everywhere you go. You can't shop, enter anywhere or pretty much do anything without your markings." "Markings, what is that?" "Everyone who is approved to be free has to be sworn to them. They are marked with the numbers, 100-200-6-100-60-200." "What the hell do those numbers mean? I do remember in the bible the devils mark was 6 6 6." "Good for you, Jimmy. Your right and if you add those numbers up, they add up to 666." Jimmy takes a second, "Yeah, they do. Is that to fool the people?" "Not sure, why they do anything. Come I want to show you something else." They walk over to multiple monitors all showing different areas throughout the region. "Yeah, I was looking at these before." "Well there is one over here is my personal favorite." Jimmy looks at it and smiles, "Wow, that's beautiful." "Yeah, that's the lighthouse on Montauk Point. There's the Ocean behind it and you can see the waves." "Yeah, I go to it all the time. It gives me a sense of peace. It calms me and brings back warm memories. My Parents used to bring me there when I was a kid. We would go on family picnics. Then we would go to the Lighthouse and take pictures. They used to have a ranch out there and we would go horseback riding. I loved to ride. Look I have a picture of me and my brother riding." "Nicky takes out a picture from her back pocket and shows Jimmy." "It's about all I have left of my personal stuff. Everything was left behind when we escaped." "Jimmy saw a few tears drip down Nicky's face. He took his hand and gently wiped her tears. She looked at him and smiled, "Sorry, just sometimes those memories get me down. I miss my Dad, my family, my friends and the way life used to be. I had a lot of friends and some great times." "Were you ever married?" "No, I did have a boyfriend and we were pretty serious. He was taken away right before we fled. I saw him executed on those monitors along with hundreds of others. They would line them up on their knees and one by one shoot them in the back of the head. They would show this on every station on every TV in the world. They wanted to send a message to fall in line or else. That image is in my mind all the time." "I'm sorry, Nicky." "Thanks, hey at least I survived, for now anyway. This is what keeps me going. It gives me a reason to get up in the morning. One day I want to be there when we can blow up these bastards. I want to witness their death as a small retribution for all the deaths and destruction they caused. I'm not sure this is possible but it keeps me going." "I am willing to do anything I can to help you see it." "Thanks, more coffee?" "Yeah." "Tell me more about yourself or at least what you remember." "Well, that's a tough one. I have so many memories, it's confusing. I remember having some type of car accident. I was cut off and ran off the road. There was my wife and our two boys in the car and they were all killed. I see this but I don't remember anything about them. I seem to know they were my family but that's about it. The other crazy thing is that when I was pinned in the car, I see this face smiling at me. It was my old friend Stevie staring and smiling at me in the window. This is really nuts, because he was killed in a night club when we were just kids. This part I remember well. The rest seems almost more dream like." "What do you mean killed?" "Yeah, me and a few friends were in a club and Stevie was with this girl. It was late and the club was kind of empty. He was getting her number when these two other guys came in. They knew the girl Stevie was with and this one guy started hassling her. Stevie and this guy got into a fight and he shot Stevie. I was there holding him as he bled out. I know this happened; I mean I remember it very well." "Oh, that's horrible." Yeah, it was pretty bad. The thing is that happened when we were twenty. Then

I see him at the accident that had to be twenty something years later. Now that makes no sense. Plus, how could have he been there and why would he be smiling? We were great friends. I don't know, it's all a mess in my head."

CHAPTER 29

"You said you were a veteran; do you remember any of that?" "Definitely, I was in Viet Nam did like thirteen months of pure hell." "You see a lot of action?" "Plenty, to many buddies killed. I lost a real dear friend who shouldn't have been there. Look we were all kids but this kid Andy he was a sweet guy that wouldn't hurt a fly. They threw him out there gave him a gun and told him to go kill some Viet Cong. He was lost, he would follow me around like a puppy dog. I got to love the guy like a brother in a few months. Then one day on patrol bang, he takes a bullet right through his head. Nineteen and dead. For what? a senseless war. Not one of us ever heard of that shit hole before we got there. Yeah, this I remember really well. After beating a case of malaria, I was sent back to the field and that's when I got hit. We were sent into a Viet Cong village and things got ugly. I was part of some shit that I would like to forget. I saw some buddies get killed and then it was my turn. I had very little time left and I thought I could make it out of there in one piece but I was wrong. Don't get me wrong, I did make it out." "Were you hurt bad?" "Bad enough but that's a long time ago." "Did you keep in touch with any of your buddies?" "Yeah, I did of what I can remember." "You seem to remember a lot." "I do but then the most recent past gets all messy. Most of this was twenty years ago. All except the car accident." "That's it, maybe in the car accident you suffered some kind of amnesia?" "Could be but how does that explain me showing up here? All that I remember there was not any of this shit going on." "What's the last memories you have?" "Well that's when it gets crazy. I have these flashes of being with a priest. I can see myself traveling with him in England to some distant monastery. Then we go to Italy and there are murders that we are involved in. Some type of meeting that we are supposed to go to. Then I can see this church up on a hill and we meet another priest. I'm down in some old ruins of some kind. Then I'm in a hospital operating room. After that I'm hiding and you call out to me." "It is very confusing, not sure what to say. I'm sure there's a reasonable explanation for all of it. Somehow your recent memories have been wiped out. I'm sure in time it all will come back." "Yeah, I guess your right. You don't have a shrink down here, do you?" "No, sorry." "When will the rest of the group be back?" "They will be back soon. They visit different cells, exchanging information. The Docs make rounds and then go back to their makeshift hospital. I can take you there, when their back. Maybe they could examine you? Till then we have some time to kill. I'm sick of watching these monitors, let's do something different. Take your mind off all those questions you got running through your head." "Like what?" "I got some movies, cards, or a board game." "What kind of movie?" "War, drama, comedy, we have a decent collection." "Comedy sounds perfect." "Okay, let's see what you like. Come with me. Check these out." "Wow, not bad. Even alphabetized, I'm impressed. How about you pick one." "Okay, I could do that. Let me see, hmm, how about this?" "Splash?" "Have you seen it?" "Yeah, now that I remember. John Candy and Tom Hanks. I love those guys." "Great, it's my favorite. I have a crush on Tom Hanks." Jimmy watches the smile on Nicky's face. He can't help thinking how pretty she is. She had a way about her making him think he knew her for a long time. He felt relaxed for the first time since he popped up here. She inserted the VHS tape and they sat next to each other. "What about the monitors?" "We have sensors all over the area. If anyone comes close to our location, we have alarms that will sound. We have some heavy hi-tech guys with us." Jimmy smiles and sits back and watches the movie. He loves to hear her laugh it's contagious. Even though he remembers the scenes well but he can't help from laughing with her. He is seated so close to her he can't help thinking how good it feels. He feels like a school boy with a desire to just hold her hand. As the movie winds down to the end Nicky looks at Jimmy. "You liked it right? You were laughing pretty good." "Yeah, I did see it but it's a great movie. As they get up, they here sound of people walking in. "We're back, hey Nicky what have we missed?" "Not much, no activity around us. What came out of your meetings?" "Well we're waiting for the announcement when the trio of darkness will be coming to the U. N. Everything we hear is that it's a definite. Who is this?" "Sorry Mike, this our newest guest, Jimmy." "Hi, when and how did you end up here?" "That's a long story. Nicky saved my ass outside and brought me here. I seem to have some amnesia and I'm not sure how I got here." "Amnesia? Wow, that's something. Nicky, can I talk to you?" "Sure, Jimmy why don't you relax and I'll be right back." Jimmy watches as Nicky walks away. He sees about a dozen guys checking the monitors and sitting around exchanging notes. He takes a seat and waits. "Nicky, what do you know about this guy? How do we know we can trust him?" "Look he was running from the cops; he's a veteran and I believe his story. You know I'm careful and I wouldn't bring anyone down here if I wasn't sure it's safe." "How do you know?" "I've been talking to him, I know, trust me. He is willing to help. He could be an asset and bring us some needed intel. He was in Viet Nam; he's seen plenty of action. I trust him. When's Dan coming back?" "He should be back in a day or so. I'm sure he's going to want to check this guy out." "No problem." Nicky walks back to Jimmy, "Sorry about that but we don't get many visitors down here. We have to be careful who we trust." "Hey, I get it. I would be concerned about my story if I was him." "Come on, I'll introduce you to the crew." Nicky walks Jimmy around and introduces him to everyone." "I don't want to be dead weight around here so what can I do." "Okay, before your cleared I can't give you any real involved tasks but we do need help in here." "Ladies this is your new helper, Jimmy." Jimmy smiles as Nicky introduces him to the staff. "This is Ellen, Jeannie and Sue." Sue walks over to Jimmy, "I have a good job for you. You know how to use a knife?" "Yeah." "Good, then you can cut up these chickens, we're making chicken stew and soup. This should keep you busy for a while." "Okay, no problem. After working in the kitchen for a few hours Jimmy washes up and goes to his bed and sits. "Hey, come on we're all eating now. Jimmy follows Nicky to a large table where about fifteen of them are seated. There is some light conversation and then Jimmy is asked to help clean up. He helps and then goes back on his bed and lays down. Nicky comes in, "Look, I know this isn't what you had in mind of helping out but until Dan comes back, that's all I can have you do." "It's all good, I get it. Who's Dan?" "He is the lead guy. He has a lot of experience and sort of became the unofficial leader. He kind of calls the shots. When he comes back, he will spend some time with you and give his blessing. Then you will be accepted." "What if he doesn't accept me?" "Then, well you know" "Yeah, I do know." "Don't worry, he's a cool guy, he'll know you're okay, I know it." "Thanks Nicky. I want you to know how much I appreciate all your help. I know there are some out there that don't trust me and you've been protecting me. I really owe you." "You don't owe me anything, Jimmy. I like having you here and I know Dan will like you. I'll make sure of that. Now get some sleep there could be some more tough chores for you tomorrow. Good night." "Good night Nicky." Jimmy sits on his bed and he sees a few books on a shelf. He looks through them and picks up the bible. He lays back in bed and reads. The next day Nicky comes to him with a big cup of coffee. "I thought you could use this." "Thanks, just what the doctor ordered. Nicky, do you have a minute?" "Sure, what's up?" "I want to read you something." "Okay." I read this last night, "He will go out and fool the nations who are over all the world. They are Gog and Magog. He will gather them all together for war. There will be as many as the sand along the sea-shore. 9 They will spread out over the earth and all around the place where God's people are and around the city that is loved. Fire will come down from God out of heaven and destroy them. Then the devil who fooled them will be thrown into the lake of fire burning with Sulphur. The wild animal and the false preacher are already there. They will all be punished day and night forever."

"You know my father was a preacher, I have read the bible many times. Why are you reading it to me?" "Well, it gave me an idea. If these two, as you call them devil kids can't be stopped why not do God's plan. Fire and Sulphur, some type of explosive that will burst into flame and Sulphur." "Yeah, maybe that will work. We'll run it by Dan when he comes back. I'm glad you're doing your homework." "Trying to earn my keep." "Have you had experience with explosives?" "In Viet Nam it was my job to call in fire power when we needed it. One night I had to call in a White phosphorus hit on an enemy position. I saw firsthand what that shit can do. So, I was thinking that you can make an explosive that would cause fire and Sulphur, just might do the trick." "You know, I like the way you think. I'm kind of like having you around here." "I kind of like being here to, Nicky." Nicky smiles and walks away.

Later in the day:

"Hey Nicky, he's back." From the back of the room a few more men walk in. "It's good to be back. I need you all in here for a quick briefing. Everyone goes into another room. Jimmy waits outside looking at the monitors. "We have confirmed that Wilhelm and the evil ones will be addressing the U.N. We are looking into a plan on how we can get to them. They are well protected but there is always a way. This is all for now but we will have an update and more details soon. Everyone leaves the room except Nicky and Dan. After a while they come out, "Jimmy, I want you to meet Dan." Jimmy gets up and goes over to Nicky. "Jimmy?" "Danny, holly shit it is you. I don't believe it." "I can't believe it either." Both of them hug and Nicky says, "You two know each other?" "Yeah, we grew up together. I haven't heard from you since the army." "Yeah, sorry about that. After I was wounded, I went in to hiding. I really cut off everyone. Now that I look back it was stupid but I was in a bad place." "What happened after the army?" "This is going to sound crazy but I don't remember much. Just like I landed here, it's all a blur." "We've been talking since Jimmy got here. Seems like he has some type of amnesia." "I have all these mixed up flashes of memories that come and go. It's a long story but bottom line is I'm not sure which of these memories are real. It's like I've had a few different lives. Hey enough about me, how the hell did you end up here. Nicky tells me you're the big man around here." "It's something I kind of fell into. I was knocking around from one job to another and my brother talked me into being a cop." "A cop?" "Crazy right? but I did it and it worked out. I was kind of good at it. I made detective and was working in some pretty heavy stuff. Then the world fell apart. I got lucky when the NWO came to New York. I had a buddy from the department that made a deal with them. He became one their informers and they put him on their force. I didn't trust him but I went along with him. I had to do some shitty things to get their trust. I became one of their hunters. It's my job to find anyone they mark as a threat. I'm part of a task force that hunts, captures and bring them in. Believe me it's not something I want to do but it's a trade-off. I catch some guys that will be caught anyway and gain their trust. Gives me access to a lot of important information. It's not just being there but I have become friends with one important high-ranking member of their community. This guy loves the ladies and the booze. He calls on me to take him to some meetings, that's what he tells his wife. I have become his private security and confidant. I have covered for him many times and also make sure I get him home in one piece. He is not as bad as many of the others he just has the right connections. He also looks the other way when I do some things that are not approved. Plus, when he drinks, he gives me some good information. That's where I've been the last few days. He got in some trouble with his wife and I had to stay with him in a hotel for a while. I also escort some of his bimbos to and from his room. He finally got his wife to forgive him with some expensive jewelry and he went home. I'm back on regular duty for a while. He got me some time off as a reward. He will dry out and be a good boy for a while. Jimmy, you don't remember how you ended up here or where you came from?" "The only thing I remember was hiding in an alley way and there were cops looking for me. Then Nicky called me and brought me down here. I've been telling Nicky the last memories are all crazy. From traveling through Europe with a couple of priests to being in some car accident. Then I'm in an operating room looking up at this bright light. Then I go out and wake up in the alley." "Shit, that is weird. Could the car accident have caused your amnesia?" "I guess so but even that was weird. "Why?" "I don't think it was an accident. I was run off the road by some crazy driver on purpose. This I'm sure of. Then I'm pinned in the car and see my wife and kids. They were not breathing and I'm sure they were gone. Then I see our old friend Stevie staring at me in the window. He was smiling like he was happy about what happened." "Stevie, Stevie Bracken?" "Yeah, it was him. Look I know that's crazy but that's what I remember." "Why would he want to hurt you we were all great friends? You said your wife and kids?" "That's another thing, I believe they were. The problem is I don't remember them either." "Man, I don't know what to say. That thing about Stevie too is weird." "Of course, being he is dead over twenty years." "Dead, twenty years, what are you talking about?" "He was killed at the club remember?" "Stevie wasn't killed." "The girl Stevie liked and then this guy came in and him and Stevie got into a fight. He pulls a gun and shoots Stevie. I tried to stop it but I was too late." "Jimmy, Stevie was never killed. You got in between Stevie and that guy and dragged Stevie out the door. I was in touch with him up till a few years before the NWO took over. He was living in Syosset with his wife. After the NWO I tried to find him but they left and I guess went into hiding. He was a veteran too and had to run." "This is screwed up; I remember that night well and he was killed." "Didn't happen Jimmy, I'm positive." Now, I'm really confused." "Look, you've been through a lot and I think you should get some rest. Maybe your memory will start to come back. Give it some time." "That's the problem, I have a lot of memories I just don't know which are real." "It's okay, you're safe here. Just get some rest and we'll talk more." "Okay." Nicky looks at Danny and then at Jimmy, "Come on Jimmy, let's go back to where you can get some rest." Jimmy follows Nicky almost in a trance. They get to his bed and he sits. He looks up at Nicky, "I don't get it, how could I be so screwed up. I mean everything is so confusing. The Stevie thing really blows my mind. Nicky, I saw him die. He bled out in my arms. How could he and Danny have two different memories of what happened.?" Nicky sits next to Jimmy. I don't know but there has to be some explanation. I agree with Danny, try to get some rest. Things have a way of sorting themselves out in time." "Thanks Nicky, you've been great. I hope your right." Jimmy lays down on the bed and closes his eyes. Nicky walks out and over to Danny. "You two guys grew up together?" "Yeah, we knew each other from little kids. We went to school together and pretty much did everything together. Jimmy went into the army and was shipped to Viet Nam right away. We wrote each other all the time. He used to tell me all the shit he was going through. He went through a lot of bad situations. Seen a lot of action and then his letters started to change. I would write and not here from him in weeks. I kept writing but then he stopped completely. I knew he was wounded pretty bad. I tried to get in touch but got nowhere. After a long time, I just kind of gave up trying." "What do you think about what he says about your friend Stevie?" "He's wrong, like I said. I kept in touch with Stevie for years. I don't know what to think why he has these memories. The accident, a wife and kids he doesn't remember. Stevie running him off the road and smiling at him. None of this makes sense. I don't know what to think. Hopefully he'll come around." "He seems like a great guy." "He is, he was my best friend. I feel terrible we lost touch all these years. I can't help feeling guilty. I should have tried harder to find him. Maybe I could have helped him." "Come on, you must be beat. Want a cup of coffee?" "Sounds good."

The next day when Jimmy awakes. he keeps thinking about all

that has happened. Waking up in an alley, running from police. Nicky calling out to him. Bringing him down here. The world has been taken over by evil demons. People being killed because they were veterans, religious leaders. Reuniting with Danny and Nicky taking care of him. Plus, the haunting fact that he can't remember anything before this. How he ended up here. Where he came from. Anything about his life that makes sense. All these flashes of multiple lives. The car accident is the one thing that stands out in his head. That's the one memory that keeps coming back. Not the details but he could feel the pain from the accident. He decides to get up and find Nicky. She is the one thing so far that makes him feel good. He hardly knows Nicky but somehow, he feels a connection. He feels very attracted to her. He likes being with her. It's crazy but he is happy to be here because of her. When he is around her, he feels like a kid wanting to hold her hand. He feels excited, as he decides to get up and find her. He walks out to the large room. "Hey, you seen Nicky?" "Yeah, she is in with Danny." "Thanks." Jimmy walks over to another small room and sees Danny and Nicky hugging and kissing. He is taken by surprise and just stands there. Nicky sees him, "Hey, good morning." "Good morning, I'm sorry didn't mean to interrupt." "No, don't be silly. Can I get you some coffee?" "Yeah, that would be great." He smiles at Danny as Nicky leaves the room. "You and Nicky are together?" "Yeah, we been together for about two years now. Have to tell you she is great. She keeps me together and gives me a reason to go on. This world is so screwed up but she is my rock." "Hey, that's great. I'm happy for you." Nicky comes back with the coffee. "It's amazing that you two grew up together. "Yeah, me, Jimmy, Stevie, Sal and Ray were like brothers. We knew each other since we started in Grammar School together. We lived all around each other, the farthest away was Sal and he lived two blocks away in the same development. The crazy thing that our town it was predominantly Jewish but the only one of us that was Jewish was Ray. The rest were all Italian Americans and were very proud of it. Stevie's mom was Italian his dad was Irish. Ray the only Jewish one loved to eat with any of us Sundays because all our families made lots of Italian dinners and Ray loved it. All of us took turns watching out for Stevie but for some reason I was the one that always felt that it was up to me to take care of him. Stevie was different than the rest of us. His Father was an alcoholic and he was a real nasty drunk. There were many times Stevie would call me and the other guys to come over and get him because his father was drunk and started punching everyone around him. He hit Stevie's mom, his two younger brothers. He was big, mean and violent when he was loaded. We bailed Stevie out many times. I would get Stevie and he would come with me and stay at my house until a few days went by and his father would dry out, for a while. Although his father would hit all of them, it was Stevie, maybe because he was the oldest that he really went after the most. The last time his father went nuts, I was the only one who could get there. Just as I pulled up to Stevie's house, a big TV came flying through the front window. His father also loved to bust up all the furniture and throw it at Stevie. I told them to call the cops but they would never do it. It was a really bad situation. Most of the time Stevie was normal and his family life had some weeks of calm. The bottom line was Stevie needed help and I loved the guy he was special so I always was there for him. He would be a hand full at times but he had a great heart and would do anything for me and the rest of us. Stevie was the one kid that even when he did something wrong and got caught, he would just look at you with a scared puppy dog face and you would forget about what he did. Of course, Stevie knew it and played that card many times. My parents loved him he was so polite and cute. The girls would always be drawn to him with a devil personality but he had an angel look to him. Sometimes he just wouldn't think things through before he went and did something stupid. Like a job! He bounced from one to the other. He never had any money and when he did get some, he would give it all to his mom. That was the thing about him he would do anything to make a buck, any way possible except holding a regular job. As soon as he got the money, he would give it away. The money meant nothing to him but when he gave it to his mom and made her happy, he was happy. Like I said he was a handful but he had a great heart. Every time he met a new girl, he would fall in love with her.

After the first date that's all he would talk about that this one was the most wonderful love of his life. The problem was that love affair would last about three more dates and Stevie would fall out of love just as fast. He had such a way about him that, when he ended the relationship the girl felt so bad thinking it was her fault and everyone, including myself, would console him. Stevie was a special combination of lovable, funny, conniving, gambling, walks on the edge and a guy that you wanted to choke, hug and then help him. I loved the guy like a brother, the fact he was ten months older than me meant nothing. I still looked after him like he was my kid brother." "Did you guys have a lot of girlfriends back then?" "No not really. We were always hanging out together and none of us had steady girlfriends." "There was this one girl we both liked when we were really young." "Oh yeah, did you fight over her?" "No, matter of fact it was kind of funny. Her name was Janet, you remember her Jimmy? "I do, these memories are clear. You met her first." "Yes, I think we were about thirteen or fourteen. I met her at Stevie's cousin's house party. She was like a distant cousin of Stevie. They had a big finished basement with a bar and piano. I actually got the nerve up to talk to her. Just little stuff like where you from, what school you go to. She was real sweet and pretty. I fell for her in about two minutes. It was like my first puppy love. She lived in Cambria Heights, Queens. After the party all I could think about was her. I used to play records and think I was dancing with her. I was smitten." They all laugh, "So, did you date her?" "Date her, I didn't have the nerve to call her. Believe it or not I got her address from Stevie and I wrote her a letter." "You're kidding?" "No seriously, I didn't have the confidence or the nerve to call her. A few days later I get a letter back from her. She said some nice thing like she liked meeting me and some general questions. You know stupid stuff like what's your favorite song, group, movie. We wrote a few more letters and then she sends one that smelled like perfume and says why don't I call her and maybe come visit her. I get up the nerve to call her. She says she has two girl fiends, so why don't I come over with Stevie and another friend. We can hang out at her house. She has a finished basement with a record player. I set up the date for that Saturday. She lived in Queens and we didn't drive yet so we had to take the railroad to Jamaica and walk. I tell Jimmy and Stevie and they were excited about it. I take three records from my older brother Alex to bring with me. Do you remember them, Jimmy?" "Yeah, there's a Moon out Tonight, by the Capris, Baby oh Baby, the Shells and I can't remember the other one." "It was Once in a While, by the Chimes." "How do you remember that?" "Easy, they were three slow records. Janet had all fast records. We were down her basement and her mom stayed upstairs. She came down at the beginning and gave us some homemade pizza's and sodas. Then she went back up and didn't come down. Later I found out that Janet was the only child and she was a spoiled princess. After we ate, we sort of paired up and started to dance. We started with a couple of fast records but then we put on the three slow ones. She dims the lights and it turns into a make out party. The three records were the only slow ones, so we played them all day long, over and over again. That's why we never could forget them. The day was great, so we made the same date for the next week. We go down the basement, same story but we did bring a few other records. The day is going well and then she asks Jimmy to dance. This goes back and forth, me and him taking turns dancing with her. She tells Jimmy she likes him and to call her. At the same time, she tells me she likes me and to call her. A few days go by and me and Jimmy get together and say we want to call Janet for another date. We tell each other what she said. We decide to call her together and let her choose which of us she wants to be with. We go to a phone booth and call her. I get her on the phone and I ask her does she like me or Jimmy? She says she likes us both. Jimmy and I start pushing each other to be the one that dates her. We get in this argument back and forth, that I don't like her that much, so you should date her. Well this goes on for about ten minutes and she gets disgusted and tells us she doesn't want to see either one of us and hangs up. We laugh and tell each other we were too good of friends to be played against each other." "That was probably the closest we ever got into an argument." "What's crazy is how I remember these things. It's like a have been through multiple lives. I'm just not sure which are real." "That's funny but it's so nice that you guys were so close." "We could tell stories for hours but we have to take care of some business. Jimmy that idea of yours that you told Nicky sounds promising." "Idea?" "Yeah, the bomb fire and Sulphur." "Oh right, you think that can work?" "Maybe, your referencing the bible makes sense. Look if you told me all this stuff about devil kids taking over the world, I would have laughed.

I haven't been the most religious person around and I wasn't into reading the bible much. Now with all this, it seems all these prophecies are happening. So why not go with it. I ran this through our bomb guys and they said they could rig up a device that can work. I'll be going out there and will try to get the latest intel. Once I get that information I'll come back. Then we will put a plan together. We won't have much time. I'm sure the window of opportunity will be short. You know Jimmy, I feel bad we haven't had the time to really catch up. Hopefully we get through this and we can spend a lot of time together. I can't stay down here too long. I can't risk blowing my cover." "No problem, I understand. I want to let you know anything I can do in this operation I am willing to do. I have seen plenty of bad situations and I know how to handle them that part of my memory in Viet Nam is very clear." "Great Jimmy, I know you can handle it. Let's see what we come up with and then we'll go from there. Keep an eye on my Nicky for me. She likes you and she can fill you in on how things work around here. There's not many women down here and none as attractive as Nicky." "You're a lucky guy Danny, she is a real keeper."

CHAPTER 30

Pompeii, Italy:

Father Thomas looked at Brother Aiden, "What happens now? What did the Vatican say?" "They are leaving it up to me. They know it is very dangerous to go to their meeting. They also know that we are their only hope of getting the information on what happens there. They feel that this meeting there is a ceremony that will be taking place that could affect the whole world. They are extremely concerned that if they don't have immediate information that their plans cannot be stopped. At one time they believed I could interfere with their success but now they are not sure. The signs are that this is the beginning of the final battle. They have gathered the most powerful people in their society to be there. They feel I can't stop them or interfere but that I can get them the information of what they accomplish and their plans. Father I under estimated the danger involved in this. The serial murders around the world, the killing of Father Regis proves these people are ruthless. I cannot ask you to go into this with me. I appreciate you coming but it is too dangerous for you." "What are you going to do Brother?" "I have been around a very long time. A lot longer than you can imagine. I have fought this evil over and over again. I have been blessed with a gift and a curse. I have had the power to call on messengers and angels to help me stop many forms of evil. I have no fear of death. I also feel they want me there because they want me to witness their ceremony. They want me to go back to the Vatican and tell them what I see. They are very confident they cannot be stopped. They want their word to spread. They have no fear of me. For that reason, I believe they will not harm me because of this. I could be wrong and that's why I think you should go home. You have been a great friend and I want to see you safe." Brother, I know how you feel and I appreciate our friendship. I too have been around a long time and devoted myself to God and the church. I not only feel it is my calling but also my life's work to be with you now. There is no going back for me. I want to come with you we will see this through and report back to the Vatican." "Are you sure this is what you want?" "Yes, Brother, I am sure." "Well, then we go and may God be with us."

Deposit NY:

After dinner Stevie sits at the bar waiting for Mandy. After a while she comes back. "Hi, you miss me?" "Sure, want a drink?" I do but why not come up to my room where the drinks are free." "Sounds good, let's go." They walk up to the second floor and into Mandy's room. "I hope you don't think I do this all the time but this town is so boring especially in the winter." "Why do you stay?" "Good question. I moved into the city a few years ago. I wanted to be a performer. I had this idea I could dance and even act a little bit. Maybe hook on to something in show business. That of course was a pipe dream. The rents were insane. I ended up sharing a small apartment with this girl I met. She was from Ohio and had the same ideas I had. The place was a dump and the area was even worse. Junkies all over the place. I got a job in little Italy, busing tables in a small Italian restaurant. The money was bad but that's all I could get. My roommate gets a job dancing. Yeah, you guessed it in a dive strip club. Same old story, am I boring you?" "No, it's okay, I'm good." "You want a drink?" "Sure." "Vodka or beer?" "Beer sounds good." "After a few months where I could hardly make the rent, I let her talk me into dancing. After a month of doing that and the scum I had to deal with I hit bottom. My roommate was getting hooked on pills and bringing these dirt bags back with her I got sick to my stomach. I decided to come back here and work for my Aunt and Uncle. They are good people and they welcomed me back. I do a lot of complaining but I am happy here. The lifestyle is quiet but compared to where I was it is home.

""Your parents?" "My Mom left when I was four and my dad was a drinker. He would go on binges and would leave me with my Aunt and Uncle. Then One day he left when I was ten and I never saw him again. So, it was just me and thank goodness for my Aunt and Uncle. Hey, I'm being a downer, tell me about you. What kind of work brings you here?" "The last thing I want to do is talk about me. I'm interested in you. You plan on staying here long term?" "Yeah, I guess so. At least until that shiny knight comes into my life and sweeps me off my feet. Takes me away and we get married have a beautiful house and three beautiful kids. Of course, he's a doctor or something like that and is madly in love with me." As Mandy keeps talking Stevie begins to feel a strange sensation. His body like many times before begins to vibrate. He feels the urge to be violent. He has been through this before. He tries hard to stop it but it can be so overwhelming. "Can I use your bathroom?" "Sure, it's right over there." Stevie goes in and runs the cold water. He splashes his face and looks in the mirror. The familiar voice penetrates his head. "What are you waiting for. I handed you a lamb to be butchered and your sitting there chatting. I have warned you before you will do my biding. I want you to kill her and carve into her. You have failed me one to many times. This will be your last chance. Kill the little bitch and do it now." "I'm not a killer." "But you are, you have killed many times. You are what you are. You can't run from it or me." "Why can't you just leave me alone." "No, you fool, you were brought back for this to kill and kill again." "Okay, I will do your sick command but that's it for me. After this I'm done. I can't do it anymore. I won't do it anymore." "Stevie hears the voice laughing, "Oh but you will." More laughter. Then a knock on the door, "Stevie, are you okay?" Stevie, reaches in his pocket and pulls out a wire and holds it in his hand. "Sorry, I'll be right out." He grabs the wire and stretches it between his two hands and pulls. He takes a deep breath and swears to himself this is the last time. He opens the door and Mandy has her back turned at the kitchen sink. "I'll be right there Stevie just cleaning up. Sorry I hate messes.

Make yourself comfortable. Want another beer?" She says without turning around. Stevie approaches her from the back wire stretched out with an evil look in his eyes. He slowly approaches her and then in a split second he lets out a scream. "No." He puts the wire in his pocket and bolts out the door. He runs back to his room. He quickly grabs his bag of clothes and leaves the room. He goes directly to his car and drives off. Mandy can't believe that he just left. She sits down and laughs, "I know how to pick them." Stevie drives south headed back to Long Island.

Jamie sits by Gulli, "What do you think?" "I'm not happy with you going undercover, if that's what you're asking." "What are you my dad? I can take care of myself. I want to catch this creep before he strikes again." "He could be anywhere by now. Look, I'm not your dad. I'm way too young for that. I want to catch him as bad as you do. I got the boss's word we will get the first call on any hits on him. If you are out somewhere else you might not be able to respond as fast.' "Bullshit, come on Gulli don't give me that. We are equal partners and you can't worry about me. If you do, we can't do our jobs." "Okay, your right but my hunch if he is still around, I think he will go after Lisa. I'm not sure of the reasoning but that's what my gut tells me. They took away the patrol car but I say rather than work the bar scene we stay close to her especially at night." "I can see that and you might be right. Look I'll talk to the boss and see what he thinks. If, he lets us follow her then I'm in on it. Plus, I'm not that crazy about the bar scene anyway." "He has unfinished business with her. I think he fought off his instinct to kill her and run out the door. The reason is I think he has feelings for her. Either way I believe he will return to see her for one reason or the other." "Okay, I'll be right back.

After driving five hours Stevie pulls into a fast food restaurant. He orders a coffee and pulls into the back of the lot. "I need to see her one more time. Lisa makes me feel almost normal. I don't want to hurt her. I just want to talk to her. I want to explain that I'm not bad. I never wanted to hurt anybody. It wasn't me. That shit voice in my head made me do all those sick things. I'm done with that. I don't know what to do but I know the first thing is talk to Lisa. If she will listen to me? I can't tell her everything but just enough to try to make her understand. I really enjoyed being with her. She made me feel good. If I don't talk to her, I'm going to lose control. I think she really likes me. We had feelings for each other I'm sure. I can't believe what has happened to me. I hurt people and that makes me sick. I can't go on like this. Lisa is my last chance. She can help me. I hope she'll talk to me. I know I can change. That urge and the voice telling me to kill Mandy I stopped it. I didn't give in. I know I can be good. Just need to see Lisa." A worker sees Stevie talking to himself and knocks on his window. Stevie rolls down the window. "Are you okay?" "Yeah, I'm fine." Stevie puts the car in reverse almost running over the worker and peels out the drive way. The worker goes back inside and talks to another worker. I think I saw that guy that's been in the paper. You know the guy they want for possible some murders." "You're kidding right." "No dude, I'm not." "Then you should call the cops." "You think?' "Yeah, if you think it was him, definitely." "Yeah, I'm going to call." A few minutes later Gulli gets a call on a possible ID on the POI. "Some kid at McDonalds thinks he saw our boy in the parking lot." "Let's go." Gulli speeds off and goes to McDonalds.

Stevie pulls into Lisa's parking lot and walks to her apartment. He knocks on the door. Lisa gets off the sofa and goes to the door. "Who is it" "It's Stevie I just want to talk." Charlie comes over, "Who is it?" "It's Stevie." "Oh my God. Oh, don't let him in. Lisa don't let him in." "Lisa, please, I just want to talk. Just let me in for a minute. I promise I will be only a few minutes." "No Lisa, Don't," do it. I'm freaking out. I'll call the police." "Wait Charlie, please. Stevie I'm sorry but I can't let you in. It's late and I have to get up early tomorrow." Stevie pleads, Lisa listen to me. I just want to explain why I left and ran out that night. I was feeling sick and I had to go." Charlie runs to the phone and dials, 911. "Stevie please leave, I'm sorry but I can't let you in."

Gulli gets the call that Stevie is at Lisa's door. He speeds out of the Mc Donald's lot and heads over to Lisa's.

"Lisa, I'm sorry. I never would hurt you. I felt we had something special going. I've been so confused. I just need to be with you, just to talk. You have nothing to worry about. You're the best thing I have in my life. Please let me in." "Stevie go away. Lisa can't let you in. I just called the police so you better go." "I'm sorry Stevie but Charlie's right please go. I think you need help. I can't help you, I'm so sorry." Stevie falls to his knees in tears. "Lisa, please help me. Help me."

Gulli pulls into the parking lot he and Jamie pull their guns and come running to the apartment. They spot Stevie at the door. "This is the police turn around and put your hands-on top of your head" Stevie gets up slowly and reaches into his belt and pulls out his gun. He turns and fires at Gulli. Jamie and Gulli return fire and Stevie is hit in the arm, chest and stomach. He falls to the ground holding his chest as the blood pours out of him. He lays face up and he hears a voice. "You're a fool. I could have protected you but you wouldn't listen. Now you will pay. The pain you are feeling now is nothing to what awaits your soul. You will be mine now and you will beg for mercy." Lisa comes out the door and screams. Charlie holds her back. Stevie looks at Lisa and whispers, "I'm sorry." Stevie's head falls back and all goes black.

Sirens blasting and police cars encircle the entire area. Jamie turns to Gulli, "He is mortal. Looks like you were right. He did come back for Lisa." "You get lucky sometimes. You know with all the tools we have sometimes you just go with your gut. An in most cases like this you have to get lucky to." "I still don't get it. We never got any prints, no DNA, and we still don't know who he is." "When the reports come back, we should get the whole story."

"He definitely looks like this Stevie Bracken. The picture of him in the yearbook is weird. If I was picking him out of a line up, I would say it is him. He might have come back from the dead but maybe he was a time traveler?" "A dead time traveler? He was killed when he was twenty." "Well, what about a different reality he could have crossed over in one reality and then was killed in another." "Jamie, you're reading to many comic books or watching some Twilight Zone reruns. Look it's just a coincidence he looks like him. You know we all have a double somewhere. The bottom line is we got him. Dead, end of story." "If you say so."

Two days later:

"The reports on our buddy are all back." "Okay, Jamie, what do we have? "Nothing." "What do you mean nothing? No matches." "No, just what I said, nothing. His blood work was all zero's, no prints, it's like he wasn't human." "That's crazy, let me see that." Gulli stares at the reports, 'Holy shit!

CHAPTER 31

Jimmy sits as Danny addresses the group. "This is our opportunity to hit them. We have an explosive that should do the job. We're not looking to blow up the entire building just to target Wilhelm and his devil kids. If we take them out their organization will fall apart. The problem is to get close enough to them to make this work. Wilhelm is going to appear with them in the middle of Times Square. They have a mass execution scheduled at twelve noon. They have a few highly wanted fugitives that they will execute. Then He will give a little speech. He has put a liquid enclosed explosive that if we can deliver it to a few feet from where they stand it will explode into fire and Sulphur. Hopefully this will be enough to send these demons back to hell. We are going over a few options on how to deliver it. Once we decide then it will be a go. I am going to a meeting later this afternoon and hopefully I will get the date it will happen. We've been waiting for this opportunity for a long time. Wilhelm has been very careful in his public appearances. This is the first time all three will be in public together." Nicky stands, "To me it sounds a little too obvious that this is going to happen. I mean this type of public happening leaking out to you makes me worry." "Nicky, my source has always been right on. I have been gathering information for over a year. I have no reason to distrust it now." "Sorry Danny, but I just have a bad feeling. Please be careful." "I always am. I should be back late tonight hopefully with the details." Jimmy walks out and gets a cup of coffee. He watches Danny and Nicky together and he can't help feeling a little jealous. He knows it's crazy but that's the way he feels. Danny walks away and Nicky comes over. "What do you think?" "I'm not sure. The explosive could work but how they are going to deliver it seems like a big problem." "Here's the thing, as an organization we have kept most of our cells separate at all times. This is the one time that our most experienced leaders have been gathered. I know this is a big effort but I just get this feeling something is wrong." "You mean their setting Danny up." "Yeah, could be. I know what he says about his asset out there is always been right on. The problem is I don't trust anybody out there. You never know when they can turn so to benefit themselves. I realize that we would have not had some small successes without the information that Danny gets. Still nothing as dramatic has gotten to Wilhelm and the demon kids. They are well aware of that every underground operation all over the world is after the same thing. A way to destroy the three of them. This is why they never appear in public together. They have enough intel on us that we are one of the biggest and well-equipped operations. It would be a relief for them to expose and eliminate us. They then would see other operations start to fall apart." "I haven't been here long enough to give you any real help on this. Danny seems sure of his contact and he knows you have to take chances to succeed. I understand your worry but it's not like you guys have too many choices. From what I see so far, it's only a matter of time until they find you. You've been lucky so far but you never know when it could end. If Danny feels this is the one opportunity to get them and blow their organization apart, I think you have to go for it." "I guess your right. Danny knows the score better than I do. If he believes it will work then it will work. Jimmy, I'm happy you showed up. I kind of like having you around. Danny spends a lot of time out in the field and I don't have any real friends to talk to. A lot of the guys are good but I can't really talk to them. For some reason I can talk to you. It's strange but it's like I know you a long time. I like talking and spending time with you." "Same with me Nicky, you make me feel like I belong here." Nicky gives Jimmy a big smile, "Come on let's get something to eat."

Danny drives with a big smile on his face. "Yes, this is it. We're going to blow these bastards to hell. He pulls into the deserted lot that he always parks in. He approaches the secret passage to the underground location. He can't help smiling as he will tell the crew the news. He enters the room and shouts," Meeting hall now! I got the exact time and schedule. Nicky and Jimmy get up and head over. The rest of the group head into the meeting area. "Okay, great news the ceremony is in five days. It will be at Times Square just as we thought. The three will be there. Wilhelm will give a speech and then the executions. They have five leaders from our underground cells. They also have as many as sixty other operatives from many different cells. It will be at noon. We now have five days to finalize how to deliver the explosives." There are cheers from the group and smiles all around. "Stan, get your team together and get us a special delivery plan. Mitch you and your group get the explosives finalized." Danny comes over to Nicky and gives her a big hug. "Baby, this is it. This is finally the day we get to fight back. Jimmy I'm happy you're here. When this is over with maybe we can all have a life back." As Danny continues talking a large explosion blast rocks the room. Then another explosion from another area. Then sounds of bullets being fired from all sides. Black uniformed police with automatic weapons firing at everything and anything. Screams and chaos follow. Danny grabs Nicky's hand and pulls her along running. Jimmy follows. A loud speaker bellows out, "Lay on the floor face down with your arms around your head. Do not move." As Danny, Nicky and Jimmy are running they are met by a line of NWO police pointing automatic weapons at them. "On the floor face down. All three lay on the floor. Danny out of the corner of his eye sees the black high boots and the NWO insignia. He recognizes the voice immediately. Captain Beckett. The commander of the area. "Danny, I always knew you were not one of us. I've been waiting to put all your lead operatives together. I have good news and bad news for you. The good news is that the information we have been feeding is true. The bad news is that you and your playmates are part of the mass executions. We told you we had some very important fugitives and guess what? You are one of them. Your operation down here has been a thorn in my side for quite a while. I could have taken you down a long time ago but I waited for you to bring all your little helpers together. Guess what? You did. I am a little disappointed in you, I have to admit. I thought you were a little smarter than this. I thought you might catch on and disappear on me. Fortunate for me and not so good for you. Your desire to destroy our leaders got the best of you. You followed your heart and not your head. That's a shame. Well, all's well that ends well. That's what I always say. Sargent, takes these pathetic creatures into the van."

As Danny gets up, they begin to walk through the rubble. Dead bodies of his friends that he has worked with for years. He watches as the police finish destroying any equipment that was still intact. He looks at Nicky as they walk, "I'm so sorry." Nicky looks back and gives him a warm and loving smile. Jimmy follows as they go out to the waiting vans. Hundreds of people stand by watching. Some laughing and others silently shaking their heads. Captain Beckett walks triumphantly through the crowd. The vans drive off.

CHAPTER 32

Pompeii, Italy:

Father Thomas asks Brother Aiden, "What does it say?" "It's a warm invitation to Oliver Wilhelm's meeting. He even put a little hand written note," Looking forward to seeing you there." "It's obvious that he feels extremely confident, that we do not pose any threat to him or to the success of their ceremony. He wants us there as witnesses to see firsthand what will take place." "Do you think he will harm us in any way?" "No, I do not. As I said before, you do not have to come. I understand if you want to stay away." "No, I'm coming." "Well, I will notify the Vatican of the plans. Let's pray that our prayers can interrupt their madness and we survive."

Days later Danny looks out a small barred window. He sees an incredibly large crowd completely covering the area for as far as he can see. He can't believe that he is jailed in what once was Macy's Department Store. They converted this wonderful building into a jail and God knows what else. He remembered all the times his mom would take him on their annual Christmas trip into the city and to Macy's. She had a way of filling his Christmas toy list with him and he never knew it. She had to be part magician how she fooled him. He was only eight or nine but still. All the years he would watch the Macy's Thanksgiving Day parade that would pass by this wonderful building. The bands and entertainment would stop right in front and perform. Children laughing with their parents and waiting for the big moment when they would see Santa Claus come. Now as he looks down, he sees a stage with twenty guillotines lined up. He can see camera crews all around the area. Photographers and reporters everywhere. This is so hard to believe this is happening. As he looks out the window, he hears footsteps coming down the hall. Armed guards open the door and Captain Beckett walks in. "How are you doing this morning my friend?

Hope you are enjoying the sights. I purposely put you in this cell because of the view. I thought you would appreciate that. It's a beautiful morning a perfect setting for all our festivities. Just so you know there is about a million people out there. We have large screens all over the area so that all can witness the event. We have clowns circulating with balloons for all the children. Free ice cream for the kiddies, under ten of course. I am told that every country in the world will be covering it live." "You are a very sick man, Captain." "No, I'm a general now, thanks to you. I'm not sick at all. I am in the best of health. Just so you know after the event we are putting on a free concert with all the latest recording artists. Sorry you and your friends will not be around to see it. Well, I'll have to leave you now. I am off to have a personal pre-game meeting with Mr. Wilhelm himself. I will give him your best regards. It's amazing how bringing down the largest terrorist network will do for you. By the way, I did stop by and give my personal farewell to your girlfriend. She is such a beautiful young woman. She has a beautiful face and a body to match. Of course, after today not so pretty anymore. Oh, your other little friend Jimmy, I believe, sends his best too. Any last requests before I leave?" "Yeah, go fuck yourself."

An hour later the guards come for Danny, Jimmy, Nicky and seventeen other prisoners. They march them down to the street. As they walk up to the stage the crowd cheers. Across from the stage a TV booth is set up. Over the loud speakers blasting out for all to hear. "Wow, what a sight. I have never seen anything like this. We want to welcome all of you out there to this amazing event. I haven't seen anything like this in all my years in broadcasting. I have covered seven super bowls, three world series and three Olympic games. This is by far the most exciting event ever." Yes, Cooper, I have to agree. I have covered presidential ceremonies, political conventions, debates, you name it but this tops them all." As the crowd roars Jimmy, Danny, Nicky and the other prisoners are placed in front of the guillotines. As Danny watches in amazement, marching bands surround the stage and begin to play. They continue playing and marching around the stage. From up high in the balcony overlooking the stage Oliver Wilhelm, Aaron, Lilith and their two-faced dog Cerberus stand. They are waving to the people and smiling. After a few minutes of ecstatic cheering Oliver speaks. "It is a pleasure to see everyone enjoying this monumental occasion. We are pleased to have captured these terrorists. I want to thank General Beckett and his force for a job well done. These terrorists have been disrupting your lives for too long. Now they will receive their just reward. Let this be a warning to any other terrorist organization that this is what awaits you. It's only a matter of time when we will eliminate every last one of you. On behalf of Aaron, Lilith and myself, we hope you enjoy this reckoning. Immediately following we will have a fabulous concert for all of you to enjoy, thank you." More thunderous applause and cheers. The guards place Jimmy, Danny, Nicky and the rest one by one into the guillotines. The band plays again and this time cheerleaders and dancers perform in front of the stage. "What a sight. This is a spectacular show. Now we're going to our on-stage reporter, Sarena. "I'm approaching the leader of the terrorists Danny. "Danny, can you tell us how you're feeling right now?" Danny just closes his eyes and does not reply. "Are you sorry for all your terrorist acts?" "Well, I guess he has no comment. What about you Nicky, from one woman to another, can you tell me what is going through your mind right now. Nicky softly speaks. "Sorry sweetie, I can't hear you? Can you speak louder?" "I hope and pray you all rot in hell." "Whoa, not very lady like. I don't think our terrorists have too much to say. Back to you Cooper." Jimmy, tries to look at Nicky but he can't move his head. He just shuts his eyes and prays. General Beckett stands in the front of the stage and yells into the microphone. "Are you ready for some action!" The crowd roars. The announcer says, "Here we go." General Beckett signals to the guards and one by one they release the guillotines. One by one the blade slices a head off.

Each time the crowd roars. "Wow, will you look at that!" Jimmy can't help to open his eyes as one by one the guillotines fall. "This is amazing, those heads are rolling." Jimmy, knows this is the end, as he prays harder and harder. The guard stands in back of Jimmy and awaits the general's signal. Jimmy, forces his head to the side just enough to see the blade. A second later the general gives the signal and the blade comes swooping down. Jimmy finishes his last prayer and then nothing.

Pompeii, Italy:

Father Thomas and Brother Aiden follow the instructions to the meeting place. The car service leaves them off on a remote and isolated road. The sign at the front gate has the address that they were given. The driver looks at the address to make sure, "Are you sure this is where you want to go.", "Yes, this is the address. I hope they have a phone and I will call you when to pick us up." "Would you want me to wait?" "No, that won't be necessary. I have no idea how long this will take." "I will go into the village and it will take me about a half hour to return. I have never seen any place this close to the volcano before. This villa must be right at the foot of the mountain?" Yes, you seem to be right. We will be fine and I'm sure I will be able to call you when we are done." The driver nods and drives off. "I don't even see any villa. This place is quite unsettling." "I agree Father, but this is where we have to go. Come let's walk up and see what is going on." They open the black rustic gate, walk through and follow the path. After a few minutes they see the stone villa. Through the windows they see the inside glowing with what seems like candle light. They approach the front door and begin to knock. There is no answer as they again knock and call out. "Hello." No reply. Brother Aiden slowly pushes the door open, it creeks and swings open. They continue to walk in and see that it is a very small cabin. There is a small fire place and a small table with two chairs. A book case and a small sofa. A very old radio with a small end table with a lamp that has a low light to it. Father Thomas turns to Brother Aiden, "I don't understand, is this the right place?" "Yes, there has to be more to this then what we are seeing." They gaze around the room, "That large curtain over there." Brother Aiden walks over to it and slides it open. There is a large two-sided door that opens from the middle. He looks at Father Thomas and slowly opens the doors. They walk slowly through the doors and see a very large room. The room is narrow and then widens dramatically. The walls are wood and this area was of new construction. "This had to be added on to the original stone villa." In front of them they see about twenty figures all with black robes and hoods, in a large semi-circle. They are all facing a large alter like stage. Behind the stage there is a very large floor to ceiling glass door looking at Mount Vesuvius. There are candles all over the entire room. At the front of the stage there is one-person chanting facing the outside. He is chanting in a strange language that neither Father Thomas or Brother Aiden understand. After the one on stage chants the other twenty repeat the chant. Father Thomas looks at Brother Aiden and speaks softly, "What should we do?" Before Brother Aiden could answer the hooded person at the alter turns. "It's Oliver Wilhelm." "Yes, so it is." Just at that moment a hooded man comes from the side of them, "Please join us and rejoice as the Master will be present" They look at each other and Brother Aiden whispers, "We must pray to stop whatever is happening here. Pray Father, like you never have before." As Father begins to pray, he hears Brother Aiden chanting in Latin. As if they knew what they were doing, Oliver and the society chant louder and louder. Oliver then stops, "He is upon us, the master is present. There is total silence and then a loud voice penetrates the entire room. ***These are my children and they will lead you till I decide to return. Do as they say and obey every word. The world will be yours to enjoy. This is the beginning of the end of times. For years to come the world will kneel to these chosen ones. Those of you that expected armies from the underworld are fools. There is*** *no need for any armies. The chosen ones will force their will on all the world leaders. They will all bend to their rule. When the time has come, I will return and then the final battle will take place. I will force the almighty one to come and save his world. The battle will rage and I will then be the true and only ruler of all mankind."* As the voice penetrates a red fog filters down from the mountain. The volcano begins to roar. Louder and louder until the volcano erupts. The red fog becomes thicker and engulfs the whole area. Father Thomas is shaken as he turns to Brother Aiden, "What is happening. What should we do?" Brother Aiden does not answer and continues chanting. A big blast rocks the room as Mount Vesuvius erupts once again. This time spitting out flaming lava. The red flaming sea of lava rushes down the mountain. All the society starts to panic, "We will be killed." Shouts of panic fill the room. Oliver yells, no one move stay where you are and witness the new beginning with your own eyes." As the burning red fire flows down the mountain from the center of it comes figures slowly walking towards the villa. They seem to be walking in the middle of the red burning lava. As they come closer and closer the lava just stops. Father Thomas looks at Brother Aiden in bewilderment. Brother Aiden whispers, "My God help us. He has sent his children from the depts of hell. God help us all." Out of the lava comes Aaron, Lilith and their two-faced dog Cerberus. Oliver and the society kneel and bow their heads. Brother Aiden grabs Father Thomas by the arm and pulls him away. "God is the only one who can save us now."

CHAPTER 33

"Jimmy, how are you feeling?" Jimmy opens his eyes slowly, "I don't know. I feel like I'm in a fog." "Well, you've been through a lot. The operation was very delicate, long and successful." "Doctor?" "Yes, I'm Doctor Davis and I operated on you." "I don't remember what happened." "You were in a major car accident and to be honest you are lucky to be alive." "Accident? Everything is all mixed up. I'm trying to remember but I don't remember the accident." "You suffered a major brain injury but I believe we fixed you up. It's normal to have memory problems after such an injury. Also, you have been in a coma for three months." "Three months?" "Yes, it was touch and go for quite a while but we were able to stabilize you. We hoped it was only a matter of time till you came out of it. I have to say I'm very pleased you did." "I have a lot of flashes of memories circulating in my head." "No reason to push it. Just try to relax and get some rest. We will be running a few tests on you in the next few days. We will monitor your results and get a rehab program for you. Physically and mentally you're going to need some help for a while. I feel that in time you will make a full recovery. You have to be patient it will take time." "I have a lot of questions and I don't know where to start." "Give it some time I have other patients to see. I'll have the nurse come in and give you some meds." "Thanks Doc." Jimmy lays there and has flashing scenes playing out in his head. He keeps seeing himself in different situations with so many different people. Some he thinks he knows others he doesn't. He also has visions of places he doesn't recognize. He shuts his eyes and tries to hold back his frustration. "Why can't I remember? Where was I?" A few minutes later two nurses walk in. "Hello Jimmy, how are you feeling this morning?" He watches as one nurse comes to his bedside with some pills and water. The other has her back turned looking at his charts. "Try to take some water first. Don't drink fast small sips, okay?" "Okay." My name is Connie and I will be checking on you and so will a few other nurses. Now take these and I'm take some vitals." Jimmy does what she says and keeps on trying to remember what happened to him. Connie smiles, "Looks good, you're doing just fine. There are a few visitors that want to come in and see you, are you okay with that?" "Yeah, sure." I'm going to start with just one." Jimmy nods he watches the other nurse as she puts the chart on the rack and walks away. As she walks away, she smiles, "Be back in a little bit, Jimmy." He has a strange feeling that he recognizes her but can't seem to be sure. "Jimmy, thank God you came out. We been worried sick about you.' "Danny, is that you?" "Yeah, it's me buddy. I'm so glad you woke up. How you feeling?" "I'm okay, I guess. Danny I can't believe you're here." "Of course, we've been here for months. We take turns coming to visit you. The girls have been reading to you. They say that could help when someone is a coma." "The girls?" "Yeah, Maria and Jennifer." "Maria and Jennifer, I'm confused." "No problem the doc said that you will need time for your memory to come back. Maria is my wife and Jennifer is Stevie's wife." Your married?" "Of course, you're the Godfather to my first daughter Lucia." Jimmy, holds his head feeling the heavy bandages. "Sorry, my mind is all screwed up." "It's okay, Jimmy, you're going to need some time. Hey could I bring in the rest of the guys? They are dying to see you." "Yeah, sure." Maria, Jennifer and Stevie walk in. "Jimmy, so good to see you." Maria and Jennifer hug Jimmy. Jimmy is totally confused. "It's great seeing all of you. Stevie is that you?" "Hell yeah, it's me. Wow, we were all so worried you weren't ever coming out of that coma. So glad you're back, baby. We have a lot of catching up to do." As they were all talking the nurse comes in. "No, this is not going to work just one of you for now. Jimmy needs some time so off you go." She shuttles them towards the door. "Hey, we will be back tomorrow, get some rest." "Love you Jimmy, see you tomorrow." Jimmy grabs Danny by the arm. "Can you stay awhile?" "Sure." The rest leave along with Connie the nurse. "Danny, I know that this going to sound strange but Stevie, I can't believe he is here." "Of course, he would be here.

We're all like brothers. Why wouldn't he be here to see you?" "I don't mean that he came but that he is here. You know, alive." "Jimmy, what are you talking about, of course he's alive." "Danny, the one thing I do remember he was killed in the club when we were kids." "No man, you saved him. You saved both of us. If it wasn't for you, we both would be dead. Don't you remember? Stevie got into that fight at the club over Jennifer. That ass hole ex-boyfriend of hers comes in and starts a fight with Stevie. Stevie and him go at it and I go in to break it up. He pulls a gun and you grab him. You guys both fall to the floor the gun goes off and shoots him. You take the gun away and then the cops came in. You're a hero and you saved us. We both owe you our lives." "Danny, I don't how to explain any of this but my memory has all these different things. One thing is that Stevie was killed. I mean I see these memories of me and you in this crazy world where this evil ruler took over the world. I could see me with two priests traveling through Europe looking to stop some evil plot. I see parts of an accident that I am in. The crazy thing is that I have a wife and two boys killed in that accident. I see Stevie laughing at me while I'm pinned in the car. Plus, so many other weird visions keep flashing in my mind." Wow, hey you were in a coma for three months. You probably had all these hallucinations, nightmares and dreams. Who knows what else you went through? You're here now, Stevie and me are both alive because of you. I have a great wife and two daughters. Stevie has his wife Jennifer have two boys. All because of you. I'm no doctor but I'm sure all these hallucinations you have had will clear out. You just need some time. You should tell the doctor what you told me but I'm sure he will tell you the same thing. After a while you will be your old self." Just then the nurse walks in, "I think Jimmy can use some rest now." "Yeah, look Jimmy I'll be back tomorrow and every day until you're ready to get out of here." "Thanks Danny, see you tomorrow." Danny walks out the door. Jimmy looks at the nurse and notices how pretty she is. He also feels like he has met her before. "She says there is one more person outside that has asked if he can see you for a minute, okay?" "Yeah, no problem." In walks an elderly priest, "Hi Jimmy, I'm Father Thomas." Jimmy can't hide the shocked look on his face. "Are you okay, Jimmy?" "Yeah, I'm sorry but do I know you?" "Well, I don't think so but I have been doing some praying for you on my visits." Father, I'm sorry but I have been dreaming and I'm certain you were in them." "You have been in a coma and I have sat and prayed by your side. I guess it's possible while you were in the coma somehow you saw me. The funny thing is that when I was doing my rounds here, I passed your room. I noticed you and for some reason, I had that same feeling that we knew each other." Father, I think that all these dreams I have had, are not some types of hallucinations or nightmares. I get the feeling more and more they are real. I know this sounds crazy but it seems that somehow, I have been living like three separate and different lives. I am becoming more aware of them. I can't quite put them all together yet but I feel that I actually have lived through them. Just as one comes to an end, I seem to pop up in another one. Sorry Father, I don't want you to think I'm crazy." "Not at all son. You know it's funny you say all these things because I have had a lot of these same feelings. I have been doing a lot of research and there are a lot of newer theories on this subject. A multiverse is a theory in which our universe is not the only one, but states that many universes exist parallel to each other. These distinct universes within the multiverse theory are called parallel universes. This could mean that you can be in separate dimensions or realities at the same time. I know this can be very confusing but who knows if your dreams were real or just dreams." "I agree it is all very confusing. One more thing Father, does the name Brother Adam or Raymond mean anything to you?" "Brother Aiden?" "Yes, that's it." "Yes, he is a very close friend. He is in a secluded monastery in the northern part of England. Why do you ask?" "I seem to remember him in one of my dreams." Jimmy smiles, "I'm happy you stopped in and I hope we can spend more time together." "Yes, I will defiantly come back and we can talk more." The nurse comes in and says visiting time is over. "Jimmy, I have some personal items we kept safe for you." She hands Jimmy a plastic bag with his wallet and a small box. Jimmy opens the box and takes out a gold-plated pocket watch. "Nurse, I don't think this is mine. I don't remember having this kind of watch." "It's yours it was in your pants pocket when you were brought in." Jimmy looks at the watch and sees it opens. He pops it open and sees it's inscribed. He reads it out loud, ***"Multas vitas, sed unum Deum aeternum novit omnia."*** "Father, I think it's Latin, do you know what it means?" Father Thomas looks at it, yes, "Many lives, one eternity, God knows all." Jimmy and Father Thomas look at each other, "Jimmy, this looks very familiar to me. I really have to go." "Okay, Father but please come back." "I will my son." Father Thomas quickly walks out the door physically shaken. Jimmy takes a deep breath and feels a strange feeling run through his body. The nurse comes close to the bed, "Jimmy, are you alright?" "Yeah, I guess. It's been a very strange day. The nurse smiles, well, you've been through a lot. Now it's time you get some rest. "Do we know each other?" "No, I don't think so but I have been here taking care of you for three months." Jimmy smiles and notices her badge on her uniform, "Your name is Nicole?" "Yeah but everyone calls me Nicky.

END

"TILL WE MEET AGAIN"

ACKNOWLEDGEMENTS

I want to thank my oldest and dearest friend, John Celano for all his help in writing this book. All the Vietnam stories are based on John's personal experiences in the Vietnam war. John and I grew up together and have remained closest friends for over fifty years. What John and his fellow soldiers went through in fighting for our country in a thankless war, should never be forgotten. I did take a few creative licenses in some areas, especially in eliminating the offensive language that was common place with soldiers.

"It's something unpredictable, but in the end it's right. I hope you had the time of your life."

__ Green Day

www.ingramcontent.com/pod-product-compliance
Lightning Source LLC
Chambersburg PA
CBHW070926190726
48292CB00004B/1124